GRACE MONROE

Broken Hearts

MIX
Mixed Sources
FSC

FSC is a non-profit international organisation established to promote the responsible management of the world's forests. Products carrying the FSC label are independently certified to assure consumers that they come from forests that are managed to meet the social, economic and ecological needs of present and future generations.

Find out more about HarperCollins and the environment at www.harpercollins.co.uk/green

AVON

AVON

A division of HarperCollins*Publishers*
77–85 Fulham Palace Road,
London W6 8JB

www.harpercollins.co.uk

A Paperback Original 2009

1

First published in Great Britain by
HarperCollins*Publishers* 2009

Copyright © Grace Monroe 2009

Grace Monroe asserts the moral right to
be identified as the author of this work

A catalogue record for this book is
available from the British Library

ISBN-13: 978-1-84756-046-9

Set in Minion by Palimpsest Book Production Limited,
Grangemouth, Stirlingshire

Printed and bound in Great Britain by
Clays Ltd, St Ives plc

I am very lucky and I would like to thank everyone who gave me a chance; Jenny Brown, my agent who was always on hand with support and advice, Maxine Hitchcock, Keshini Naidoo and the team at Avon who are the best at what they do. Thanks, girls!

Maria

Many thanks to anyone who has helped with this process.

Linda

To Auntie Theresa who made this world a little better.

Maria

To Paul for being so splendid.

Linda xx

Prologue

The middle of a November night in Scotland is rarely a happy time. For any poor sod in a PVC miniskirt and corset standing in an Edinburgh alley waiting for a punter, it was even worse. The wind was whistling down the Shore and right up her backside, even through her thermal knickers and the thin coat she had thrown on top of her outfit.

It had better be worth it.

She knew how to protect herself, but this weather was wearing her down. It looked as if she wasn't the only one who was affected – the streets were quiet, particularly lacking the type of man she was looking for. She'd seen a girl who looked to be no more than fifteen disappear with an old bloke about ten minutes ago. You'd think that the ancient ones would rather be at home having a cup of tea than spending the gas money on a quick fumble with an underaged girl. She laughed quietly to herself. Not her type. Not her type at all.

She wanted a nice car, with the heating on full blast, and a bit of comfort while she did what she had to do. Classy car; classy guy. She laughed quietly again. The ice

1

moon actually suited her purpose, even if she was freezing. She could see almost everything right down the Shore to the Docks. If she had moved a few hundred yards, the Queen's old yacht *Britannia* would have been in her line of vision from just beyond where lights from the local restaurants glimmered on the Water of Leith. During the day, and all through spring to autumn, there were swans swimming there. She remembered this from an earlier visit to Edinburgh, but, wisely, they were at home tonight as well.

A car engine revved in the distance, creeping towards her. There was ice on the cobbles where she stood and the punter was obviously a careful man, which she could see both in the way he was driving in the treacherous weather and the manner in which he was scanning the women. A thought flew into her mind – maybe he was too careful. She screwed up her eyes; she didn't want to be stopped by any of Lothian and Borders' finest. Mind you, the cops in Edinburgh were tolerant of vice girls, and the official line claimed that they had 'created a safer environment'. She'd read in the local paper that the residents weren't quite so broad-minded and the flat owners around the gentrified area were no doubt less than happy to be part of this safety campaign for whores. She'd have to go on gut feeling – you couldn't tell a cop by looking at him, and you couldn't tell whether any man was going to be fit for the purpose until way beyond the stage when it was too late to turn back.

The Mercedes drew up alongside the kerb. She teetered along in her heels to the window – it wasn't the latest model, but it was close enough. Salesman probably.

Away from home, away from the wife, needing a bit of recreation and able to justify that it's meaningless. She saw in him what she was looking for – what she needed. She threw open her coat and gave him a look at what was on offer. 'Evening, darling,' he grinned after rolling down his side window, letting her feel the warmth away from the streets behind her. She smiled back and wiggled her way round the front of the car to the passenger door.

Inside, it smelled of stale sweat and cloying pine air freshener. The back seat was littered with empty crisp packets, a discarded boy's football boot and a teddy wearing a Newcastle United strip. She smiled at him again as if she hadn't noticed, as if his treachery didn't turn her stomach. She needed him as much as he needed her. More.

Locking onto his eyes, she ran through a quick menu, making sure that the prices hovered somewhere between a bargain and a promise of satisfaction. She didn't want to be too cheap or he might suspect that she was a beginner; she didn't want to be too expensive or he might prefer to take his business somewhere less pricey. It was a balancing act, and the customer needed to get the sense that his luck was in. She offered a lot for twenty quid, and gave the excuse that it was a cold night.

Price agreed, she and the punter drove off; he was headed for a secluded spot where they could conduct their business unobserved, or so he told her. She wasn't frightened; her heartbeat was slow and steady, and her mind was focused. He seemed to know what he was doing. Experienced. Been here before. Good. A smile creased her face as she stroked her handbag. In another life, given different circumstances, she might have been married with children. She might have been the one waiting at home for this balding lump of lard as he risked everything.

The car drew to a halt on a deserted road that ran alongside the Docks; no CCTV that she could see. A fine film of sweat had broken out on his brow; his breathing was heavy and expectant. He leaned in to kiss her and she got a whiff of fabric softener from his shirt. Some woman cared for him. She recoiled from the image as she shoved him back into the driver's seat and leaned over. Her hand reached for the zip on his suit trousers. It wouldn't take long. A few quick strokes and hopefully she wouldn't have to go any further. She smiled as she pumped away at him – but his eyes were closed and he was paying attention to nothing but the actions of her left hand.

He certainly didn't notice as her right hand slipped into the back seat to the handbag lying on the passenger side beside the seat-belt clip. Her fingers slipped into the bag as he wriggled with delight, panting heavily and moaning some woman's name inaudibly. Stupid bastard; two-faced, hypocritical slime-bag. As she leaned in closer to his face, she could have sworn he was puckering up for a kiss.

What he got instead was a syringe filled with pure heroin.

His eyes widened in surprise as she pushed the plunger down, filling his right jugular. He started to struggle, but she knew that there would be no surprises here. He just had to wait it out. As did she.

4

She opened the passenger door and stepped outside. Taking a battered cigarette from her pocket, she drew in a lungful of smoke that warmed her chest. Blowing rings into the freezing night air, she knew that the man inside the car would be struggling to hold on to life. She heard a noise and assumed that it came from his death throes as his arms flailed against the driver's window. He was guilty, guilty, guilty. There wasn't an innocent bone in his body. Married, obviously. Or at least living with someone who cared enough to make sure a capful of fabric softener had been thrown into the washing load. A parent, obviously. Or at least with a kid in his life so close to him that football training and kicks around the park were part of normal life. And what was he doing behind their backs? Screwing around. Messing everything up. He deserved what he got. He did. And there were plenty more like him.

Glancing at her watch she felt irritated; he was taking too long. She opened the door and reached over the passenger seat. He had stopped thrashing and his eyes were closed, his breath shallow and laboured. But . . . he was still breathing. She didn't have time for this. Reaching into the back seat she dug her nails into the soft fur of the teddy; shoving it into the man's face, she held it against his mouth and nose, and waited – until any sign of life was gone.

Good.

Glad that was over, she started on the real work. She delved into her bag again, this time pulling out an ultra-sharp boning knife and poultry cutters. She rifled through his CD collection, quickly looking for something that meant nothing to her, something to muffle the sound of bones shattering, before realizing that heavy music coming from a parked Merc could arouse suspicion, even in a quiet street near the Docks.

She cracked through his ribs. She was proud of her strength. Strategic planning aided her attempts every time. Still, both were means to ends. Plunging the boning knife in, she severed the superior vena cava and neatly removed the organ. She double-bagged it in cling film and popped it into her handbag.

Stepping outside the car, she reached into her bag, lifting out a handheld car vacuum. Her work here was almost done. She reached into her bag again. With her thumb and forefinger she removed a hair, a single hair, from inside a plastic freezer bag.

She left it where she was sure even those idiots from the identification bureau would be sure to find it.

The sooner the better.

PART ONE

Edinburgh
November 2008

Chapter One

'Have you reached a verdict?' Judge Neil Wylie asked the five women and ten men of the jury.

Show time.

I breathed deeply and steadied myself. I always hated this bit, this time in a trial where everything you've worked for hangs in the balance. If I was to live up to my reputation as some sort of Ice Queen, I had to keep my act going – but it was hard when I was bricking it. I stared unblinking at the jury box, thanking God for my poker face and Boots for the six inches of make-up that was hiding any emotion that might be lurking there. In truth, all I wanted was someone to hold my hand and tell me I'd done well and that everything would be fine. I'd be as well hoping for Santa to make an early appearance.

To keep my hands busy, I pretended to scribble down notes on the yellow legal pad in front of me. It had been a long, tiring murder trial, but this moment was where everything was so exciting yet so terrifying. It was out of my control and I hated and loved that feeling. Would I have changed anything? Would I rewrite the script if

I could? What if I'd fucked it up? My mind was flooded with all the little things I could have done better. There was also a part of it that was trying to remind me of all the things I'd done well. Really well. My mother's voice wanted to sneak in there – Mary McLennan wouldn't want me to get too confident in case I was heading for a fall. My mind was a busy place.

A stout, pigeon-chested woman in her mid-fifties struggled to her feet. With her beige hunting gilet, green tweed skirt and reading specs hanging from a gold chain round her neck, she was a perfect advert for *Horse and Hound*. I rechecked the chart I'd drawn up two weeks ago during jury selection. This was Miss Agnes McPhail, breeder of Rhodesian Ridgebacks. My stomach tightened a bit – I felt somewhat uncomfortable with the thought of Miss McPhail as the foreman. She was only on the jury because I had run out of challenges. I remembered the old adage that dog owners end up looking like their pets – well, she must have been housing a few mutts that looked like well-skelped arses. The sound of the odd nervous cough was the only noise as the court macer took the verdict from Miss McPhail and handed it to the judge. I couldn't take my eyes off the white sheet of paper. The judge unfolded it as I studied his face for a telltale sign. There was none. He was as good as me at this lark.

I stole a glance towards my client, Kenny Cameron. An ugly, skinny wee shit if ever there was one. He was five feet five inches tall and, in his boxers (Christ, what a thought), he tipped the scales at just under nine stones. Cameron stared straight ahead; only the bobbing of his

Adam's apple indicating he was still alive and kicking. He was submissive and reconciled to his fate, as he had been throughout the trial for the murder of his wife, Senga. The only time Cameron showed any emotion was during direct examination, when he explained why he had bludgeoned big Senga to death. When asked to describe how his partner had sustained head injuries, Kenny Cameron began to sweat as he haltingly told the jury about hitting the ball hammer off his wife's skull, over and over again until he was covered in her brains. When he was finished, his hands shook and his body heaved with great dry sobs. The jury looked a bit green too. I only hoped they still remembered why he had done it.

'Will the accused please stand?' Judge Wylie shouted.

My client staggered to his feet. I remained sitting, staring ahead with a lack of emotion that was very hard work indeed. The press would be watching for any sign of weakness, to see if the Ice Queen was melting.

'In the case of Her Majesty's Advocate against Kenny Cameron, the verdict reads as follows: We, the jury, being duly empanelled and sworn, do find the accused Kenneth Michael Cameron, not guilty . . .'

The courtroom erupted. I couldn't hear the rest of the verdict because of the din. One of big Senga's sisters screamed obscenities while Billy Boyle, festooned with chunky golden necklaces and a Benidorm tan, tried to jump into the well of the court to stand up for the innocence of his dead sister. Ma Boyle's eldest son held my eye as he was beaten back by a police officer. To be honest, I didn't know who Boyle was coming for – Kenny

Cameron or me. My client clearly thought it was him and collapsed in the box. The two court policemen standing guard by his side rushed to give him first aid. It was basic stuff – a quick, harsh slap on the face to bring him round. I made my way to Kenny knowing that he had won the battle but lost the war.

'Calm down,' I ordered in a voice much calmer and steadier than it should have been, given that I was dictating to Scotland's first family of crime as much as I was to Cameron; they could hear me as clearly as he could. 'Just relax . . . everything is going to be okay.' The lie slipped out of my mouth and I put my arm protectively around him as the Boyles looked on. Someone tapped my shoulder. I half turned. Ranald Hughes, the prosecutor, handed me a glass of lukewarm tap water. He was ten years older than me, a senior member of the legal hierarchy who had been assigned what had looked like an open-and-shut case. Politeness was bred into him, and as an officer of the court he would want to do his bit to restore order and behave appropriately towards a lady. 'Would this be of any use?' he asked, looking doubtful. I took the glass and handed it to Kenny Cameron. Ranald Hughes watched my client sip the water. When the colour returned to Kenny Cameron's face, it was time for the prosecutor to speak, which he did in the tone of a Church of Scotland minister.

'Mr Cameron,' he said, 'the law must be seen to be done.' He coughed, drawing himself up to his full height to deliver the abbreviated sermon. 'I prosecuted you because no one can take the law into their own hands.' I was itching to tell the prosecutor to raise his voice because Senga Cameron's family still looked nasty, but that was pretty normal for them. I was out of luck just when I needed someone other than me to be loud and noticeable – maybe it was my imagination, but Hughes seemed to say the next bit in a whisper, so much so that I had to strain my ears to listen. He drew in like a conspirator, but not until he'd checked over his shoulder to gauge the distance of the Boyles, who by now were fighting with the police and refusing to leave court. They probably felt right at home, given how much time they spent there as a matter of course. 'But I also want you to know I don't think your wife had any right to treat you the way she did, and if you had overcome your fear of ridicule and shame then you would never have ended up in Edinburgh High Court, my man.'

Ranald Hughes coughed, nodded in my direction, turned on his heels and left for the judge's chamber – well out of the way of any trouble. I, on the other hand, had to push through the melee of Boyles and journalists. As Kenny Cameron's friends and supporters made cautious moves towards us, I put my hand out to him. He shook it. He looked and probably felt like a sick fish. His mob was no match for the Boyles. 'I hope you can put this behind you, Kenny.' I held his eyes. 'Get on with your life. Everyone deserves a fresh start.' Through gaps in the crowd I could see Senga Cameron's mother, Ma Boyle, point in the direction of me and Kenny and draw her finger across her neck. She was a sly cow; no one else saw it. Nodding in my direction, she allowed the policeman to escort her out of court. Now that the verdict was in, and the trial was over, the lawyers were redundant.

Ranald Hughes and the prosecution team came back into the empty court to collect their papers. He shrugged his shoulders in sympathy. 'A Pyrrhic victory I fear, Miss McLennan.' I smiled. I had a reputation to maintain, as did all lawyers – society would surely crumble if I'd fallen at his feet and started crying, telling him that he was right; but we both knew that he was.

I wouldn't get out of this without paying a price of some sort.

Chapter Two

She loved how he looked when they were having sex. Staring at him, with his arm muscles supporting his full weight, she couldn't care less about whether or not she was getting what she wanted or needed. Instead she wondered how they looked together – what other people would think of them if they could see them at this moment.

Kelly Adams thought a lot about the opinions of others. She lay on her back beneath him and did what she could to satisfy Dr Graham Marshall's every desire. Her jet black hair (straight out of a bottle) fanned out on the pillow, just as she'd arranged it. She lifted her legs higher round his shoulders as he growled and shut his eyes. Kelly was out of breath; this was bloody hard work, but it was worth it. She watched his body for signs that he was close to orgasm; every sinew in his neck tightening as he strained before the collapse came and he took his body out of hers. As his face came to rest on her shoulder, she made a few dramatic groans herself and gave quite an impressive shudder. To be honest, she'd never had an orgasm anyway, so she wasn't quite sure how it should be, but men always appeared quite satisfied with what she'd learned from DVDs and magazines and friends. She wasn't bothered – as long as he'd enjoyed himself, and as long as she could get him to herself, what else mattered?

Graham Marshall lay for a moment and listened to Kelly's heart race with her exertions. His nose wrinkled at the smell of her deodorized sweat interlaced with too much sweet perfume. He stroked her skin lazily and peered across her thighs at the clock on the hotel bedside table. It was one in the afternoon. Marshall sat bolt upright and threw his feet onto the floor, making the springs in the bed creak. Kelly watched her naked lover walk towards the bathroom, picking up his sports bag on the way.

'Please stay, Graham,' she said, unable to conceal her neediness. She knew that he hated that sort of thing, but sometimes she just couldn't help it. They were so good together, so perfect, and she just wanted him to recognize it. 'Why don't you take the afternoon off? Why don't you stay with me? Please?' she whimpered again.

'I've got a consultation at two thirty,' he replied without turning round, the coldness in his voice unmissable.

The hot water washed away the sweat he had just worked up and he ran his soapy hands over his firm pectorals, taking time to admire his own body. He towelled himself dry in the cramped hotel bathroom. Condensation from the shower had fogged up the mirror so he took the end of the towel and wiped the glass. Haunting blue eyes in a chiselled tanned face stared back out at him. Even he thought they looked cold. His mouth

16

was thin and hard. Women were either seduced or cowed by it; the ones he liked best were both.

He rubbed his hands through his thick dark brown hair; artfully messy was the look he was going for. Everything was artful with Graham Marshall. When he eventually came out of the bathroom, Kelly was still naked. On more than one occasion she had tried to entice him back into bed after he was ready to leave. He knew she was trying to control him with sex – he also knew how unlikely it was that she would succeed.

'Kelly, Kelly, Kelly,' he whispered seductively as he moved towards her and sat down on the bed. She smiled at him, waiting for the words that would make her feel worthwhile, words that would recognize just how perfect and special she was. Graham Marshall paused, then bent down to tie his handmade shoes as he sat up and looked at Kelly, leaning forwards to face her. 'This, this my darling . . .' He twirled her hair around his fingers as she gazed at him. 'This . . . is the last time I'll be seeing you.'

Kelly jumped out of bed almost at the same time as he stood up, a stunned expression on her usually confident, unremarkable but mirror-perfect face. 'You are joking. You are joking! Tell me you're joking, Graham?' she said, her voice cracking.

'Why would I be?' he asked, casually.

'Because . . . because . . . well, why would you not see me again? What's wrong with me? Why wouldn't you want me? I just don't understand,' she whined.

He stopped halfway through fixing his tie and stared at her. 'No. You probably don't. But you see, Kelly, you do nothing for me. You look like a hundred other stupid tarts. You have no brain to speak of. You lie there like a dead fish when we're in bed, only showing some sign of life when you remember that you have to pretend to be enjoying it. You've been convenient, I'll give you that – but what *are* you exactly, Kelly? What are you?' Marshall kept his back to her so she would not see his grin as he finished his speech.

'What do you expect me to say? I don't know what you want me to tell you,' she said, pulling at her hair and pacing the room. He half turned and stared into her eyes, enjoying the play of emotions on her face. 'Okay. Let me give you something – your little eyes lit up there, didn't they? You're not bad to look at in an overdone, fake sort of way, and you have never asked for much really, but . . .' he tapped his forefinger off his temple as he spoke, '. . . you're stupid, stupid, stupid.'

Kelly's mouth fell open. She glared at him for a moment before her jaw tightened with anger. 'You bastard! You think you can use me, and then just decide it's over?' she spat, anger flushing her skin again. 'I'll tell your wife. I'm going to phone her now. Watch me.' She reached into her handbag for her mobile. His laughter filled the room as he picked up his briefcase. 'Why don't you care? Why don't you care, Graham? You're joking . . . tell me you're joking!' Her fury passed swiftly, and there was a pleading note in her voice.

He shook his head. 'Actually, I never joke.'

The smile slipped from his lips and he looked at her in a way that she'd seen before but always tried to ignore. This time it frightened Kelly and she stepped back and fell into the headboard. Graham Marshall prowled round the divan until he was standing over her. He studied her impassively for a second, in the manner of a lab technician observing an experiment. Suddenly, he grasped her ankle and painfully twisted her leg until she was face down on the wrinkled sheets. He took a moment to admire the length of her neck and the curve of her shoulder as she cried out in agony. He ran his free hand through her long black hair, and then he pulled it so hard that a clump came out in his hand, exposing a small patch of bleeding scalp. Her body trembled as he flipped her over onto her back again, still holding her leg.

'I will only say this once.' He spoke to her slowly, as if she was incapable of taking in anything but the most simple of messages. 'You will never phone my wife.' He yanked her hair again. 'What will you never do?' he asked. The smile had returned to his lips.

'Phone your wife,' she said, trying to keep the fear from her voice, hoping that he'd just hear obedience. 'I will never phone your wife.'

He caressed her cheek with his forefinger. 'Be a good girl and tell me why you will not contact my wife.' He spoke slowly and clearly, enunciating every syllable. He twisted her ankle again; she winced in pain as the tears streamed down her face.

'I won't phone . . . I promise I won't phone.' It was hard for Kelly to speak as she was sobbing so loudly.

'You didn't listen to me,' he whispered, squeezing the fingers on her left hand now that he had let go of her leg.

'I won't phone!'

'Tell me why.' His voice was soft and understanding.

'I'm a good girl and you told me not to.' Kelly tried to smile as the excruciating pain coming from her fingers threatened to make her lose consciousness. Had he broken them? 'I always do what you want . . . please stop hurting me.'

He let go of her and kissed her – gently – on the forehead.

'Not bad,' he smiled. 'But a smarter reply would be that you won't do anything to piss me off because I can hurt you – really, really hurt you.' He crouched down beside Kelly and opened his briefcase. He paused for a moment, his back to the shaking woman, before taking out a scalpel. The blade shone so that he could see his own reflection in it. He placed the tip of the blade to his own cheek and closed his eyes at the coldness of it. 'Really, really hurt you,' he repeated, never taking his eyes off her as he put the scalpel back in his briefcase and walked away from the bed. Kelly wrapped herself in the duvet, trembling. He watched her reflection in the hotel window as he adjusted his tie. Could he convince her that this had all been a sick joke? Would she open her legs for him again? There was no doubt she would – she was dim to the core and she was crazy about him. These thoughts caused him to grin, and for a moment he played with the image of Kelly grateful to have him back because he was right – she was stupid.

'You know, the room is paid for . . . you should rest, stay till the morning if you wish,' he said.

'I'm sorry,' Kelly cried. 'Please come back after your

consultation! Please! I'll be good, I promise!' she pleaded, but he was already on his way down the corridor.

The cold air hit him as soon as he left the hotel. The sky looked threatening, dark grey snow clouds rolling in over the Firth of Forth. He turned off the alarm on his black Porsche. Maybe one day he would do something for Kelly. Something delicious, a reminder, a keepsake. He drove off, smirking with expectation.

Maybe she was a good girl after all.

Chapter Three

Dr Graham Marshall drove down Lothian Road where, on his left, Edinburgh Castle, shining black with rain, dominated the landscape. The miserable November weather was keeping the shoppers at home and off Princes Street, but a busload of Japanese tourists was decanting at the Caledonian Hotel. Waiting at the traffic lights, he could smell the sugar from the doughnut kiosk. His lips crumpled in distaste as a fat scaffolder stuffed fried dough into his mouth. Graham hated obesity. It was just one more thing on his list of likes and dislikes; a long list. The lights changed just as the radio reporter began the lead story on the two o'clock news; he turned left and headed towards Haymarket.

'This is Tony Baxter at Edinburgh High Court speaking with Brodie McLennan, defence agent for Kenny Cameron, who has just been acquitted of murdering his wife . . . Miss McLennan, why do you think the jury accepted the defence of battered husband syndrome with regard to Kenny Cameron?'

'The jury returned a not guilty verdict simply because they heard the evidence . . .' said a clear, educated Scottish voice. 'Mr Cameron was hospitalized four times by his wife's temper. A battered wife rightly gets a great deal of sympathy, but there are a significant number of men who are subject to domestic violence.'

'If that's the case, why don't we hear more of it?' asked the reporter.

'The "henpecked" husband is as much a joke as the mother-in-law . . . these men not only suffer at the hands of their spouses but their plight is wrapped up in shame.'

'Not everyone would agree with you, Miss McLennan. Some women's groups are angry at this decision, saying that you've set back the cause of zero tolerance by twenty years. One group said that this decision is simply a return to the days when it was assumed men had a right to hit their wives – because now, if they do, they can claim it is self-defence.'

'Violence is violence, Mr Baxter, and, if you don't mind me saying so, your argument is muddled in the extreme. Mr Cameron's wife threw a pan of hot chip fat over him in a drunken rage. She had a metal umbrella and the tip of it had been sharpened. Her usual practice was to stab him with it if he didn't work fast enough. I could list many more instances, but it sounds to me as if your mind has already been made up.'

'Miss McLennan, Kenny Cameron beat his wife to death with a hammer – and he never denied that. Some people are saying that he walked free today because of a clever lawyer's tricks.' Listening to the radio, Marshall could hear the sharp intake of breath from the lawyer. When she spoke again there was no disguising the iciness of her tone.

'It was a simple decision for the jurors to make once they understood how repeated beatings affect the human mind. This isn't about gender, this is about violence, and I'm sure every women's group in the country will be more than happy to educate you about that if you have some spare time, Mr Baxter.'

To his credit, the reporter didn't miss a beat. 'You've been critical of the Crown Office for taking this prosecution from the start. Do you think they would have prosecuted a woman in these circumstances?'

'I think they would have accepted a plea of culpable homicide . . . but today I'm pleased they didn't offer it.'

'Miss McLennan, you've had a string of high-profile victories in recent years – how do you handle your celebrity?' The car filled with the deafening silence of dead air before Brodie McLennan replied in a softer voice, 'Trust me, Tony, I'm run off my feet visiting clients in Saughton Prison and jointly managing a law firm . . . life's too hectic to think about anything else. Thank you so much for your time and interest.'

His mobile phone bleeped to indicate an incoming text as he turned the radio off. Christ, he thought, Kelly again with her desperate clinginess – he hated that sort of woman, but they were just so easy to get. What would she be offering now? When would she get it into her thick skull that women like her had absolutely nothing *to* offer? They thought that sex was such a bargaining tool, but they had never realized that Graham Marshall had sex with himself, not with them – they were just there at the same time, and by far the less interesting partner. As soon as he parked, the message shone: *Ur sins will catch up with u. Rag Doll pub in 1hr or i go to papers*

This must be her idea of intelligence. Laughable really. Marshall shuddered at the spelling rather than the content of the text, and flipped the phone closed. He sighed wearily before switching the mobile off and putting it in the glove compartment. What was this? Did Kelly think he was going to become the perfect boyfriend because she was pretending she knew things about him? She knew nothing. A scalpel held to her in a hotel room, a bit of rough sex in the afternoon; she probably thought the papers would be lining up to take her picture if she went public.

As he walked towards his office, he reflected on why she was doing this now. He knew that the few words, the few gestures he did make that she could interpret as 'warm' were enough – no doubt she had visions of them sharing dinner with his parents, choosing an engagement ring, having babies. It was slightly intriguing to wonder whether she was actually willing to play the game a little – had she involved someone else? Was silly little Kelly trying to get what she wanted? The thought that she might have told someone else about them set Marshall thinking about other possibilities. It could be a blackmailer after easy money. It wouldn't be the first. He'd had dealings with greedy men before and he wasn't the one who came off worse. However, this time he suspected it was nothing more than Kelly Adams thinking she could make him do whatever she wanted. Really, the notion that calling his wife would be a disaster was laughable. Still, some credit was due to Kelly – she'd recovered rather quickly from the blubbering mess he'd left in the hotel room not so long ago. He had been working hard, so he called his secretary to postpone his afternoon appointments until later that week. A few easily rescheduled sessions would give him the chance to relax with a drink anyway. He rubbed his temples for a few moments, and collected his thoughts before turning the car round and heading back into town. He had time to play.

Chapter Four

The afternoon trade at the Rag Doll was brisk, but it didn't hide the fact that it was a down-at-heel drinking den that Dr Marshall wouldn't normally be seen dead in. The regulars turned to stare at him as he entered the gloomy pub – for a moment he wondered whether it had been a good idea to park the Porsche outside. The owner of the bar was a huge man in a kilt who was hardly making the atmosphere friendlier as far as Marshall was concerned. He heard a customer refer to the man as Glasgow Joe; he was still behind the bar, not serving, just keeping his eye on the place, keeping his eye on Graham. It made Marshall uneasy; what was he looking at? Surely his money was the same as anyone else's, so why did the huge man keep looking at him – was he a friend of Kelly's? Is that why she'd asked to meet here? Was he in on all of this with her? Marshall told himself that he was an intelligent man, that there was no point in thinking of things that were probably nowhere near the truth. If Kelly was behind this, it was very straightforward. She just wanted money to make her feel better.

He ordered a sparkling mineral water and took it to the table in the furthest corner from the door where he could see the comings and goings of the pub, switching his mobile back on as he sat down. Despite the stern talking-to he had just given himself in his mind, he couldn't help but feel a wariness as he realized that the man he had heard called Glasgow Joe continued to look at him. Marshall tried to concentrate on the near-naked pole dancer who shimmied like a bowl of jelly to some vaguely identifiable Seventies disco nonsense. All of the other tables were empty; what customers there were in the place were crowded around the stage, and, unlike him, they didn't seem to have to feign interest in the stripper. She wasn't attractive to him and she wasn't a potential client, so what was the point in looking? Graham wondered.

Marshall's phone rang and he stood up and made his way to the front door to avoid anyone eavesdropping on the call. Wisely, Kelly had obviously had second thoughts about a face-to-face confrontation and was going to try it all anonymously. The door slammed shut behind him and he pressed the green button to answer.

'Pull the scarf more tightly round your neck,' a woman's voice purred. 'We don't want you catching your death, do we?'

He didn't reply. His eyes scanned the horizon for Kelly. It didn't sound like her, but she would no doubt try to disguise her voice or get a friend to call for her. If only she had put this much imagination into her perform-ances in the bedroom, he might not have got bored so quickly. She was close by, watching him, he was sure of it. His ears were tuned into her soft, steady breath. He closed his eyes, just for a second, and imagined his hands around her throat, squeezing every last drop of air from her lungs. What would that be like? Would he enjoy watching as her eyes bulged and she gave up trying to scream?

'Cat got your tongue?' she said, interrupting his reverie. 'We can be nasty or nice, it's up to you.' She hardened her tone. 'It's no skin off my nose. Either way, you'll pay.'

'I don't know what you're selling,' Marshall replied, tightening his jaw and listening to the nuances of her breath. This definitely wasn't Kelly – there was no accent as such, it was unlikely such a caller would have given anything away in such a manner, he supposed, but there was no trace of Kelly at all from what he could tell. So, she'd brought a third player to the table, had she? If they were as stupid as she was, it wouldn't make any difference.

'Wipe that innocent look off your face: your play-acting doesn't wash with me,' the caller said snippily. There was a pause before the woman continued, and the words she came out with seemed to have meaning for her, seemed to matter more than they would to a two-bit blackmailer only after enough spare cash to buy a new handbag, if it indeed was Kelly behind all of this nonsense. 'My mother always said a leopard can't change its spots.'

Marshall drew breath but said nothing.

'Do you hear me?' she asked. 'Do you hear me? Don't you think I deserve an answer?'

'You didn't ask a question,' he said, smiling to himself.

'I thought that maybe you were so smart that you might have guessed it by now,' she told him. 'Isn't there a question that you've been avoiding for years, Dr Graham Marshall?' She emphasized his name as if she was spitting it out of her mouth. He answered with silence. 'Why don't you tell me the answer to this, then,' the woman continued. 'How would you like people to know? Would you like that, Dr Graham Marshall?'

This didn't feel like the sort of prank Kelly might play. This had an edge, but was it the edge he had peered over in the past? In spite of himself, Marshall was intrigued.

'You clearly have a lot of time to waste, haven't you?' said the woman. 'I've been to London, Dr Marshall, spoken to your old neighbours. They were very helpful, told me about you, your habits – they even showed me photographs, wasn't that nice? You're older, of course, but who isn't? I took the snaps to a specialist – isn't it amazing what they can do? It turns out that, with computer age progression, you can't cheat Nature really. You've been caught, Dr Graham Marshall. Caught. Your lies and your cleverness – none of it matters. I know it's you.' The woman's breath was getting faster, rushing towards him as the words fell out of her mouth towards his carefully constructed life. She was rustling paper so much that he could hear it. There was no point telling himself that it could all be fake, that she could be rustling today's *Daily Record* and some supermarket receipts.

She knew.

30

So what? he asked himself. He was Dr Graham Marshall and he would not be taken down by some lowlife scheming blackmailing bitch. Not now. 'I'm sure you think that your points are terribly interesting, Miss,' he said, 'but really, it's rather old news, don't you think? Now, I'm assuming that this is all about money and that you'd rather have cash, as opposed to a cheque or money into your bank account,' he laughed quietly, 'but I do like to keep things civilized – who am I dealing with? What's your name?'

'Names only matter to some people,' she hissed at him. 'They're not everything, are they? For some people, they can be changed as easily as a pair of socks; for others I guess they can be the key to their whole world collapsing around them.'

He felt cold. This needed to end. 'Name your price,' he said.

'You've earned a fortune over these last years, haven't you, Dr Marshall? And, in your game, reputation is everything. If you're so sure that this is about money, why don't you tell me what *you're* willing to offer?'

'Have you told your . . . employer what you've discovered?' Marshall asked, playing for time until he felt more confident. His voice was cold and hard. He needed to know who had instructed her to delve into his past. All he heard was a slow clapping start from her end. A steady, irritating sound that only told him she was using a hands-free and that she was getting stronger, more confident as this conversation went on. It was a long time since anyone had treated him with such disrespect.

'Well done, good question. What's the answer, do you

think?' she asked. He heard her drumming her fingers impatiently on a hard surface.

His eyes searched all the parked cars, but from what he could tell she was nowhere in sight. Marshall stared unblinking into the distance and shook his head slowly from side to side. 'The answer, my dear, is . . .' He raised his forefinger to his lips. 'That I suspect you're too smart to share this tidbit with anyone else. You're not working for anyone else at all, are you? Let's just say I still think it's our little secret.' The blackmailer was quiet but her silence revealed nothing more to him. 'One thing does bother me, though . . .' He pushed a stray hair out of his eye as he spoke. 'You seem very confident about all of this. About dealing with me.' Marshall paused before he said the next words and they formed a question for himself as much as for his would-be blackmailer. 'Why aren't you scared?'

The woman seemed to wait forever before laughing into the phone. 'When you want something so badly, so desperately, you don't really care about anything else. You don't feel fear, you don't feel anything.'

He had no idea what her game was, but was very keen to believe that she was actually just a money-grabbing lowlife. If so, she would presumably have worked out how much would keep her going for life. Well, let her believe it. 'I think that five hundred thousand would be fair, don't you?' he asked, to no reply. 'I don't have that kind of money just lying around,' he continued, hoping that he sounded convincing enough to buy some time. 'I need a few days to raise it, to liquidate it. How much time do I have?'

'Once you've paid me exactly what I need, I'll be out of your life. The sooner the better.'

She switched the phone off just before he whispered, 'But I won't be out of yours, sweetheart.'

Once you realised he couldn't
it was obvious. He pushed the button
the light, and the noise and the machine descending
from the ceiling ...

Chapter Five

A bare tree branch lashed against the kitchen window. The drumming noise made Pauline Pearson even more impatient to see her husband, to hold him, and tell him she was sorry. Very sorry. When he was away, she genuinely did feel guilty about the constant arguing – when he was there, she was more than happy to blame Alan for his fair share of it. But she really did miss him when he'd been on the road for a while and, each time, she would decide to make a renewed effort.

The Edinburgh to Newcastle road was a bugger at any time of the year, and in this weather it was even worse. She hoped a traffic accident wouldn't make him even later. She peered out into the garden; it was a typical wet, windy November – just the type of night for staying indoors and snuggling up before a roaring fire. The boys were bathed and ready for bed. Pauline had prepared a special meal and romance was on the menu. Hopefully. She smiled. It was a long time since she'd done that – any of it: meals or sex. Even if she said so herself, the smell was delicious. She was supposed to be on a diet but tonight she'd make an exception for him. It was her way of apologizing. Pauline shuddered as she thought of the way she'd treated Alan over the last ten months or so. After all, as her mother had said this afternoon, the credit crunch was affecting everyone, and in Alan's line of business as a financial consultant specializing in mortgages, it went without saying he would be one of the hardest hit of all.

'The good times will come again,' her mother had promised, before warning that this would only happen if she kept her man happy. Pauline blushed, even although there was no one around to see it. Keeping Alan happy in or out of bed had been the last thing on her mind since his income had dropped. It wasn't just the money. He'd stopped taking care of himself, the pounds had piled on around his waist, and his hair had started to fall out. The doctor said it was stress. Pauline knew that sex would probably relieve the stress he felt, but the simple fact was she just didn't fancy him any more. Who would? There was no sexual spark now and, unfortunately for their marriage, it was obvious. If only he'd try to get himself sorted out, do some sit-ups, cut back on stuffing his face in front of the telly every night when he was at home. He'd never been God's gift, but surely it wasn't hoping for too much to not have her stomach heave when she thought of him touching her? It was hard to know when she had stopped wanting him, but she was determined to do all she could to get things back to normal.

She walked to the window again and pulled back the curtain. Where was he? The boys wanted to kiss him goodnight and Jason had left his Newcastle United teddy in the car. Although he was seven, he slept better when he was cuddling it. Pauline tried Alan's mobile again. No answer. She poured a glass of wine to calm her nerves. He wasn't answering his phone because he was driving: he couldn't risk the automatic points and fine and she didn't like him using a hands-free kit because it might still affect his concentration. In spite of their recent difficulties, she did love him deep down.

The doorbell rang.

At last. Why wasn't he using his key? Maybe he'd forgotten it; he was always losing things. She took another sip of wine, deliberately not answering the door, and tried to calm down; she didn't want to snap at him just as he was coming through the front door. Pauline could feel her irritation rising; his finger was back on the bell and the noise was going right through her. She could feel her romantic mood dissipating.

A blast of cold air hit her in the face as she opened the door.

It wasn't Alan.

Two police officers stood where he should be; one of them was a woman – that wasn't a good sign, she thought.

'Can we come in, Mrs Pearson?' the female officer asked gently.

'Well, I'm a bit busy, pet. My husband's been away on business and I'm expecting him in any minute now,' she replied. 'So, no. No. I'm afraid not. No.' She wanted them to go away. If they had something to say, she didn't want to hear it.

The woman reached out and took hold of Pauline's

damp, very, very cold hand. Pauline Pearson thought she felt her heart stop.

'Aye well, it's Mr Pearson we'd like to talk to you about . . . can we come in now, pet, do you think?'

Pauline heard herself whispering 'No' over and over again as they came in. It made no difference whatsoever.

Chapter Six

Lord Edward Hunter took a deep breath as he stepped inside the front door of 10 Downing Street. He had waited for this moment ever since he had first been called to the bar in 1974.

It did not disappoint.

He was still holding his breath as his eyes took in the entrance hall on which many famous feet before his had trodden. This invitation was only the start, he told himself. As he climbed the grand staircase, the portraits of past prime ministers smiled down at him. The lackey had already advised him that the prime minister, Andrew Lairg, was waiting for him in the study. Lord Edward Hunter was excited to see this room, so full of history and promise. Winston Churchill had slept in it and the present PM had restored the tradition of working there. Hunter had long suspected that he still had a bit of the innocent child about him, and he found enjoyment in the fact that he could continue to be impressed by such environments. The fact that he was part of this world often amazed him, and he hoped it would long continue to do so.

'I'm glad you could make it, Edward.' Andrew Lairg smiled and held out his hand. The PM's grip was firm and dry but not painful. 'I think you've met Connor Wilson, haven't you?'

'Yes, Connor and I have met,' Lord Hunter replied. How could he forget the in-depth grilling the prime minister's right-hand man had given him in the Garrick only two weeks ago? Lord Hunter sat in the seat that Andrew Lairg had motioned towards and stared into the fire which roared in the white marble Adam fireplace. The prime minister sat opposite him whilst Connor Wilson poured the drinks. He didn't bother to ask how Edward liked his whisky. They knew everything about him – or they thought they did.

Andrew Lairg looked preoccupied. 'How's the family?' he asked his guest.

'Its just Mary and me now that the children are off to university,' Hunter replied, hoping that this small talk would not go on for long.

'Are you both in good spirits?' the prime minister asked.

'Fit as fleas.' Hunter had already been through a thorough medical check and MI5 would already have given Downing Street a copy of the report.

'Good, good.' With those words, the gentle, family-man image of the prime minister vanished, and sitting opposite Lord Hunter was the hard-nosed politician who had steered a Labour government through two general election victories in hard times. 'The party cannot afford another cock-up like the Weatherby scandal. He sat in that chair and bloody lied to me.' The prime minister's eyes were cold and hard. 'When that reporter from *The Sun* found her . . . found his bloody wife . . .'

Lairg went quiet and started brooding again. He didn't need to finish. Everyone in the country had seen the pictures of Lady Weatherby and her lover. The scandal was not that she had cuckolded her husband, or the fact that her lover was twenty years her junior. It was the fact that the toy boy was an up-and-coming defence lawyer and she had judged a number of his cases whilst she still sat in the High Court. More worryingly, he had always won. These cases were now all subject to appeal. Lady Weatherby had held the post of Lord Chancellor of England, the highest judge in the land, and her actions meant the whole legal system was now facing one of its worst crises in living memory.

'Is there anything, any fuck-up, no matter how tiny it seems to you, in your past, that can come up and bite us on the arse, Edward?' The PM was known for his language when stressed. 'When you were a High Court judge, did you ever take a bribe? Did you ever knock up a secretary? Do you have a cocaine habit?' These questions were not entirely ridiculous – they were specific rumours that had circulated about the last men to call themselves Lord Chancellor. The reason they were still referred to only as rumours was entirely due to the machinations of Connor Wilson.

'I can wash my dirty laundry in public, Prime Minister.' Lord Edward Hunter held the prime minister's eye as he spoke. 'And I can assure you there will be no bombshells. Although I rather suspect you know all of this already.'

The hush in the Downing Street study was oppressive. The prime minister finally spoke. 'You've been briefed on why you are here, Edward. If I ask you to be Lord Chancellor, will you accept?'

'Yes, Prime Minister.' Lord Hunter could not stop the grin that had spread across his face.

'Good, then we'll make the press announcement tomorrow. You'll be a great Lord Chancellor, an honour to us all.'

'I am your servant, sir,' he nodded at the prime minister. His response was rather formal but he felt elated – even if he had known that he would be offered this position long before he stepped over the threshold.

The serotonin continued to pump round his body long into the night. He was unable to sleep. Throwing his legs over the side of the bed he felt his toes dig into the deep carpet; he inched them along the floor until he found his slippers. His wife, Mary, always a light sleeper, tossed and turned beside him. He wandered down to the kitchen and made himself a warm, milky cocoa. He rested his fine bone-china mug on the arm of his Chesterfield chair in the library, blew on the drink and then sipped cautiously. In the small hours of the night, he could be honest with himself. It wasn't only the excitement of his appointment that prevented sleep. When Lord Hunter had told the prime minister that there were no skeletons in his past he was telling the truth.

But there *was* a secret.

Few people knew about it, and those who did would not speak. Nonetheless, it bothered him that he'd had

41

to hide it from the man who was fulfilling his ultimate ambition.

Lord Hunter took another sip. The cocoa was having the desired effect and he felt sleepy and relaxed. There was no way he could change the past; the secret had remained hidden for twenty years and the chances that it would surface now were remote. The more sleepy he got, the more he convinced himself of this.

The cocoa grew cold as the new Lord Chancellor fell asleep in the chair.

Chapter Seven

DI Duncan Bancho rested his head on his cluttered desk and lightly banged his forehead off it until an unpleasant ache made him stop. The pain took longer to come than it had the last time – or the time before that. He knew that he was pathetic; his life was shit, no money, no promotion and no sex. It was the latter that was really bothering him just now. Peggy had been his last serious fling, and that had been disastrous. Actually, disastrous didn't even come close. The lies and betrayal had cut him deeper than he cared to admit. Well-meaning friends tried to set him up on blind dates, but he wasn't a man who enjoyed sex with strangers. He missed the dull, domestic routine: sitting in on a Saturday night with a carry-out pizza and a cheap bottle of plonk watching crap telly with someone he liked would be his idea of heaven.

Bancho acknowledged that his current attitude was affecting the team; even the assistant chief constable had pulled him in for a pep talk. Given that the actual words were, 'Pull your fucking socks up you miserable bastard, you're getting on everybody's nerves,' he wasn't too sure how helpful it was, but he had to recognize that things were bad. He needed to socialize more, extend the hand of friendship to his colleagues, and all that bollocks. The detective pushed back his chair and wandered out to the operations room to grab a coffee. He put a smile on his face, which he hoped didn't look as forced as it felt – otherwise it would frighten those of a weak disposition.

The chatter in the operations room didn't stop when he walked in the door – that was always a good sign. He wasn't an official weirdo yet. His colleagues were hard at work and looked just as tired as he felt; a few of them even raised their heads and nodded in his direction. Bancho straightened his tie and ran a hand through his hair. PC Tricia Sheehy didn't look too shabby in this light and, even in his miserable state, he had started to notice that she was the one thing that was keeping him going at work. Sometimes the thought of her even cut a few seconds off his banging-head-on-desk routine. She poured him a cup of tar-black coffee out of the percolator.

'Where've you been hiding?' she asked as she tucked a stray blonde hair behind her ear. She was medium height, medium to look at, but with a spark in her brown eyes that penetrated his deadened senses – a bit.

'Bancho! The ACC wants you to call,' shouted a secretary.

Bancho didn't acknowledge her. He sipped his coffee and continued to look at Tricia Sheehy.

'I said, where have you been hiding? You deaf?' Tricia asked again.

'He says it's important,' the secretary bawled even louder this time. 'And I thought he sounded like he actually meant it.'

'I heard you've already been in to see the boss this week . . . you know he doesn't like to be kept waiting. You best go – sir,' said Tricia. She briefly placed her hand on his arm to emphasize that he needed to move, and a quick tingle spread through his body.

Bancho refilled his cup and took it back to his office, which seemed to have got dirtier and lonelier in the five minutes he'd been in the ops room. He put his feet up on the desk, opened the bottom drawer, took out a chocolate digestive biscuit and dialled the ACC.

'What's the problem?' he asked, no preamble necessary between the two men, who knew that formalities only wasted time in the real world.

'Another one's turned up.'

Bancho stared into space. Christ.

'His name is Alan Pearson, thirty-six, he was a mortgage broker,' said the ACC.

'Suicide then? Money problems?'

'Well, that would be bloody convenient, wouldn't it, Bancho? But why the hell do you think I'd be calling you about that? Not a snowball's chance in hell. This is yours now; you and your bloody fancy training sessions in America need to come to the fore, my man. Get this solved, sorted, ended, whatever you want to call it – fast.'

Bancho got over his quick bout of wishful thinking and asked, 'MO? Is it the same as the others?' If so, this was the third in the series of killings.

'Yes. No sign of a struggle, a syringe filled with pure heroin in the right internal jugular, massive overdose, leading to a coronary . . . then the heart was removed post mortem. We've managed to keep the removal of the heart out of the papers, but it's only a matter of time. You're going to have to take over on this one, Duncan, it's definitely a series.' The ACC said it in a way that left no room for objection. Bancho swore under his breath, regretting the day he'd ever let Lothian and Borders Police send him to Quantico for a residential course on serial killers. He'd hated it, hated the bloody Americans, all looking as if they'd stepped out of a film with their chiselled jaws and perfect hair, and hated all the serial-killer profiling stuff which he couldn't see translating to Edinburgh. America was different, too different he thought, the geography, the people – none of it was the same over here; even while on the course, he'd constantly questioned whether there was any point to him being there.

'Right sir,' he said, sighing deeply. 'I'll get the details into the system, see what we can come up with.' Both men fell silent, sending out an outspoken prayer that the updated version of HOLMES – the Home Office Large Major Enquiry System – would come up with something. Anything.

'You up to date with the victims so far?' asked the ACC.

'Surface details – men in their thirties with good jobs, married with kids. Bodies left in their cars. We're still checking to see if there is any connection between the first two men. I take it the new one falls into that pattern?'

'Yes, he does. What about the small stuff on the other two? Do they support the same footb ll team, go to the same bookies, escort agency?'

'The team are going down those avenues and a million more besides,' said Bancho, not holding out much hope, given that nothing had been turned up so far. 'So this is the third body in as many weeks . . . he's working fast. We'd better hope he doesn't accelerate. Forensics is baffled. Even the lab boys are stumped. The bodies are clean except for a stray hair, they've analysed it, but whoever it belongs to is not on any database.'

Bancho wasn't surprised; he knew better than to rely on someone coming up with an instant answer. When this case was solved it would be as a result of legwork and good old-fashioned detective skills, he told himself – no matter what the public thought.

'I want results before the press know what we've got on our hands. Someone out there must know some-thing . . . You find the bastard. That's an order, Bancho. Find him quickly.'

Chapter Eight

Edinburgh castle was floodlit. I stared up at it and daydreamed. The night was black, making my reflection in the glass all too obvious – Brodie McLennan, aged thirty, and feeling ninety. I glanced across at the huge mirror that took up the wall opposite my desk. Contrary to public opinion, I am not a narcissist, but it was a good idea to be able to practise my court speeches in advance. The mirror was actually the idea of my grandfather, Lord MacGregor, a former Lord Justice Clerk. He had very strict ideas on the standard of pleadings in court and he was determined I would meet his exacting standards, and that meant paying attention to the superficial as well. The fact that he was on a round-the-world cruise with the second wife that I hadn't yet met didn't mean that he wasn't still interfering with my life, even if it was via the presence of the mirror that constantly reminded me of him. Still, I wouldn't have it any other way. I loved that old man, even if I never told him.

There are events that change the course of your life, and the trial of Kailash Coutts was one. Not only did I find my grandfather but my birth mother. Kailash was charged with the murder of Lord Arbuthnot, Scotland's top-ranking judge – and my father. She walked free at the end of the trial and they walked into my life. If I wasn't already screwed up by then, this put the tin lid on it. Kailash had been notorious throughout Scotland, and further afield, for a long time. What was in the public eye was that she was a dominatrix who pretty much ran the sex scene in Edinburgh – she'd probably tell me to emphasize that she ran the *classy* side, one of the many things she and I disagreed on. Kailash had been involved in a cause célèbre that had almost ruined the firm I worked for, given that one of the senior partners had found himself and his 'preferences' splashed across the front page of all the tabloids, thanks to his dominatrix of choice, Kailash again. When she was accused of killing one of Scotland's top law figures, I was staggered to find myself defending her at her request – however, that paled into insignificance as events unfolded and I discovered she was my birth mother . . . and that the man she was thought to have killed was my child-abusing, rapist father.

The mirror showed me that I had inherited his looks and her brains. It wasn't as disastrous a combination as it sounds at first – Kailash was one smart cookie. Long dark auburn hair hung in curls – or rats' tails, depending on the weather – around my shoulders. I didn't have the usual redhead's complexion because Kailash is mixed race and I had taken some of her skin tone. None of her dress sense, though, as she constantly informed me. In her words, I looked a bloody mess. A wave of self-consciousness flooded over me as I peered at the espresso stains on my blouse. I was a messy eater; it's why leathers were so right for me.

The buzzer sounded.

'Brodie? A Dr Graham Marshall is on the phone and he says it's urgent,' said Lavender. She was in the third trimester of a much-wanted pregnancy and she sounded exhausted. I was surprised she was even answering calls – she had suffered from morning sickness so badly that she rarely made it out of the ladies' these days. She had been grasping on to the fact that all the books her husband Eddie read assured them both that most women kissed goodbye to the nausea and vomiting once the first three months had passed. Lavender always did have to be different, though – and, at nearly seven months, it looked as if she might be one of the unlucky few who was going to throw up for the whole time. I felt sorry for her – but, after watching her and Eddie go through the misery of a miscarriage last year, I was secretly giving thanks every day she was sick as it meant she was still carrying that precious baby.

'Make an appointment for him, Lavender.'

'He says it's urgent.'

'Too bad. They always say that, as well you know. I've got a family dinner tonight and if I'm late Kailash will kill me.'

'He really did sound as if it was urgent this time,' she answered. 'Anyway – don't you recognize the name? He's that plastic surgeon. He's very good. Apparently.' I know that Lavender – and Kailash – thought I should know every mover and shaker in the city, but recognizing the names of plastic surgeons was surely taking things a bit far? Unless there was an implication that I might need an appointment myself.

'It's always urgent,' I repeated. 'What's it about?'

'He won't tell me.'

Dr Graham Marshall just went up in my estimation. Lavender was the nosiest person I've ever met, and if he'd managed to keep his reason for needing an 'urgent' appointment from her, he might be intriguing.

My watch showed that it was six o'clock and I had to be at The Vineyard for seven thirty. Kailash could do everything except cook, so we tried whenever possible to make her take us to restaurants. If I saw Dr Marshall, it would mean I wouldn't have time to change and Kailash would give me a bollocking. No, it wasn't worth that. This meal meant a lot to her – when Grandad got back from his cruise, she and my half-sister Connie were all going off skiing, so it was the last time I'd see them for a while. I still felt pretty pissed off that I couldn't go due to work pressures and money worries. If I missed the meal, too, I'd pay the price.

'I collected your dry cleaning – it's behind my desk,' said Lavender. It wasn't the first time she'd read my mind; one quick glance told me my shoes were scuffed but I'd get away with it. I knew that if Lavender was thinking ahead then she'd already decided I should talk to this man.

'Okay, put him on.'

'Ms McLennan, thank you for taking this call. When does your secretary leave?' I felt the hackles on the back of my neck rise. I could say things about Lavender, just as she could (and did) about me, but I'd be damned if

I'd let anyone else. She wasn't some daft secretary to be bundled away on a client's whim. 'I don't mean to be offensive,' he continued. 'It's simply that a man in my position can't be too careful.'

'Dr Marshall, I can assure you that anything said within these walls is safer than in the Bank of England.' I knew that for a fact, because in a former life Lavender Ironside had hacked into the bank's files. It was why she'd changed her name and moved to Scotland – I think that the bank here had so far been saved from her expertise.

'Ms McLennan, give me an appointment tonight and I will pay you fifty thousand pounds. If I agree to hire you, I will give you a retainer of a great deal more.'

I was speechless. I hated to be bought for money because it reminded me of Kailash's business, but a quick glance at Lavender's face as she listened to the man on speakerphone let me know which way the land lay. She was nodding furiously, daring me to say no.

'Six thirty will be fine, Dr Marshall. Do you know where my office is?'

'Yes,' was the brief reply before the line went dead.

'Arrogant bastard,' I hissed at the phone. There was no way I could refuse the fee. High-profile trials like the Kenny Cameron case were all very well but, even though I made a fair whack out of legal aid, they didn't pay the enormous overheads the firm carried. The cases that did were more mundane: a two-cop breach of the peace or an assault that I could farm out to another lawyer in the firm. I grabbed the phone and left a message for Kailash to stop her heading for the restaurant until my meeting was over.

'I'm out of here,' Lavender said, already putting on her coat, which was struggling to contain her baby bump. 'I wonder what he wants,' she said; a smile crossed her lips knowing she would be the one to type up my file notes. Nothing from the next meeting would be beyond her knowledge.

Chapter Nine

Six thirty had come and gone and there was still no sign of Dr Marshall. I stared out the window. Perhaps he was parking his car. Perhaps he'd changed his mind. The wind was whipping the bare branches of the trees as the rain bounced off the pavement.

I opened the door to Lavender's room where my dry cleaning hung on wire coat hangers covered by plastic. I rifled through them. Each item was, to be frank, rubbish and, really, I had nothing to wear, pathetic though it sounded. Kailash would have a field day – she'd get to inform me with her superior fashion sense and all-round personal style perfection just where I was going wrong. Deciding that I might as well take the Fat Boy, which was parked downstairs, I threw off my suit and struggled into my leathers, leaving the top button on the trousers undone until they'd eased off a bit. Switching the desk light on, I settled down to go over tomorrow's court files, but no sooner had I sat down than there was a knock at my office door. A shadow of doubt crossed my mind: recent events had made me wary and, as I recalled Ma Boyle drawing her finger across her throat, the last thing I wanted was an after-hours visit from the Boyles. I tried to settle my nerves. Although my own office suite was deserted, the building was filled with young associate lawyers working overtime trying to make partner. They weren't exactly hired muscle, but surely their talents could stretch to calling the police if needs be?

Dr Graham Marshall didn't wait for me to answer the door, walking in as if he owned the place. I watched our reflections in the mirror and so did he. He was judging me, his eyes lingering on the open button of my trousers, no doubt thinking that he could fix the fat for me for a couple of grand. I tucked my T-shirt in tightly so it was even more obvious that I'd recently packed on a couple of pounds, or ten. I took a sip of the cold black coffee on my desk. If I was going to spar with this one I needed all the energy I could lay my hands on.

'Ms McLennan,' he said, and held out a manicured hand. His hands were softer than mine, but then he'd probably never changed the engine oil on a motorbike. I noticed ruby cufflinks on his French cuffed shirt and remembered reading that rubies the colour of blood confer invulnerability on the wearer. Tough: he needed me; that much was obvious from the offer of big money and the demand for an urgent appointment. He wore a bespoke pinstriped suit with an immaculate cut and looked like a cover model for *Men's Health*. Dr Graham Marshall was incredibly good looking, and he knew it. Damn, he knew that I knew it.

'I was invited to the New Club last Wednesday. Have you been?' he asked out of nowhere.

The New Club was a very old, distinguished club where the elite of Edinburgh meet. On Wednesday nights they debate obscure topics. I wasn't sure what this had to do with whatever Marshall wanted me to help him with, but I had the right answer. 'My grandfather is a member and I've had dinner there many times,' I said.

'I didn't see you.'

'I was otherwise engaged last week. I find it filled with irrelevant old men and equally irrelevant ideas, so I don't go unless I'm dragged kicking and screaming through its hallowed portals.' I got some pleasure from being deliberately combative.

'Well, on Wednesday they were discussing something rather more relevant: should readers boycott books written by criminals when the proceeds are going directly to families of victims?' It was getting late and I was in no mood to play his games; then I thought of the fee and remembered the client is always right. I cleared my throat and humoured him.

'I take it that this theoretical book was bought by a publisher not because of the criminal's talent as a writer but because the reader would believe it was a step-by-step manual of how a crime was actually committed?'

'Oh, obviously. Lord McNair argued that such a book should not be published because of the pain and humiliation it would cause the victims – what do you think?' The silence was heavy, my stomach rumbled; I hadn't eaten since midday and my dinner at The Vineyard was on hold.

'I believe in free speech and freedom of the press. I don't believe criminals should profit from their crimes, but that wasn't happening with this theoretical case, so the book should have been published.' I wanted to stop playing games, but I also wanted the fee he had promised me. Marshall smiled at me and nodded before his hand went into his inside pocket and pulled out his wallet. He handed me a cheque for fifty thousand pounds. 'Thank you for granting me an appointment, Ms McLennan,' he said, smiling.

'You're welcome,' I said, trying to sound as cool as possible while inwardly wondering if I could possibly hide my glee at all this desperately needed money.

'I'd also be grateful – and I'd imagine you would too – if you would accept this additional sum as a retainer.' He handed me another cheque – this one was for eight hundred and twelve thousand, two hundred and seventy-two pounds, and sixty-five pence. I stared at it. The amount was bizarre . . . and familiar. Confusion reigned on my face. Dr Marshall coughed to get my attention.

'It's the exact amount of the bank overdraft of Lothian and St Clair WS as at close of business last Friday,' he said.

'How the hell did you get our bank details?' I asked in a voice much calmer than I expected. Most law firms have overdrafts – expenses are high and client fees can be slow in coming in. The banks are happy to extend credit because they have the deeds of the partners' houses, but recently Lothian and St Clair had rather overplayed this side of things. Added to a credit crunch and overall financial meltdown, we were in deep shit. I was pissed that Marshall had investigated our finances, as well as being amazed that he'd got through every shred of data protection there was, but, on the other hand, the fee plus the retainer would pay the bank off and maybe I would sleep easier at night. It was a tricky one. I didn't even want to imagine at this stage what I was going to have to defend.

'No,' I said, handing the cheque back to him. I never had claimed to have any business sense. 'No thank you, Dr Marshall.'

'Oh dear. I'm sorry, Ms McLennan. I'm sorry. I thought it was standard business practice to know about a lawyer before hiring their firm, so believed that if you agreed to act for me you could have the fifty thousand pounds consultation fee and put the rest in the firm, account as a retainer.' This time there was no smile on his face. I said nothing. 'I may not need your expertise – one can only hope – but if I should, then I would expect you to drop everything and act on my behalf.'

'Do you have a case outstanding?' I asked, unable to stop myself from trying to find out more.

'I'd prefer not to discuss the potential legal action until it happens. You do have my sincere apology if there was anything about this whole business that you might have found distasteful. Do we have a deal, Ms McLennan? One thing I can assure you of, if I am charged I am innocent.' He held out his hand again. I'd cooled down and needed to think about this second chance, not that I wanted him to know that.

I imagined Lavender's face – and words – if I turned down this much money.

And Kailash.

And Grandad.

And the other partners.

Shit, shit, shit.

'Deal.' I shook his hand.

When the door closed behind Graham Marshall, I waved the cheques in the air and did my victory dance. I was slightly disgusted at myself for being bought, but I was also delighted that things might be on more solid ground with the firm. And, as Marshall had said, he might not even need me – in which case, it would be the easiest fifty grand I'd ever made.

The office clock showed it was late – there was probably no point in going to The Vineyard. I picked up the phone and called Kailash. I didn't even get to speak before I heard her imperious voice snap, 'It's late. Get over here now. Another wasted evening.'

She closed the phone on me and I sighed deeply. I didn't want to go to my mother's but I knew I had to. Kailash would still have been working, waiting for my call. Glasgow Joe took care of the casino, so I would have to break bread with my mother in her Danube Street brothel. Did all families work this way? I wondered, knowing the answer full well, even as I thought of the question.

There was something much more obvious on my mind, though – who in God's name was Graham Marshall? I couldn't help but think he must be guilty as sin if he was offering me this much cash for an appointment without being accused of anything. That wasn't the lawyer in me talking – that would be the thought of any sane individual faced with a well-known figure and a stash of money being thrown at her. Now, all I had to do was wait and see exactly what it was I would be expected to do.

Chapter Ten

The door was no different to any of the other respectable doors in the road. It was painted a conservative black in accordance with planning regulations, and the brass plate beside the bell gave the number of the house but not the identity or occupation of its inhabitants.

Thankfully.

When I parked the bike outside it I was in a good mood again. The cheques from Graham Marshall were in my pocket and I was certain they wouldn't bounce. I had Googled Marshall before I left the office and his fame was more widespread and greater than even Lavender had led me to believe. The man was world famous. He operated alone in a small private hospital in Edinburgh; celebrities and the filthy rich came here from all over the world, just to be nipped and tucked by him. I had decided that it was a good sign that he chose me; my reputation was known amongst the criminal fraternity but he was an outsider. Naturally I was curious about the nature of his potential case – not to mention his manners – but many professionals and businesses retain legal firms for all sorts of reasons. The mistake 'respectable' people often make when getting into trouble is to instruct one of the big-name commercial firms, who may be excellent at drawing up a lease, but don't know their arse from their elbow when it comes to court work.

I rang the bell and waited, but not for long. Kailash's staff knew better than to keep a punter hanging around on the doorstep. Malcolm opened the door. He looked well. As usual his make-up was impeccable. His eyes flicked over me and I was found wanting. Helmet hair and unidentifiable squashed things on my leathers meant that I didn't pass his grooming test. I handed him my helmet and walked in.

'You're in trouble,' he warned as I marched down the Georgian hallway. The brothel (or 'club', as Malcolm preferred to call it) was very upmarket, more like a chic boutique hotel than a sex joint. In my mind, no matter what colour the paint job was, it was still a knocking shop. I half turned to face him. Like a child I pulled the cheque out from my inside pocket and waved it in his face. He shrugged his shoulders.

'She won't be impressed. Kailash could write you a cheque for twice that amount from her housekeeping and never even notice it was gone.' He reached out and held my elbow. 'You only have to ask her, Brodie – she'd love to help you if you need it. She doesn't want you to struggle like she did.' Only Malcolm could compare the financial struggles of an Edinburgh lawyer with Kailash's past. He had been Kailash's dresser for decades. They'd met in Amsterdam when she was an underage runaway. He patched her up when the punters got too rough, and

61

he was with her when she made the momentous decision to become a 'top', the one who wields the whip. I had become acquainted with the world of bondage, domination and sadomasochism when we were reunited.

Malcolm moved ahead of me and removed the thick blue rope that barred the stairs down to the private quarters. I followed him down into the kitchen, where Kailash sat at a substantial oak table surrounded by shiny red Poggenpohl units. A couple of girls, between clients, were at the other end of the table drinking tequila. Kailash poured me a mug of tea and passed it across. I sat down beside her, feeling like something stronger than tea – but having seen the look in her eye, I wasn't going to ask.

'So . . . who is this VIP client, the one who ranks above us?' she asked immediately.

Kailash had a golden rule – never betray or let down family or friends. It was one that she had only taken to relatively recently, but she was now a true convert. What had happened to and between us in recent years had made her convinced that we would never be apart again, even if we were still learning about each other, but it was hard going at times. Clients and work were way down her list of life's priorities, and she made that clear to everyone. The girls and boys she employed were the family she'd made herself, so although she spent long hours in her businesses, she didn't consider it work. I didn't want to say too much because Graham Marshall clearly wanted discretion, but there was no harm in saying he'd come to my office; besides, he might be a friend of hers. I leaned forward, my voice hushed.

'Now this is top secret.' I glanced around at the girls but a flash of annoyance crossed all their faces. In their line of work, they knew how to keep their traps shut. 'Don't breathe a word of this unless I give you the say-so.' The girls nodded. Kailash rolled her eyes and feigned disinterest.

'Dr Graham Marshall,' I said.

Even Kailash perked up at the sound of his name. 'Really?' She thought for a moment. 'He's good, Brodie, very good – I've used him.'

My mother rarely spoke about what she'd had done. She was beautiful, and naturally so – but she wasn't shy about enhancing and investing in what she already had. I looked at her in the warm glow of the real fire in the kitchen. Gorgeous dark hair – but filled out with extensions. Perfect figure for someone in her forties (a damn sight better than mine) – but undoubtedly helped by impossibly pert implants, something Kailash would never deign to speak about directly. A face to launch a thousand fantasies – fantasies that were helped by veneers, acid peels, Botox and plumpers. She was encased in a business suit that probably cost as much as one of the procedures she saw as an investment, and was walking in five-inch heels, looking as if she was enjoying a level of comfort that most women could only manage with a pair of Crocs. Kailash Coutts was a product. She had created herself after her early years were ruined by others. Raped as a child, left for dead by one of my father's minions after she gave birth to me in chains, my mother had found strength from God knows where, and she had turned what men had used her for into her fortune.

'So, what did he do for you?' I asked, knowing she wouldn't answer.

My mother stared at me as if I'd just asked the last time she'd picked her nose and eaten it. 'For the girls,' she said, 'I've used him for the girls. He's discreet and he treats them well.'

'And he's gorgeous,' said Dina, one of Kailash's favourites, a tiny little redhead from Dublin.

'How does that help?' I asked. 'I think I'd prefer it was some ugly bloke cutting me up rather than one who I was going to embarrass myself about. I'd want to know he knew what he was doing rather than just been making himself look good.'

'He does,' said Dina, 'he knows exactly what he's doing. But where's the harm in having someone who you wouldn't kick out of bed?'

'Who wouldn't you kick out of bed?' asked Rochelle, an Amazonian New Yorker who was one of Kailash's newest acquisitions. Kailash had been on a bit of a spree lately, bringing in quite a lot of new workers, and I liked this girl a lot – she still seemed as if she was in control, as if she could walk away from this life any minute. 'If they pay enough, they get to stay even if they look like . . .' She paused. 'A shitey arse. Right?' Kailash had an international operation. Listening to this United Nations of whores always made me laugh: it was like foreign footballers on the telly suddenly coming out with Glaswegian accents just because they'd been at Celtic for a month. 'This guy? Your mom put me in touch with him when I first got here,' she told me. 'I knew a few surgeons back home who were okay with working girls, but this one – he's actually a nice guy. Doesn't want to turn us all into porno lookalikes – looks at what you've got and makes it even better.'

'What's he like off duty?' asked Dina.

'Arrogant,' I said.

'The best surgeons are . . . Why has he retained you?' Kailash asked. 'You don't do commercial work.'

'I don't think it's commercial.'

'Well, you don't do medical negligence cases either,' she said.

'For the sort of money he's offering, I could learn. Anyway, I don't know what his exact problem is and if I did I wouldn't tell you . . . client confidentiality,' I said. All I knew was that Marshall had seemed to hint that it would be a criminal charge. 'I'm sorry I wrecked the dinner. Was Connie disappointed?'

'Yes, she was, but she'll get over it. She's all drama and hormones just now anyway.' I looked closely at my mother when she said this, but there was no sign of resentment. I was born when Kailash was only thirteen – she hadn't had the luxury of being a stroppy teenager like my half-sister Connie.

'What about you? Do you forgive me?' I asked.

'I've got work to do,' Kailash answered. 'Good luck with Dr Marshall.' She planted a cold kiss on my forehead, giving me a taste of my own medicine. Kailash was a harsh disciplinarian – it was the quality she had built her fortune on. I should have known better than to break the golden rule – family, family, family. But, if this was my family, they were all telling me one thing – I shouldn't judge Marshall too quickly. These girls weren't stupid, they could read people, and he seemed to have their vote. I had my own little research group here. I could only assume that Marshall was about to be sued by a client for some sort of malpractice and, if he had fucked up someone's face or whatever, they must be even richer than him, given the amount of money he'd offered me. This might be interesting after all.

Chapter Eleven

She knew that the body had been found by now and she assumed that the police were treating it as a serial case. Actually, she could only ever make *assumptions* about what the police would do. All she knew for sure was that they were stupid. That they screwed up. That, even when they had a cast-iron case, they still got things wrong.

She needed to leave them in no doubt.

Ever since she had got here, she had known that this was where it would end. The years of waiting, of being used and being treated like a victim – it all stopped here. There were things that she couldn't get out of her mind, images that wouldn't go away, but these days she had other pictures to put in their place. When you knew what you were doing (as she undoubtedly did), there was a comfort to be found in killing. She felt that she had found her purpose in life – and God knows she had needed one for so very long.

There were those along the way who had helped her to get to this place, and they were often good people. They had no idea that they were assisting her to do what she needed to do, but they were part of it, nonetheless. However, there were others, of course there were others, who had been the real impetus. She thought about it for a moment. She had no way to describe what had been done to her. There were no words. There were no emotions. No one could understand. No one could empathize. But *it* had happened. *It* was done. Now, all she could do was make sure that the payment was exacted from the right place.

She had her methods by this point. There had been a lot to organize and it had taken a while to do it, but she was exactly where she needed to be. She thought back on the three men already dead at her hands. She laughed to herself, a low, soft noise that made her seem gentle and warm. She had read all of the books on how to do this, on how to avoid being caught, and on what killers do. She couldn't believe that some of them kept mementoes, trophies. She had all of that in her head. She had nothing against those men as such – yes, she hated them, and had taken their lives, but it wasn't personal. What on earth could she have taken from them? They were just symbols in themselves. Was she expected to fill her handbag with cufflinks? Locks of hair? Photos of them in their final moments? She had what she wanted from them – their bodies, their deaths; and the absolute knowledge that they had helped her.

Since she had arrived here, it had all been so easy. These men, they all thought their needs were so important. Each of them so easy to spot. She always looked for particular cars – single businessmen were no use, she needed to make sure that they were guilty beyond her own certainty. Bigger cars, expensive cars, but ones with baby or booster seats. Little triangles on the back saying 'baby on board'. Mr Men sunscreens that had been rolled up but were still identifiable. Good men, good fathers. Making sure their children were safe, happy and provided for. And while they themselves were away from home, what was wrong with a few minutes of downtime?

Every businessman in every city in the country knew where to go. If they didn't, there were websites to tell them. There had always been so much publicity about the red-light district in Edinburgh that it wasn't hard to find. Even if the girls had been moved around a bit, it didn't take much to discover where. The drugs were everywhere, too. Edinburgh had changed. There used to be less dependency amongst the prostitutes in the capital than in other cities, but in the last couple of years it had got as bad as anywhere. Cheap rates for everything. That worked well for her on two levels. She could get heroin easily and for next to nothing. And because she was clean, good looking and articulate, she appealed to the better class of punter as soon as he rolled down his window.

The first one? He couldn't believe his luck. Neither could she. It had been so easy for both of them. When she approached his car, she had expected to be nervous, but there was actually an amazing feeling of calm. She had been without true purpose for so long that this felt like the real thing, as if she was finally doing what she should be doing. His accent was closer to hers than she felt comfortable with, so she'd had to make adjustments there, but she had learned from that point not to be so worried. It wasn't as if her victims were going to be around to give the police clues. She laughed softly to herself again. Her stomach had lurched at one point – not when she killed him, but when she had to . . . do what she had to do. The next two were easier. She was getting better, and she'd keep getting better.

Now – now she had to find the next one. Time was pressing on. This had to end.

Chapter Twelve

I was driving slowly because the rain-soaked cobbles were dangerous, and lack of speed meant my helmet visor was steamed up. By the time I reached Suzie Wong's in George Street I needed a stiff drink, or six. The weather had forced people off the streets, and even Edinburgh's premier night spot – as described by its totally unbiased owner – looked deserted.

Music echoed round the cavernous cellar, but the bar staff outnumbered customers. Moses Tierney, club owner and leader of the Dark Angels, looked pissed off at pretty much everything. It didn't appear my welcome here would be any warmer than at Kailash's but I was proved wrong very quickly, and not for the first time. Moses waved at me as soon as I came into his line of vision, and pulled a bottle of champagne out of the fridge.

'I hope that's not the watered-down stuff you sell to your customers,' I said, accepting a glass, knocking it back quickly and indicating that I needed an immediate refill.

'It's not watered down, Brodie – it's just a brand no

one quite appreciates yet. This is the real McCoy though.'
Moses was celebrating my result in the murder trial. He
hated the Boyle family for reasons that were not entirely
known to me, so anything that upset his rival, Ma Boyle,
was a source of rejoicing for him. A rumble of high heels
and raucous laughter weaved into the bar in the guise of
a huge hen party. Moses's eyes lit up. His night had just
got even better. Left alone to prop up the bar, I watched
the staff spring into action. They shook and stirred sixteen
cocktails in record time, which was just as well, because
the girls looked as if they would swallow them as fast as
the barman could make them. The party would definitely
have passed Kailash's scrutiny test. Spray-tanned to within
an inch of their lives, I hated to admit they looked gorgeous,
young, and vibrant. It would have taken a good chunk
of Dr Marshall's cheque to have paid for their hair
extensions alone, and I wondered how they could afford
it – then one glance in the mirror at my own sorry reflection told me that their money had been well spent.

Moses ignored me, continuing his banter with the
girls as he filled up my empty glass at the bar. The bottle
was almost finished: surely I hadn't drunk that much?
My empty stomach growled and the drunken dizziness
hit me like a sledgehammer just as Glasgow Joe walked
in. He didn't acknowledge me. I'm not sure he even had
time to notice I was sitting there as the hen-party girls
swamped him, sticking their hands up his kilt in a
desperate bid to find out if he was a true Scotsman. He
didn't put up a fight. Behind the drinks dispensers were
smoky mirrored tiles. I couldn't avoid my reflection, and
it wasn't a pleasant sight. I looked old. My ex-husband

looked gorgeous and every girl in the hen party agreed with me. I'd split up with Jack Deans, my sort-of-boyfriend, three months ago, and I was having romantic thoughts about the spin cycle on my washing machine, so the sight of Joe combined with all the champagne I'd glugged on an empty stomach was having quite an effect.

Glasgow Joe was the bad boy from my childhood. I'd hankered after him for years as we both pretended to be just friends, and then I married him in a cheap Vegas ceremony that lasted longer than the marriage itself. I still hankered after him.

He came up behind me, hooked his finger in the loop of my trousers and whispered, 'How about you and I get out of here, gorgeous?' I guess he must have noticed me after all. I swivelled round to face him. Joe was about twice my size when I was sitting, and he had to bend down to speak into my face. He had a broad face with chiselled cheekbones and a couple of faded scars above his brow. Like an old tomcat he wore the marks of previous fights well. His collar-length hair was swept back from his face; a couple of stray grey hairs were obvious at his temple. His skin was clear and tanned and he had a touch of stubble on his cheeks and chin. He was untouchable – nobody who didn't have a death wish messed with him – and I'd thrown him away on more than one occasion.

God, the drink was getting to me.

Glasgow Joe held my chin with his free hand, and his dark eyes stared into mine. He didn't blink. They say that people in love stare into their partner's eyes for eighty per cent of the time – it stimulates the sex hormones. Mine were certainly beginning to stir.

'There's a lot to think about,' I slurred.

'What's there to think about? I'm promising you more booze, a carry-out pizza with up to three toppings of your choice, and any sexual position you can think of – within reason.'

'The pizza sounds good.'

'Don't kid yourself, darlin' – you like the sound of the rest of it too.'

'I need time to think,' I said, guzzling some more champagne and trying to sound ladylike. The truth was that I would have jumped on Joe quicker than the pizza order would have been ready, but, even in my drunken state, I knew that he didn't do one-night stands. At least, not with me. Anything more was a scary prospect, at least for me. Every reconciliation we'd ever had had broken down because he'd wanted to get married again, have children, and settle down. The more I learned about my own history, the less likely that seemed to be an option. So I pushed him away. I insulted him and bristled at him. I told him I wasn't interested in anything but casual sex, and then flaunted Jack Deans in his face. And all the time I was desperate for him.

He could probably see my forehead furrow with all of these thoughts.

'You're thinking too much, Brodie,' he growled, kissing my neck. 'Let me go over the high points for you – food, drink, sex.' His finger was still hooked into my trousers. I inadvertently glanced at the door – and that's how I ended up with Glasgow Joe back in my bed again. As if I didn't have enough trouble in my life.

Chapter Thirteen

Kailash keeps telling me that I need to act more like a lady – usually I tell her to piss off (which seems to highlight her point), but sometimes I see what's she's getting at. What went on between me and Joe when we first got back to the flat stays between me and Joe. Afterwards? Well, that's a different matter.

By the time I'd managed to drag myself out of bed, he was snoring softly and the first rays of morning were creeping in through the wooden blinds of my bedroom windows. I crept through to the kitchen, pulling his T-shirt over my head as I walked, smelling everything I liked about him on it. I didn't know whether to wake my flatmate Louisa up as I guessed she'd probably been listening all night anyway – maybe I should just get the postmortem over and done with. I decided against it. I wanted to keep this to myself, even exclude Joe, just for a little while longer.

When I was with him, when it was just the two of us, everything seemed so right, but as soon as I started thinking about things, I went down the road that had caused us to split up more times than I could count.

Where could this possibly lead? I wasn't the type for settling down. I wasn't maternal. It would be obvious to anyone who knew the tiniest part of my life history that what I had come from was never going to make me average wife-and-mother material, but the truth was that I did actually have lots of strong women in my life – they just weren't enough to convince me that I could do what they had done in their own ways.

My mother, Mary McLennan, had been my rock. I had been through the time of worrying whether I was being horrible to Kailash by still thinking of Mary as my 'real' mother, but Mary had done everything for me and I missed her more and more as I got older. Kailash? She had given birth to me, and she had saved my life, but she was hardly the perfect Mum. How much of that was my fault, I don't know. Malcolm had been right when he had said that she would do anything for me, but I still reacted against that. What sort of mother could I possibly be when my own background was so fucked up?

I knew that it was what Joe wanted – was that enough? On top of everything, I'd watched what Lavender and Eddie had gone through last year and it had broken my heart. They had wanted that baby so badly, we all had, and when Lav had had the miscarriage, I had felt so hopeless. Now, every day was a day closer to the baby she was desperate to have – but the pain wouldn't stop there, would it? She'd be terrified all her life, never knowing if she could truly protect it. I didn't think I was strong enough to cope with that, and I didn't know whether I had enough love in me.

Joe wouldn't give in. He persevered, told me we were

made for each other, and I wanted to believe him so badly – and every so often we fell back into bed again. Were we going to follow that pattern forever? This was part of it – me, alone in the kitchen in the early hours of the morning, thinking about things too much and being torn between those thoughts and yet wanting to just think about how much I . . . loved him. I did. I loved him. I'd be buggered if I'd tell him, though.

'You thinking about me?' came the voice from behind my left shoulder.

'That you, Louisa?' I asked, refusing to let myself soften at his words.

'No offence – but do I look or sound like that weird wee lassie? Nice weird wee lassie that she is,' Joe answered.

'Want a coffee?'

'No. I want to talk to you.'

'Want a coffee?'

'You're not funny, Brodie,' he answered. 'Well, you are – but not at times like this.' He pulled me back from the kettle to the barstool I had just left. 'Sit.'

'Woof,' I barked back at him.

'Remember. You're not funny.' As I sat on the high seat, I was closer to his eye level than usual and my feet dangled nervously, knowing the lecture I was in for. 'We can't keep on doing this. *I* can't keep on doing this. Do you want the whole speech or just the highlights?' he asked, not waiting for an answer. 'We're not getting any younger. Life isn't getting any easier. But it could be, if we were together. You could have everything, Brodie – so why won't you let yourself?'

'I've got everything I need, thanks,' I muttered.

'You're not a bloody teenager. Christ, there's not much to choose between you and Connie sometimes. You after a new mobile phone or something with all that pouting that's going on? I've tried it every way with you. I've bought you lollipops when we were kids. I've battered the bullies in the playground. Christ, I'm still battering the bullies – it's just a bigger playground. I've run away from you, I've married you. I've ignored it when you bring shit like Jack Deans back to your bed; I've hit the roof when you bring shit like Jack Deans back to your bed. What's left for me to do? What is it going to take?'

'Before what?' I asked him.

'What?'

'What's it going to take before what? Before you leave? Before you give up?'

'Is that what you think's going to happen, Brodie? Is that what you're scared of?'

I snorted. 'I'm scared of nothing.'

'You should be,' Joe said quietly. 'You should be.'

'Because you *are* going to leave, aren't you?'

Joe whirled the barstool round to face him and wrapped his huge arms around me. I was shaking and I hoped he'd have the manners to ignore it. He lifted me down from the seat and wrapped me up some more, moving my mess of tangled curls from my left ear. 'I'll never leave you, Brodie,' he whispered. 'Never. I can't. But by Christ, can you make it all a bit easier? Please?'

I don't remember what happened after that.

Well, I do – but I'm trying so hard to be a lady now . . .

Chapter Fourteen

After some more ladylike bedroom action, I was on my way to a routine visit of the cells in St Leonards, a courtesy call on the flotsam and jetsam I call my clients who were picked up on a variety of charges. None of them was particularly serious, and they could have been handled by Lavender's husband, Eddie Gibb, who also worked in the practice, but I needed time to think about the consequences of my lust-driven actions of the night before. Glasgow Joe had a meeting at the casino with Kailash, and our business commitments and lack of sleep meant that we both had an excuse to leave the flat quickly without talking about anything in any more detail – that was par for the course with us, and the fact that we had almost seemed to be getting somewhere in the early hours of the morning didn't really mean anything; I was sure we'd be back to square one next time we met. And I was sure that I would get the blame for it.

The streets were deserted as I kicked the Fat Boy into life, turning left up the hill to Hanover Street where the black top was as shiny and black as Moses Tierney's nail varnish. It meant only one thing; any cobbled road in

Edinburgh would be as slick and dangerous as if it were covered in ice. A quick mental calculation meant I would have to take a detour through the Grassmarket. The Grassmarket is a half-trendy area filled with boutique hotels and expensive restaurants, but for years it was the haunt of the hopeless alcoholics, down-and-outs, and the homeless. A few shelters for these men and women are still there, and they manage to stop the area gentrifying into what it wants to be. It's not a bad place – there are some nice shops and clubs, but I wouldn't want to hang around there at night any longer than I had to, outside of Festival weeks. There are usually cops hanging around, though, so I stopped at a red light, even though there was hardly anyone about to potentially run over. As the engine idled I looked around, remembering it was Kailash's birthday soon. I was trying to squint into the window of the cashmere shop. I had to shake my head at what I saw, not quite able to believe it.

Dr Graham Marshall was the last person I expected to witness wandering through the entrance door of the Mission hostel. I was so shocked the bike wobbled beneath me, and for a sickening moment I thought I was going to lose control. Last time I came off the bike I broke my arm – I couldn't afford to let that happen again. Lavender would kill me, for starters.

What on earth was Marshall doing here? He was hardly homeless, or the do-gooder type, and, unless there was more money in begging than I'd ever imagined, he wasn't going to pick up any new patients by hanging around here. Not only did I want to know why he was here, I needed to talk to him. The morning had come with a lot of questions I wanted answering. Despite last night's activity with Joe, I had woken up needing to get more information on my new client. I was still burning to know how the hell he'd got the firm's bank details for one. I parked the bike. What I had to say to Marshall would only take a minute; nonetheless I put the lock on the front wheel, remembering my own concerns about the place.

A man and a woman stood on the steps outside the hostel smoking thin roll-ups. The man seemed to be wearing every piece of clothing he had ever found; none of it fitted, and a grey overcoat tied with a piece of string covered it all. Black dreadlocks hung around his shoulders, and on top of his head was a big Jamaican knitted beret. His age was indeterminable, his face covered by a salt-and-pepper beard, but he smiled at me and pointed to the bike. Harleys were a great icebreaker. The woman held a tin of super-strength lager in her hand. She was the size of an undernourished ten-year-old, but in spite of the abuse she'd clearly been through, her body had a youthfulness to it. I have to admit that my jaw slackened when she revealed a completely toothless grin. I smiled back at them and moved inside the door, where heat and the smell of food hit me. I hesitated for a moment, wondering whether I'd made a mistake. It was incredibly unlikely that Marshall would be here – but there also weren't many men who looked like him in Edinburgh, so who could I have possibly mixed him up with? No, it was Marshall I had seen, and I needed to find out what he was up to.

'If you've two hands and are ready to use them, come

in. If not, stop cluttering up my lobby,' a Leither shouted from inside the Mission. The owner of the voice, a wizened pensioner in an oilcloth apron, smiled at me and held out her hands. She looked as tough as leather but her eyes were calm and contented. 'Ina Gibbon,' she said, and touched my elbow as if she wanted to share her world with me.

My nose wrinkled at the smell of the place. I wasn't sure I wanted any part of this, but I did need to speak to Graham Marshall. I allowed myself to be taken to the kitchen. Industrial-sized vats of soup were being mixed by this thimble-sized woman; she was struggling, so before I'd even had time to remove my leather jacket, I started stirring the ham and lentils. I expected her to ask what the hell I was doing there, a stranger in this world, but she took a different tack after having a good look at me, maybe also just a bit pleased that she had another pair of hands in the place, however temporarily.

'What's your name, hen?' she asked.

'Brodie. Brodie McLennan.'

'Brodie? What kinda name is that?' I smiled again, not really knowing how to answer such a question, and waited for a moment when I could ask about Graham Marshall. A shadow of recognition passed across her face before she smiled back at me. I wasn't prepared for what came next. 'Brodie!' she chortled. 'Oh, aye. I only remember one wee lassie with that name. Wis your mother Mary McLennan from the flats?'

Ina Gibbon had managed to link our worlds after all. Everybody in Leith knew my mum, and the flats where I'd lived. And the fact that my mother had chosen to name me after the tea factory that could be seen from our window had been a source of amusement to everyone as I was growing up. I nodded. 'A very nice woman, your mother . . . what brings you down here, Brodie?' she asked, suspicion still written all over her face. 'You're no' a journalist, are you?' she asked.

I shook my head; she said nothing, waiting for me to reveal my profession. I remained silent; one thing I *was* sure of was that being a lawyer wouldn't go down any better than being a journalist.

The canteen was filling up. I couldn't see the patrons because the shutters were still down, but I could hear them and, most of all, I imagined I could smell them. Dr Marshall was still nowhere to be seen and I saw no escape. Ina was watching me like a hawk and my lack of an answer hadn't helped matters. If I wanted anything from her, I'd have to give something back. She'd thought of it before I did.

'You're in charge of ladling the soup. Keep it stirred; there'll be a riot if you give them thin, watery muck. They need the kind of stuff that will stick to their ribs. It's cold out there at night, very cold. God bless them, we've even lost a few of the laddies and lassies recently – poor souls must be freezing to death,' Ina said as she opened up the hatch.

They came with empty bowls on their trays. I sloshed soup into them and Ina gave them a bread roll. I never thought it would happen, but the line did eventually come to an end. 'Go out and speak to them, hen,' the old woman commanded when we'd finished serving. 'Join them at their tables and make them feel human – that's even more

83

important than food.' She shooed me out of the kitchen clutching a bowl of soup. I stood for a second like the new kid in the playground, and then I spotted the pair from the front door and began to move towards them.

'Hey! Brodie!' I was distracted from my potential new friends at the shout and I half turned to see where it had come from. A client of mine, known as Wee Elvis, who'd just been released from prison waved at me. How long would it be till I was visiting him at St Leonards again? He motioned to me to join him but I was still waiting for Dr Marshall. The dreadlocked man from the step tapped his chest. 'I'm Mack and this ... this is Lucky,' he pointed to the dog at his feet. He'd saved the choicest pieces of ham from the soup and the dog was lapping it up from his fingers. 'We're Siamese twins,' he smiled, pointing to the dog. 'Where I go, he goes – this is the only shelter that gives Lucky house room. That's why I always slept rough, so we could be together. But at Christmas we woke up and my mate was gone – I think he's dead – and I couldn't take a chance with Lucky's life, so we came here.'

The dog was busy trying to sniff my crotch as his master gave me a potted life history. Out of the corner of my eye I spotted Dr Marshall walk into the dining room. It *was* him! He was jacketless, his shirtsleeves rolled up, and a stethoscope hung round his neck. My best guess was what I would have thought pretty unlikely, given the arrogance I had thought ran through his blood, but it seemed pretty obvious that he ran an informal clinic here as the last patient trotted along beside him, talking animatedly into his face. Ina came round from the kitchen with a bowl of soup. It was placed before Marshall as if he were royalty, but from the look in Ina's eyes he was higher up in her estimation even than that.

I sat down across from him and he stopped eating. He didn't seem at all surprised to see me – it was his innate good manners that had caused the pause. 'How was your first visit?' he asked.

'You spotted me?' I replied.

'Long before you got off your bike . . . that machine makes some racket.'

'Why didn't you say something?' I asked.

'My work here is important . . . not just to me. I knew if it was vital you'd hang around, and if you were hanging around Ina was going to make you work. We can always do with an extra pair of hands.' He smiled at me. 'Did you enjoy it?'

I looked at the clock on the yellow canteen wall and I smiled. Time had flown. 'Yes, I did actually,' I said.

'Do you feel good about yourself for the first time in ages?' he asked. I thought about it. It might be clichéd, but it was also true. When I'd parked the bike, I'd intended to ask Marshall a few questions, then maybe return his cheques – tell him categorically that Brodie McLennan could not be bought. Seeing him here, in the Mission, I'd changed my mind again.

Didn't everyone deserve a second chance?

Chapter Fifteen

Dr Gerry Cornwell screwed his eyes against the daylight as he climbed up the five steps of 17 Belgrave Square, London. The address, one of London's grandest, borders Knightsbridge and lies at the heart of Belgravia. The headquarters of the Royal College of Psychiatrists never failed to thrill Gerry Cornwell every time he walked through its hallowed portals.

'Morning,' said Doreen, secretary to Dr Cornwell, Head of College. 'You look rough. Been on a bender?' Cornwell took two paracetamol out of his secretary's bottom drawer and swallowed them without water. He ran his hands through faded ginger hair. The small round spectacles that he'd been forced to wear in recent years were perched on the end of his nose. His bespoke navy pinstriped suit had been made for him when he was two stones heavier and his shirt had been worn for three days in a row. 'Is it that obvious?' he asked. There was a worried note in his voice. One quick glance over her boss's appointments diary and Doreen decided to lie – using her discretion was a habit she utilized as well as her ability to anticipate Cornwell's moods. 'No, no – I'm the only one who could tell. You look fine. Was the celebration for anything special?' she asked.

Doreen's curiosity about his personal life was a source of some irritation to Dr Cornwell, but he really did feel rough this morning, and he might need Doreen in a good mood to help him out later in the day. His eye lingered on her coffee cup; she sprang to her feet and poured him a hot, freshly percolated brew. He perched on the edge of her desk. 'You know Lord Edward Hunter?' he asked.

'The judge? You meet him for lunch sometimes?' Doreen nodded. How could she remember some details like that and then forget to enclose reports with his letters? The woman's jumbled sense of priorities never ceased to amaze him.

'Yes . . . well,' he struggled to keep the irritation out of his voice, 'he's about to be announced as the new Lord Chancellor of England, and I cracked open a bottle of malt to toast his good fortune.'

'Any excuse,' Doreen mumbled under her breath. Dr Cornwell's drinking was getting worse. His problem had begun years before she started working for him, but she thought Cornwell was a good man, for all his faults.

Gerry Cornwell took his coffee and wandered through to his office. The oak bookcases had been in situ since the mid-nineteenth century. He ran his fingertips along the leather spines, an old habit, and made his way to the window, stopping to pick up his messages from the in-tray on his desk. The sun was struggling to be seen behind the cloud. He rifled through the pile of notes left for him by Doreen and discarded the three new research papers. They would be read this evening when he had the time to ingest the statistical information. In between a few glasses . . . There were requests for him as an after-dinner speaker and he threw those in the bin; he had no need or time for such things. He had no inclination these days, either. Nor were telephone messages of any interest to him, except the last one. He smiled as he picked up the phone to return the call. Detective Inspector Sam Jones. There was a name he hadn't heard in a few years; no doubt she was phoning to discuss Lord Edward Hunter's appointment as Lord Chancellor. It never hurt to have friends in high places.

'It's Gerry,' he said when he heard her voice, anticipating hers in reply. He smiled again. The three simple words he did hear wiped it from his face.

'He's started again.'

Chapter Sixteen

Gerry Cornwell felt that he was going to faint. Or throw up. Instead, stupid questions formed on his lips. 'Are you sure?' he asked. Silence was the only reply. Of course she was sure. She wouldn't have called otherwise. This wasn't something to take chances on, to fill with rumours and half-thoughts. He shook his head in an attempt to clear it and continued. 'Where? Where is it happening?' His voice was shaky as he tried to swallow the bile that had crept up from his stomach.

'Edinburgh.'

'Are you sure?' he asked again, desperately hoping that the simple process of repeating the words would convince her to change her mind and say it was all a mistake.

'Can you stop saying that, please? Yes, I'm sure. I'm sure about all of it. He's in Edinburgh and he's killing. Again. There was a request on HOLMES 2 from a DI there. They put in the MO from Edinburgh to see if there had been any similar murders elsewhere in the country. Some DI called Bancho,' she said.

'So, what did the computer say?' he asked, unable to keep the fear out of his voice.

'No, of course, Gerry. It said "no". We have been able to keep some things quiet. Maybe too many,' DI Jones said sadly, as her voice tailed off.

'How many have died?' asked Cornwell.

'Three. All men so far.' Sam sounded shaken and tired.

'Sam, what are you going to do about it?' His voice quavered.

'I need to go there, Gerry. I need to get a feel for it and I need to let this Bancho know what he's up against. And, before you ask, yes, I'm sure. I'm booked on the three thirty flight from Stansted to Edinburgh.' Sam Jones paused before asking what she really wanted to know. 'Gerry? Why do you think he's started again, after all this time?'

The silence between them was heavy. DI Sam Jones wondered if the psychiatrist was crying. He wondered whether she was.

'The question isn't why he has started after all this time, Sam, it's why has he waited for so long? We all knew he wanted to do it again, we knew that he had his wish list. Do these killings fit in with anything he . . . wanted?' Dr Gerry Cornwell rubbed his temples. The headache, which had been throbbing behind his eyes since the moment he woke up, was now turning into a full-blown migraine.

'I'm not sure of that one yet,' said Sam. 'I really do need to be there. I've been waiting for this for years and dreading it for just as long – but I have to find out whether they'll be willing to take my advice on it and whether they'll even consider him as a suspect.' Cornwell could hear her voice tighten. She had a battle ahead.

'When did you get the information from HOLMES 2?' he asked.

'I got an email at four fifty-five. I was just leaving for the day.'

'You know about the judge?' he asked.

'I was in the cafeteria; the lunchtime news was on and I saw Lord Hunter.'

'Sam,' Gerry Cornwell said, 'it's a bit of a coincidence. Too much of one. Have you called Hunter?'

'No. I was kind of hoping you would.'

'Christ, the timing of it . . . it couldn't be worse.'

'You're worried about the Lord Chancellor?' she asked.

'Naturally,' he said.

'What about the victims and their families?' DI Sam Jones asked, not even attempting to disguise the disgust in her voice.

'Jesus, there's only so much guilt a man can take, Sam. Of course I care about the families, but Edward is a friend. Is there any chance we can keep him out of it?' he asked.

'If it's at all possible, I will.' Her answer was cold and clinical, but he still believed that she would keep to her word.

Dr Gerry Cornwell put two fingers on his neck and took his pulse. It was so high it was dangerous; his breathing was in his upper chest and shallow, a fine film of sweat covered his whole body. The telephone felt heavy in his hand. 'Sam, when you find him . . . what do you plan to do to him?' he asked anxiously.

There was no reply. The only sound was his hammering heart and panting, inadequate breath. 'Sam? I asked you a question.'

'I'll do whatever it takes,' she replied.

Chapter Seventeen

The police canteen at St Leonards was packed. Scotland was playing in the World Cup qualifiers, and the officers on duty were trying to catch the start of the match. The volume was on full and the tail-end of the six thirty news was still on. DI Duncan Bancho tried to find a quiet corner to sit in; he pushed his fork around the stodgy plate of macaroni cheese and squeezed tomato sauce on his side order of chips. His eyes glanced up at the TV screen. The new English Lord Chancellor was being interviewed on the government's policy on crime. Lord Edward Hunter promised tougher sentences for offenders – Bancho wasn't naive enough to actually believe it. He stabbed a particularly large chip with his fork and rammed it in his mouth as a shadow fell over his plate. He looked up. A woman was blocking his view of the telly – he hoped she'd bloody move before the start of the match or the end of his chips.

'Detective Inspector Duncan Bancho?' she asked.

'Depends who wants to know?' He craned his neck, trying to see past her, to check if the match had started.

'I did try to call – a few times. They said they'd put

a call out for you? Detective Inspector Sam Jones. I'm with the Met.' She fumbled into her inside pocket and pulled out her badge, handing it to him. He took it and looked at it with interest, folding the badge over before handing it back.

'May I sit down?' she asked.

'Not there . . . come round here.' He patted the seat beside him and she sat down, affording him a clear view of the TV. The screen was showing the terraces and the Tartan Army was in full voice. He shook his head. Whoever had decided that the tartan caps with sewn-in ginger wigs was a good look must have been off their heads. He shuddered and turned his attention back to his plate. 'Care for a chip, Sam?' he asked.

She looked at the wilting potato covered in tomato sauce. 'No thanks, I'll pass – but I'd love a cup of coffee . . . black, no sugar.'

Bancho pushed back his chair and went off in search of Sam's drink, his curiosity sparked. What the hell could someone from the Met want with him? More bloody work, he guessed. His life was getting worse by the day and tonight's football result wasn't likely to improve matters. Standing at the till he observed DI Sam Jones. She was coat-hanger thin – probably one of those who lived on her nerves and the black coffee she'd asked for. Her blonde hair was cut into a short and manageable style; it suited her deep green eyes and high cheekbones. Her clothes were serviceable: raincoat, navy trouser suit, white T-shirt and plain chunky heels; she wore them all well because she carried no fat. Bancho subconsciously ran a hand over his waistline and vaguely wondered what people thought when they met him for the first time.

'I hear you have Cupid on your patch.'

Bancho stopped shovelling the cold macaroni into his mouth. 'Jesus Christ. You don't beat about the bush. How do you know about the hearts?' he asked, keeping his voice as low as possible. No one knew about this. Well, hardly anyone. This killer who had been dumped on him wasn't just a straightforward sort of maniac – this one liked to cut the hearts out of the poor bastards he murdered and then take them away home with him. As things stood, they'd stopped any leaks before they started and the media had no idea what was going on – they knew about the killings and that was enough to keep them quiet for now; but if they found out about the hearts they'd have a fucking field day. Bancho sighed at the very thought. Cupid was the name they'd come up with in the office; they always needed something to make hideous stuff like this less . . . evil.

Sam stared back at him. 'I know more about this Cupid than anyone should. I know he takes the hearts and I know who he is.'

'How?' was the only unimaginative comment Bancho could come up with.

'For twenty years I've waited for him to surface. I've scoured the papers in every region of Britain and then when I could do it online I trawled the Commonwealth countries and America. It was only natural that when HOLMES, then HOLMES 2, came into operation, I'd look at any request made that contained the words "missing hearts".'

Bancho was silent as he studied her. She was hard to read – her words came out in a very matter-of-fact way, but quickly, as if she had waited a long time to tell this story. The bags under her eyes and the pallor of her skin supported her answer. Her fingers drummed on the table. She was close to the edge. 'Who is the most dangerous killer you can think of?' she asked him, but she didn't wait for a reply before continuing, 'Harold Shipman? Peter Sutcliffe? Fred and Rosemary West?' She took a sip of coffee and shook her head. 'No, the killer who is murdering these men and taking their hearts as trophies is smarter and more dangerous than any of them, because they were caught, whereas your killer has got away.'

'And you know who he is?'

DI Sam Jones nodded. 'As I said, I've been waiting for him to make a mistake for twenty years.' The excited bellowing of the officers as they watched Scotland score didn't disturb them. They stared at each other. DI Jones was waiting for Bancho to speak but he'd decided against it. 'I knew he wouldn't be stopped. He's started again and I can arrest him – but I need your cooperation.' She looked at Duncan Bancho expectantly.

'Slow down . . . I need to get up to speed with you,' he told her.

'I'm so sorry.' Her tone was exaggerated but sincere. 'I have lived day and night with this case for years. Decades. I forget other people don't know the truth and you need to know the truth if you're going to arrest him.' She drained the dregs from her cup. 'Do you have time? I don't think we can afford to lose a second – not while he's roaming the streets of Edinburgh.'

'Are you sure you're not too exhausted?' he asked, looking at her pale face etched with nerves.

'Duncan, I'm always exhausted. For years I've needed pills to sleep. I'm better now but the flashbacks still haunt me. I won't rest until he's behind bars again.' Sam Jones took a thick brown file from her briefcase and handed it to him.

'I know who he is. So do you. Read this. I'll call you tomorrow.'

PART TWO

London
November 1988

Chapter Eighteen

The high-rise flat in Andover House, Edmonton, North London, was paid for almost entirely by housing benefit. Andover House was twenty storeys high, the lifts were out of order, and the officer was forced to climb the stairs, which smelled of piss – and she couldn't blame it all on cats. The offensive odour was the least of her problems. The house she was seeking was on the nineteenth floor and she was exhausted from the night's sleep she'd already missed.

Police Constable Sam Jones knew it was going to be bad as soon as she saw the tear-stained faces of the small group of neighbours. They were huddled outside the only door on the landing that was clean and freshly painted. She knew it was going to be really bad when she saw the grief etched on the face of the hardened police officer guarding the door.

'Any news of the little boy?' asked a small, fat woman with greying black hair in a pigtail that hung halfway down her back. WPC Sam Jones stared at the lady's red sari and shook her head. The neighbourhood had been united by sorrow. A body had not yet been found but, rightly or wrongly, all hope was gone. Matthew Cook had been missing for far too long – even the police thought so.

Sam's clothes were stained and grubby. She'd been out all night helping to search the area around Edmonton Green bus station, until there wasn't an alleyway, an empty shop doorway, or a bin that they hadn't raked through. The bus station was reasonably central, but hardly any of the CCTV worked, and the huge numbers of people seemed more used to closing their eyes to everything and everyone around them rather than actually to noticing things. Usually they wouldn't talk to the police at all, but a missing child had opened their mouths a little – they just didn't have anything to say. The superintendent had taken her off the search and ordered her to the family home to be with the mother. WPC Jones felt her heart crumble to dust, more with apprehension than cold – just because she was a woman didn't mean she was equipped to deal with this. In fact, she knew that she wasn't.

'WELCOME' was printed in dull green letters on the doormat. Sam wiped her feet and rang the bell. The door was opened by a red-eyed young woman.

'Are you Donna Cook?' she asked. 'I'm WPC Sam Jones.'

The young woman ignored the outstretched hand and opened the door just wide enough for Sam to squeeze through. They were trying to keep their grief private, but there was a thin line between the concerned people outside and the way they preyed like vultures on what was happening. 'No, I'm not Donna. I'm a friend . . . Angie Bell,' the young woman stuttered.

Sam recognized the name. Angie's short brown hair was knotted and unkempt, egg stained her pink Reebok T-shirt and the tracksuit bottoms she wore had been slept in. Angie Bell's head shook continuously, as if trying to deny the tragedy. 'Donna's in her bedroom. The doctors had to sedate her. She's been pulling her hair out by the roots since he's gone missing.'

She led Sam Jones into a small living room. A thick, red plastic easel dominated the room. A piece of paper was attached. Sticky blue and green hand-prints were plastered all over the sheet. An adult, Sam presumed it would be the mother, had written Matthew's name on it. There was a framed picture of two women – one of them Angie, the other presumably Donna, holding a little boy between them. The young women were dressed in what Sam saw as a uniform round here – ripped jeans, Doc Martens, blonde, spiky hair. It looked like a million years ago.

'We had tickets for a Bros concert,' Angie said, following Sam's eyes to the pictures. 'Donna ended up staying at home and I went with some bloke. She could never bear a moment away from Matthew. Cup of tea?' she asked. Sam followed her into a clean, tidy kitchen, the walls decorated with more of Matthew's art.

'That kid is her life . . .' muttered Angie, putting the tea bags down on the worktop, unable to continue with the simple task. 'None of us can believe this has happened, you know? Why Matthew? God, I can't believe it – it was my fault, all my fault . . .' She broke down, sobbing, as the family liaison officer came into the kitchen.

'Hi Sheila,' said Sam. They knew each other well and didn't bother to shake hands. Sheila Docherty took Angie by the shoulders and led her through to the living room, followed by Sam. She switched the television on and sat down. This was what Sam had come for. The superintendent wanted a detective to be close to the mother when the CCTV footage was broadcast to the public on the six o'clock news.

'Angie,' said Sam, 'can you just tell me again what happened?' She didn't need to know, it was all well documented and Angie Bell had never wavered from her story. It wasn't a story, though – it was the truth. This poor young woman wasn't a suspect, even though she believed she was absolutely responsible for the child's abduction. But Sam needed her to go through the story again – it would ground her before she saw the news bulletin and prepare her for hearing the story in someone else's voice. It was also in the file that she seemed to need to talk it out, over and over again, as if there would be a different ending. There wouldn't be. And, as time went on, everyone involved in the case became more and more sure exactly what the ending would be.

'Oh God, oh dear God,' said Angie as Sam moved towards her. Sheila Docherty watched both of them from the other side of the room. She nodded encouragingly at Sam – the WPC was doing well, even if it was obvious from her pained expression that she didn't feel herself particularly well equipped for this aspect of the job. 'It was all meant to be so well sorted; we had it all organized, you know?' She looked at Sam for more reassurance

102

as she spoke, and the officer held her hand as the words poured out.

'Donna would do anything for Matthew. Anything. So would I, honestly I would. We went to school together, we've been friends since nursery – God, since we were almost Matthew's age. We were mates since the day we met. I always idolized Donna – she hates me, she must hate me!' Racking sobs punctuated her words, and Sam had to remind Angie Bell to breathe deeply and steadily before she could continue. 'Boys always liked Donna, and she had plenty of boyfriends but – well, look at this place.' She waved vaguely in the direction of the window. 'What's the point of having dreams here? We both wanted to be teachers, I remember that.' She laughed a little, bitterly, but it was the first non-crying emotion Sam had heard from her. 'We played teachers all the time ... then, you know, parties, getting off your head, not Donna so much, but she still got caught. She was pregnant; she needed to get away from home. She never thought about getting rid of him for a second, you know.' The words came out in a rush, almost like a panicky stream of consciousness that she just had to get out.

Sam waited for a minute while Angie reflected on the lives the two teenage girls had lived. She knew places like this. Hopeless. 'Did Donna get pregnant deliberately?' she asked Angie.

'No, no – she didn't. Her home life was crap – her parents barely knew what day it was they drank so much, so they couldn't have cared less when she got knocked up. I don't know if they even realized it. Donna did see it as a way out, but she didn't get pregnant on purpose.

Actually, she really liked the guy she was with – you know he's dead now, yeah?'

Yes, they did. No matter how little the dad was involved in a kid's life, the father was always a main suspect. If he had been the one who had taken Matthew, they might have had him back by now. No, that line was closed. 'Donna didn't tell him she was pregnant – she found out he was a smackhead pretty soon after she did the test and she didn't want someone like that involved in the baby's life. She got this flat – shit, but at least somewhere for her to make her own life, and we decided we'd do all we could for him.'

'You were still good friends?' asked Sam.

'Yeah, yeah we were – I wasn't much use when she was pregnant, I was a bit wild back then, but once that kid was born . . . we both adored him. He was the most gorgeous baby you've ever seen. I've got a flat in the next block and I'm here all the time. Not for babysitting – she wouldn't spend a moment apart from him, but, well, I was just sort of drawn here. I loved it. I'd never seen someone love their kid the way Donna loved Matthew. All around us, there were our mates getting pregnant, having them or not, not really caring one way or the other, but it was like Donna came alive when she had that baby. And now? Now I've killed all of that, haven't I?'

Chapter Nineteen

Angie Bell's story rang true – and it had been checked a hundred times. Sam needed to stay objective – there was a reason for her being that way. Angie needed to be grounded to see if they could get any more details from her and to help her cope when the news blitz started. She had spent a lot of time on this estate, and it sounded as if Donna Cook was by far the exception to the rule. She had wanted her baby, she had loved her baby, she had nurtured him and she had now lost him.

'It wasn't your fault, Angie,' Sheila Docherty said. 'You know that. It was the fault of whoever took Matthew. Let's just focus on whether you can tell us anything else that can help us get him back. What do you remember happened at the bus station?'

'Donna wanted him to have everything. Not stuff, do you know what I mean?' Angie looked at the other two women. 'I could . . . well, I could nick anything she needed,' she whispered, remembering who she was talking to, as if it mattered in the middle of such an unfolding tragedy. 'But she wanted him to have a future. She only put him into nursery a couple of mornings a week because she'd read somewhere that it helped their development. She was always reading baby books, magazines, watching all the things that told you what stage they were at and what you should be doing for them. When he went to nursery she went to the library to read more. There were things everywhere – pictures and letters and colour blocks.' As Angie spoke, Sam remembered the easel. 'It was like *Sesame Street* in here! And he was smart – she made sure of it. He used to pick up toys in the shops like all the kids wanted, those teenage mutant turtle things and *Ghostbusters* toys . . .' She laughed at the memories, then caught herself and went serious again. 'But Donna was having none of it; they weren't educational enough for her boy. Then, one day, when they came back from nursery, she had all of these leaflets. I remember her eyes were like saucers and she was all sort of lit up.' Angie seemed to wander away in her own mind as she thought back.

Sam waited a little longer before pressing her. 'What was it, Angie? What had happened?'

Angie stared at the police officer as if she resented being brought back to reality. 'She'd got speaking to some woman at the library, told her about Matthew. This woman was there promoting some training thing and put ideas into Donna's head – that's how it all started. If she hadn't spoken to that stupid bitch that day, Matthew would be here now. She told her about teacher training, working with kids, being a classroom assistant, being a nursery assistant, all these stupid ideas about what Donna could do. And she fell for it.'

'Fell for it? What do you mean?' asked Sam.

'She decided to go. To Leeds. That was where there was funding for people like her, she was told. She could get her life on track and get a life for Matthew, too. All she had to do was go to this Open Day thing and speak to some people from a college and she'd have her life all sorted out . . . her whole fucking life sorted out . . .' Angie started to sob.

'And then?' Sam prompted, stealing a glance at her watch. Not long until the news.

'Then there were a few frantic weeks. She got someone at the library to help her find out what it was like, what the course would be, whether there would be childcare in the same place so she could see Matthew whenever she wanted. It all seemed too good to be true – that's what Donna said too. There was a crèche at the college, there were student flats for families – they were looking for girls just like her, some fresh start sort of thing. She said it was for Matthew's future, but I could tell she was really excited too. So, the next thing was to go to speak to them and see if they would accept her . . .'

Sam could sense the sobs coming before they even started and put her hand on Angie's arm. 'It was all sorted. She was going to get the coach from the local bus station into London, then a connecting one straight to Leeds.'

'And Matthew?' asked Sam, knowing the answer.

'She didn't really trust anyone with him – certainly not her family, but she knew that I loved him too. I'd been there since he was born, I went loads of places with them, I was round here all the time. So, the idea was that I would look after him. We all went to the bus station together – she wanted to see him right up till the last minute . . . she could hardly bear to get on the bus, but she did, she did . . . they waved to each other then . . .'

Angie's tears had stopped. She gazed off into the distance at nothing as Sam and Sheila waited. 'I thought I'd treat him. We walked back to the kiosk and I asked him if he'd like some sweets. He got some chocolate and then I checked the bus times for us to come back as I'd promised Donna I'd stay at the flat with him. It was a while, we were going to have quite a wait so . . . I only thought I'd go to the loo. That's all, just go to the loo.'

'And did you take him with you?' asked Sam.

Angie pulled her eyes back from whatever she was looking at. 'Of course I did. We went into the ladies' and I sat him outside the cubicle – they're so small. You got kids?' she asked Sam, who shook her head. 'So bloody small those places, you can't get yourself and a kid and a buggy in there. I told him I'd only be a second, went to the loo at the end, closed the door, stuck the buggy on the floor with the handles inside the loo – I was worried it would get pinched, and told him to sit there on the tiles outside and eat his chocolate.'

'Then?'

'You want the details? You want to know if I wiped my arse?'

'No,' said Sam, thinking that she did want to know how long Angie had been in there. 'You said that you were hardly any time – seconds; but how long were you in there, really, Angie?'

The tears started quickly again. 'Hardly any time at all.'

'How long? Thirty seconds? A minute?' Sam asked,

wondering how long it would take someone to steal a child.

'Maybe a bit more?'

'Doing what?'

'I was in the loo! What do you think I was doing?'

'I don't know. You tell me,' said Sam.

Angie Bell stared back at her, before finally answering in a low voice, almost a whisper. 'I was having a fag. Okay? I was having a fag. Donna wouldn't let anyone smoke around Matthew and I knew I had the whole day cooped up here with him, so I was having a quick fag. That's when he disappeared, dear God – that's when someone took him.'

Chapter Twenty

The news headlines were announced. Up until a few days ago, there had still been stories trickling in about the Piper Alpha oil platform disaster in which 167 people had died, still tales of the after-effects and of what would take forever for people to recover from. There had been political stories at the top of the hour about the merger between the SDP and the Liberal Party to form the new Social and Liberal Democratic Party and how that already seemed to be falling apart in the same year it had been put together. There were poll tax headlines, reports of a new wonder drug called Prozac – but none of that mattered now. All of it was brushed aside by one national horror. A toddler, Matthew Cook, aged two, had been taken from Edmonton Green bus station two days ago. The police had released footage of the two teenagers they were interested in interviewing in connection with the incident. As in every other household in the country, Sam, Angie and Sheila watched with horror as the little boy was led away. The CCTV camera's poor-quality black-and-white footage followed the hellish journey. Mouths dried up and tears fell as a nation watched, ashamed, as the little boy's cry for help was ignored on so many occasions.

Upstairs from where the women watched the footage on the TV news, Donna Cook had awoken from her drug-induced coma, alerted by some sixth sense. As she walked into the living room and sat down, she knew that she had to see this. There might be some detail only she could spot that would bring her baby back to her. No one tried to shield her from the TV – it would have been useless anyway, she'd have fought past them. She had fantasized about killing the boys who had abducted her Matthew, and as she watched the grimy film she was paralysed with hatred. Something gnawed deep in her soul, it niggled: a small detail, but it was important. If she could just sit down for a moment, and stop the pounding in her head, she would remember it. WPC Sam Jones watched as the young mother staggered to a chair. Sitting on the edge she bit a nail and watched the superintendent at the police press conference. Sam's stomach turned as she noticed the bald, bleeding patches on Donna's scalp. The police doctor had judged that Donna's mental health was too fragile to sanction a public appearance and, looking at her, Sam wholeheartedly agreed. The first nail was finished – Sam worried that Donna didn't have enough fingers to last through the duration of the press conference. The superintendent appealed to the public for help in identifying the two teenagers who had abducted little Matthew Cook.

Donna became agitated as she watched, biting her nails and pulling at her hair. She gripped the arms of the chair until the whites of her knuckles showed.

'No,' she shook her head as she struggled to get her words out. 'No . . . he's wrong. That man's wrong.'

Sam looked at her. 'Why? What has he said that's wrong?'

Donna Cook tore her eyes away from the screen and looked at the policewoman. 'They shouldn't be looking for two teenage boys. One was a girl. You should be looking for a girl and they're younger, much younger. Can't you see? They're just kids. Watch the tape! You're looking for kids.'

Chapter Twenty-One

Sam watched the eyes of the family liaison officer settle on her – she knew this was her call. Donna Cook had obviously been interviewed a number of times since her child was abducted, but more information could come out at any time, and this definitely looked like one of those times. Sam moved over towards the seat where she was glued to the television. The news had moved on, but the young mother had not. She held a picture of Matthew in her hands as she stared blankly at the TV screen.

'What do you mean, Donna?' the WPC asked. 'Do you recognize something from the footage? Do you know who they are?'

'I don't know who they are, no.'

Sam went back to her second question. 'Do you recognize something from the footage?'

'I think so. Yes. I think so. There were kids hanging around at the bus station, weren't there, Angie?'

'There always are. The place is full of them,' her friend confirmed. Sam knew what they meant. Places like that, bus stations, railway stations, shopping centres, they were magnets for feral kids skipping school, somewhere they could be anonymous. No one cared much who they were or what they were doing.

'Did you notice any in particular?'

Donna thought for a moment, but Sam got the impression she wasn't remembering, she was just confirming to herself what she was going to say. 'I'd pointed them out to Angie. There were two of them going up and down all the stances. A boy and a girl. He was sort of calling out to her all the time, making sure she was keeping up. She was dragging her heels a bit, getting distracted, smiling at people, but he was in front. I was holding Matthew's hand, getting ready to go on the bus . . .' Sam waited for Donna to falter. She didn't. 'I knew I'd never be like those kids' parents. Never let him out of my sight to get up to God knows what.' At these words, Angie Bell got up and walked through to the tiny kitchen. Donna's eyes never looked up as she kept on talking. 'You know what happened, don't you?' she asked Sam. 'They must have been looking for something to get up to and they must have been hanging about the toilets when they saw Angie go in.'

'We're only guessing at this stage,' said Sam, not willing to commit herself to anything that the young woman might cling on to at any point, especially later when she was alone reflecting on things. 'What do you think happened?'

'You must see kids like that all the time. Nothing to do. Nowhere to go. Avoiding whatever is going on at home, not wanting to go to school. Why don't you do something about it? Why don't the police pick them up? Chase the parents? Fine them? There were coppers in that bus station you know – I saw them leaving when we went in, plastic cups of coffee and sausage rolls in their hands. You lot only go to places like that when you need to for yourselves or when there's been a stabbing or something. Don't you think that if you were there you could stop things happening before they started? Don't you even believe that if you actually took an interest you could stop people doing bad things?' What had started as anger was fading now, and Sam could only hear resignation behind the sobbing.

There was nothing Sam could say. There was no point in offering Donna Cook platitudes or saying that they did keep an eye on things, or saying that the kids would only move somewhere else or saying – well, what could she say? That they would try to be more aware in case more toddlers were taken? That she was sorry about Matthew but she'd watch out for any other little boy being abducted?

She needed to get Donna back to what she had seen at the bus station that day, but she needed to be careful that the young mother didn't clam up completely if she started to see Sam as one of the enemy. 'Donna, you said that you were sure those kids on the CCTV were much younger? Are you sure it was them, and what age do you think they were?'

'Kids. They were just kids. The girl – she had a rag doll thing in her hand. I remember seeing it, thinking it was cute, then realizing she was on her own and probably old beyond her years. They'd be lucky if they were double figures.'

Sam knew it was hard to judge. The kids she knew round this part of Edmonton Green were so streetwise at such a young age that it was hard to guess what age they were from their behaviour. They were usually so malnourished, if not already on booze and drugs by the time they were eleven or twelve, that they were often smaller than they should have been. Donna Cook wasn't a reliable witness, but none of the other witnesses had proved to be much good either. Hopefully, the lines back at the temporary headquarters or the station would be ringing off the hook after that news bulletin and they would get some real leads. Her heart felt heavy – she needed to get out of here. It looked as if the family liaison officer wanted to talk to Donna anyway, as she lurked in the living-room doorway with Angie, hankie pressed to her reddened face, standing beside her.

'Donna,' said Sam, touching her hand gently, 'I need to go. I want to get back. There should be some information coming in now and I would like to see how far the investigation is going, then I can get back to you if there's anything positive. Is there anything I can get for you? Anything you want to ask me?'

Donna shook her head, staring again at the TV screen as if she was willing the story to run once more, just to see Matthew again perhaps, no matter what the circumstances. Sam moved towards the door and turned just as the woman looked around. 'How can they look after him?' she asked, weakly. 'They're just children themselves. How can they be looking after my baby properly?'

Sam left without a word – she had no answer, and she didn't want to say what she really thought. The harsh truth was that it was probably too late for Matthew Cook to be being looked after by anyone.

Chapter Twenty-Two

The following day, Sam looked out over Edmonton. The place sat at the north point of Tottenham, a sprawl of towering council estates, graffiti and crime. The most deprived area in Enfield, she knew it had some of the highest crime rates in London and some of the capital's most dangerous characters walking its streets, as Sam had experienced in her training so far. But today Edmonton Green was quiet, the gangs of hooded youths apparently silenced by the abduction of Matthew Cook. Like her, they had no doubt he was dead: a child murdered by two other children.

There had been plenty of activity after last night's news bulletin. Lots of crank calls. Lots of perverts wanting to know if they'd found a body yet. There were more calls from people who said they had seen Matthew with two kids – some of them would probably prove to be genuine, but they'd taken too long to come through. People were so concerned about keeping themselves to themselves that it had all gone too far – and now a child had probably lost his life because of it.

The hastily assembled 'Matthew Cook task force' was situated in an old storage room in the basement. There were no windows, and Sam felt claustrophobic from the moment she walked in. The fluorescent strip light flickered, inducing headaches, and the smell of stale, deodorized sweat was competing with the scent of industrial disinfectant. A high wooden table on rickety legs leaned against the wall under the light switch. The makeshift coffee table was marked by rings, scattered sugar and almost clean cups. The coffee tasted like hot black tar, but the task force was very grateful – anything to keep them awake. Six bashed metal grey desks were grouped in the centre of the room; two walls were covered with a map of the area, names and addresses of the thirty-eight witnesses they had already spoken to who had seen the toddler with the suspects, and photographs of the missing child. Sam needed to get out of here. Something was telling her there was nothing left in this estate, there would be no more clues here, and Donna Cook was undoubtedly innocent. Sam wanted to be back at headquarters. She felt more in the thick of things there, whereas stuck on the estate she would end up dealing with nosy neighbours who had nothing better to do than wallow in someone else's misery, and who hoped to be interviewed by journalists, getting their moment in the spotlight. She left the room and walked back to the pool car she had parked only an hour earlier.

On the drive back to headquarters, she faced up to what was preying on her mind in particular. The officers were out of their depth – she knew it and they knew it. This case was receiving a lot of coverage, and it was likely to go international if a body was found. They had wasted the golden period of the investigation. In the vital first hours after the abduction, they had searched for an adult, a man. That was the usual pattern, wasn't it? WPC Sam Jones clenched her jaw. She and – in her defence – everyone else had assumed that Matthew had been taken by someone he knew: his father, uncle, neighbour. When they found out that his dad was dead, they had even started to look at boyfriends that Donna had had in her past – maybe there was a different dad, maybe this was just a paternity fight. If it had been the case that a family friend or boyfriend had taken the toddler, the story would only have rated a passing mention. As she shuffled the papers on her desk, she picked up a copy of the photograph taken from the CCTV footage. And then she asked herself the question she had been trying to avoid since Donna had spoken. *Would it have made a difference? Would it have made a difference if they'd looked for youngsters right away?*

The phone rang almost as soon as she got in and Lynn, the receptionist, sounded shaken when she almost shouted, 'What?' into the receiver.

'Donna Cook is in reception and she wants to see you,' Lynn said. Sam Jones twiddled with the cord on the phone and didn't reply. 'Sam, it's the little boy's mother and she wants to see you,' the receptionist hissed conspiratorially.

'I know who Donna Cook is,' Sam snapped back, then hung up abruptly. Donna must have just assumed she'd be here rather than at the temporary office – maybe she should have stayed there after all. She didn't really want to deal with Matthew's mother when she had absolutely nothing to tell her, but she walked through to where Donna would be nevertheless.

The front desk was manned by the desk sergeant, a pear-shaped man with thinning hair, who was separated from the public by safety glass. There was a round grille at mouth height to allow him to speak across the counter. The only available seats were made of imitation leather, brown to hide the dirt, and on the pale beige walls there were posters of missing persons. A low table was placed in front of the seats and it was littered with public safety leaflets.

Donna Cook was staring blankly at the black-and-white image of a car wreck, which urged her not to drink and drive. Her eyes were still red-rimmed, but she had washed her face. There was even a hint of pale pink lipstick, and a black beret covered the bald patches on her scalp. Her white-and-black striped top and jeans were fresh on that morning. She was trying to pull herself together for Matthew's sake, Sam guessed. Tucking her top lip under her teeth, she looked as if she was doing her best not to cry. WPC Sam Jones pressed the button beside the desk sergeant and opened the door.

'Oh God!' Donna cried rushing over to her. She threw her arm around the officer's neck and just hung there. An irrational sense of guilt slowed Sam's reaction, but eventually she patted Donna on the back. Donna seemed so much more emotional than yesterday – perhaps what she had seen in the flat while they watched the news had been *too* controlled, but it had also been easier to deal with. Sam assumed that the true horror of what was happening had hit her through the long hours since they had last met. It wasn't unusual for victims' families to form an attachment with one officer in particular, and Sam knew that, as a woman, it was even more likely to happen with her.

'Oh God,' Donna said again, 'I wasn't sure if you'd be here, but I needed to get away from the estate and I needed to see you.' She stepped back. 'I hope you don't mind me just turning up.' She held Sam's eyes. Sam looked at her. She saw her absolute grief and knew that she couldn't turn away – or put up barriers.

'No, of course not, Donna, come in, I'll find a place we can talk in private,' said Sam. She turned and led the grieving mother through a maze of hallways to an empty interview room. It was a small, intimate space. Sam pointed to an uncomfortable grey plastic chair. 'Take a seat,' she smiled, but it didn't reach her eyes. 'Can I get you anything – tea, coffee, water?'

'Could I have a cup of tea, please? A little milk and a lot of sugar,' Donna said, frowning and rubbing her fingers along her lips. 'Sugar . . . I found it helps, it stops me shaking.' Sam tried not to stare at Donna's bitten, bleeding fingers. Her forefinger and thumb were covered by plasters with pictures of Mr Men characters on them, no doubt bought for Matthew. Sam was glad to leave the room, but a sense of duty made her return quickly with the tea, a sugar bowl and some digestive biscuits on a tray. Donna ignored the biscuits and proceeded to spoon four sugars into her mug. She stirred the tea, blew on it, and then sipped it gingerly, looking over the rim of the mug directly into Sam's eyes.

'How are you coping?' Sam asked, rubbing her temple, trying to ease the pounding headache that had been getting steadily worse all morning.

'I'm not,' she replied. 'I am tired, scared, and I know you're working very hard,' Donna said, half hidden behind the cup, 'but he's my little boy and I want to help. I want to be part of the task force, go out and see if I can find my baby.'

Sam reached across and held the damaged hands. Shaking her head, she said slowly, 'I'm afraid that's out of the question, Donna. You're not a police officer.' She handed Donna a tissue. 'You're too emotionally involved. Go home, try to sleep, and leave it to the experts. Is that why you came here?' Donna nodded. 'Even if you could be involved, I wouldn't be the one with the authority to make that decision,' Sam admitted, wishing she could do more. There was a knock on the door and the desk sergeant popped his head round.

'The super wants to see you upstairs,' he said to Sam, and made way for Sheila Docherty, the family liaison officer, to squeeze into the room. A chill came with her and the hairs on Sam's arms stood straight up. Kneeling down beside Donna she put both her arms around her and whispered: 'Its time to go home, Donna. I'll call you when I have any news.'

Chapter Twenty-Three

An hour later, Superintendent Geoffrey Vickers walked into the task-force room. His hair was dyed black except for precise white sideburns. He was fooling no one, and perhaps wasn't trying to. Superintendent Vickers was a ballroom dancer in his spare time and he carried himself well. He swept in, followed by a small messy man with ginger hair, suede patches on his tweed jacket and round John Lennon glasses on the end of his nose. The stranger shifted nervously from foot to foot as Vickers stood in front of the grey metal desks and shouted: 'Drop what you're doing and listen up!' He cast his eyes around the assembled group of officers and his eye fell on WPC Sam Jones, the only female officer in the room. He pointed at her. 'Two coffees love, just milk in mine.' He turned to the stranger and asked, 'How do you take yours?'

The visitor, quickly sizing up the situation, declined the invitation. Sam Jones outranked several of the men present, but the superintendent didn't pick up on the atmosphere, turning back to her and saying, 'Did you hear that, love? Just one coffee, there's a good girl.'

Sam stood up, the muscles in her jaw tight and the

little vein on the side of her head beating dangerously. She opened her mouth and prepared to answer back. Out of the corner of her eye she glanced at Inspector Davies, her superior officer. A gritty northerner, he was a rumpled man, but he had often given her good advice in the past. Davies sat on the edge of a desk, arms and legs crossed, staring down at his shoes as he pursed his lips and shook his head slowly. 'Pick your fights, lass,' had been his motto in previous situations; scrapping with the superintendent in front of most of his senior officers over a cup of coffee might not be the best career move she could make. Swallowing her pride, she went over to the rickety table and poured Vickers a coffee. She just managed to suppress the urge to spit in it.

'Right, listen up folks.' The superintendent cleared his throat and gestured with his arm at the small man standing by his side. 'This is Dr Gerry Cornwell.' He paused to allow Dr Cornwell to nod his head. 'And Dr Cornwell is a psychiatrist.' He stopped and made sure he eyeballed every man, but not the one woman, in the room. 'Now I know what you're thinking . . . you're thinking: what's a wanker like him doing in a police operations room?' He waited for his men to laugh, and a few brown-nosers managed to force out a titter. Sam Jones wasn't one of them. 'Well, times are changing, and we have to change with them. Dr Cornwell is what they call a profiler . . . it means he can look at the crime and tell us the type of person likely to have committed it. Bit like a fortune-teller, aren't you?'

You could have cut the cynicism in the air with a knife. The troops looked bored to death with this time-wasting.

Vickers stopped for a breath and looked at Cornwell, who was avoiding eye contact. Sam seized her moment, and stood up to ask a question.

'Dr Cornwell, my name is WPC Sam Jones. What about the CCTV footage? We already know it's a couple of kids who've taken the toddler; in fact, the mum told me last night that she thinks they're even younger than we first imagined. What else can you tell us from what you've seen on the recording?'

Cornwell looked at her with interest. He took his glasses off, held his right hand up to silence the superintendent, and said: 'If I may?' The superintendent nodded. 'The CCTV film shows us the suspects but it's not clear enough to identify them. They are young, so they may not have come to the attention of the police but . . .' Cornwell stopped for effect. 'The two suspects WILL be known to social services. They will be on records somewhere. These children come from deprived backgrounds. Superintendent, I'd like to go over my theories . . .' The assembled detectives rolled their eyes shamelessly. The superintendent glared at them, then turned towards Cornwell. 'Doctor, you'll appreciate that time is of the essence. I was rather hoping you would simply give us a written report that could be distributed.' And ignored, thought Sam. Cornwell didn't seem too surprised about being cut off in full flow. Besides, he had a plan B.

'I would, of course, be happy to do that, Superintendent Vickers, but I'm sure there will be questions, some discussion . . . Perhaps I could share my findings with one officer who could liaise?' Vickers, who had only agreed to have

125

the profiler in to silence critics and show the media they were doing everything possible, was delighted. Why not kill two birds with one stone? Get rid of the girl and shut the tweedy suited bugger up. 'WPC Jones? You'll do. Since you've already shown an interest in Dr Cornwell's work and you've been dealing with the mother, you are to give him every possible assistance. That's it. Meeting over, boys, back to work.'

Shit, shit, shit, thought Sam Jones, slamming her pen down on the desk as Vickers left. That was all she bloody needed. Inspector Davies clapped her back as he left the room and the other officers dispersed. 'Serves you bloody right, lass, you can be too clever by half sometimes. You need to learn when to shut up just as you need to learn when to just make the bloody coffee.' Davies smiled warmly at her as he said the words, and she knew that, overall, he was probably right.

The psychiatrist opened up his battered brown leather briefcase in the task-force room and placed his papers back into its depths. 'You came well prepared,' said Sam. 'But why give in so easily? Why didn't you stand your ground?' She was actually wanting him to admit that he needed more cops than just her, but she was interested as to why he had just given in to Vickers as well.

'I'm a psychiatrist,' he smiled at her. 'I treat the deluded. I would have been as mad as my patients if I'd tried to convert your fellow officers,' said Cornwell.

'What about me? Do you think you can turn me into a believer?' she asked, still feeling that she had drawn the short straw with all of this profiling business.

'I don't know. Let's see. What do you make of this?'

He handed her a report and she began reading.

'Although two children are shown on the CCTV footage, the boy is the dominant player in this murder. This boy will have come from a home where violence and beatings are daily occurrences. In all likelihood, he will be the youngest of a large group of siblings. The pack mentality is such that the older children will be encouraged to beat and attack him.'

Sam paused in her reading. 'You must be pretty up to date. Donna Cook only told me last night that she was convinced one of the kids was a girl. I got my report done soon after that so it was on Vickers's desk before I left last night, but, still, you're on top of things.' She was impressed – but still wary. 'How sure can you be about all this; I mean, where's the evidence? You can't just be guessing?' she asked.

'Profiling may not yet be normal police procedure, but it soon will be,' explained Gerry Cornwell. 'I'm not making it up. I'm not guessing. I wouldn't do that – there's a little boy's life at stake here. I'm a doctor, a scientist. I can't identify every trait of the abductors, but I can give you something to go on. Think of it in the same way you would use a police artist's sketch of a suspect. Maybe it's not a hundred per cent accurate, but it's all you've got.'

Sam read on, thinking that he was right – she'd take anything just now. *'There is no male presence in this house and the mother will have a history of either mental illness or alcoholism. In all likelihood she will have both. I recommend a search of primary schools and social service records for boys who fit this profile.'*

'You're right,' she said to the profiler. 'At least it's a start. And I do have more questions for you. I guess Vickers was right as well.'

Gerry Cornwell smiled. 'Good. I'm glad. But I'm starving,' he said, looking at his watch. 'I've had nothing since breakfast. And you need to eat, so why don't we grab a working dinner tonight?'

'In Edmonton?' she said, almost laughing for the first time since the Matthew Cook case had begun. 'We'd need a crack team of detectives to find somewhere that won't give us food poisoning.' WPC Sam Jones smiled at Dr Cornwell. Somehow she felt he had just given her the first push up the Metropolitan Police ladder. More importantly, with a lead on who might be the killers, he had given her hope that Matthew Cook could actually be found alive.

Chapter Twenty-Four

Sam's feeling of hope increased throughout dinner that evening with Gerry Cornwell. He seemed to know what he was talking about, and a lot of what he said was based on good, sound common sense as much as scientific evaluation – as a copper, she appreciated that. He was easy to get on with, too, with none of the patronizing attitudes or downright sexism that she had become so used to in the job. It was almost midnight by the time he dropped her off in a taxi at her flat, and Sam Jones went to bed with a belief that much of what they had discussed could be actively used to track down the children who had taken Matthew Cook – and, if they did that . . . She couldn't help her mind running ahead. He could still be safe. He might be alive.

At 5 a.m., her phone rang.

As she put the receiver back in the cradle, she put away the sliver of hope she had taken to bed with her.

A body had been found.

There was something about that moment that would change Sam Jones forever. It was perhaps the destruction of the sliver of hope she had allowed herself. As she dressed, she didn't know it, she couldn't, but she'd never be the same again.

Within the hour, she and Gerry Cornwell were at the scene. DI Davies was speaking to the nightwatchman who had called it in, and two other officers were securing the perimeter of the crime scene. The papers would no doubt say that it was every parent's nightmare. As Sam looked at the tiny body in front of her, she begged to differ – this was *everyone*'s worst nightmare. There was no denying that this was definitely Matthew Cook – his face was still identifiable from all the photographs and footage Sam had seen of him. Anyway, would it have been better if it hadn't been him? It would still have been someone's baby, someone's cherished child, stoned and beaten to death like an unwanted mongrel. A deluge of rain had landed on the toddler's body, washing away some of the dried red blood. Dr Gerry Cornwell shifted nervously from foot to foot as he looked down; he was finding it difficult to swallow and to breathe. She could see from the expression on his face that this wasn't a theory any longer, this wasn't a seminar topic – this was real. Sam wondered whether he had actually ever seen a dead body before; she hadn't seen that many herself.

'Jesus,' he said, shoving his hands in his trouser pockets. His eyes sought out Sam's. Hers were cold and laser-like, her lips pursed. She looked as if she was contemplating what she would do when she got her hands on the little bastards responsible for this atrocity.

At six fifteen on a Sunday morning, the air was cold and the sky cloudy. The full moon struggled to be seen where the perimeter was steep and muddy, scattered with tightly closed daffodil buds. Inspector Davies struggled on the rain-soaked ground. He dug the heels of his shoes into the boggy terrain; the last thing he needed was to go all the way down this mound. Davies was following the watchman to where Sam Jones and the psychiatrist were standing. There was enough light for him to see that it was a pathetic little bundle that held their attention. From the colour of the middle-aged watchman who was guiding him, DI Davies knew it was going to be bad, even allowing for the fact that the security guards didn't view scenes like this every day. And in spite of his twenty-year experience in the Met, neither did Davies.

The scrap yard hadn't accepted any new deliveries for months and was usually deserted, used as a storage facility. It was badly lit, next to an area known for muggings and assaults. Occasionally, in summer, kids would break through the wire and play among the old fridges and car parts. It wasn't exactly Disneyland and, in winter, even the bravest little toe rag found something better to do. The two nightwatchmen hired from a local security agency felt there was precious little of value to guard, and only patrolled round the site when the mood took them – once a week at most.

WPC Sam Jones scanned the skyline, her eyes seeking out Andover House. Most of the windows in the high rise were in darkness, but the lights shone out from one flat. To Sam they felt like a beacon for sadness and destruction. Her eyes flicked back to Matthew Cook. He looked cold. Irrationally she wanted to wrap him up in a blanket and finally take him home. The only thing she could do for the child and his mother was to get this murder inquiry wrapped up as quickly as possible. Sam knew that the last moment of peace Donna would ever know was when she held her little boy's hand in the bus station days ago.

Clambering towards the body, Sam said a silent prayer and fumbled for her radio. She called for the police doctor and the identification boys, even though someone had probably done so before her. They were taking their time. The rain came down even harder, making it difficult for the operator to hear through the poor signal. Sam repeated the request for technical backup, asking loudly where the hell they had got to, her voice cutting through the night air. The rain was seeping into her clothes and running down her face, but she was grateful for it, as it camouflaged her tears.

DI Davies coughed, startling Sam. She swivelled and turned her torch full into his eyes. 'Oh,' she said, her voice trembling, 'it's you.' Stepping to the side she flicked her spotlight over the body. Davies put his hand on Sam's back, as much for his benefit as hers. 'If you want to help Donna Cook, you have to suck this up and catch the little bastards.' He coughed again. 'If I know anything, Sam, unless they're stopped, they'll do it again.' Behind them, sirens wailed and blue lights flashed. Matthew had been found and Edmonton Green police force wanted to announce their progress to the community.

Police headquarters had been on tiptoes waiting for this moment, and the National Identification boys in their rusty Bedford van finally arrived at the crime scene. The sun was breaking through the darkness, painting the world red and gold; it was the first sunrise Sam had ever seen that didn't bring a feeling of hope. They came down the site embankment like the cavalry – but they were too late to do any real good. The body had lain outside exposed to the elements for a while, that much was obvious. They struggled against the wind to put up their blue plastic tent as the rain continued to hammer down on the material.

Dr Gerry Cornwell was soaked to the skin, his loafers covered in mud and his toes squelching inside. He was anxious to get away from this place. He pulled on Sam's sleeve. 'We can't do any good.' He squeezed her harder. 'Try it my way and I think you'll have them before the week's out.' Before she could answer, the police doctor, Dr McKenzie, came out of the identification bureau tent. He wasn't a morning person. His unshaven chin looked like a Brillo pad, and his bloodhound eyes blinked rapidly as he tried to see in the semi-darkness.

'What was the cause of death?' she asked, knowing from the state of Matthew that there would be a few options to choose from.

Sam didn't anticipate McKenzie's next words. 'It's hard to tell at this point . . .' he told her, before adding, '. . . the fact they removed his heart didn't help.'

Chapter Twenty-Five

Twelve hours after they had both looked at the horror of Matthew Cook's final resting place, Gerry Cornwell's stomach rumbled. Sam showed no signs of stopping. The duty social worker had provided them with copies of reports on the problem families in Edmonton Green, and the number was depressingly high. Sam had lost track of time, her nose was buried in a pile of papers, and there was a stack of notes at her elbow.

'Let's be honest, we're not going to solve this case in one night,' Gerry said. 'Are we?'

She stared at him as an irritated sigh escaped her lips. 'We can try. Or do you want to give up now?'

Gerry walked over to her desk. 'Which one are you reading?' he asked.

'An account of a seven-year-old boy who smashed every window in his school. Do you know what my first reaction was?' Sam stared at him unblinking. Gerry shook his head. 'My first thought was – that child needs a good smacking. That was before I read that his father beat him every night with a dog chain.'

'The killer in this case . . . I can tell you that his life,

134

her life, their lives hasn't been a bed of roses,' Gerry said, getting his jacket. 'You do know that, don't you?'

'Nothing excuses what they did to Matthew.'

'So, no matter what we find, you won't have any sympathy with the killer, despite what you've just said about that boy?' he asked as he threw her jacket to her. She shook her head. 'Good, because telling me about that incident at the school has given me an idea. Can you tear yourself away from the reports and I'll tell you about it?'

'Okay, I didn't realize how late it was. You must be starving,' she said.

'Just a bit.' Gerry Cornwell had a metabolism like a furnace and if he didn't keep it stoked he became light-headed and grumpy. Losing his temper wouldn't help anyone just now. 'Give me fifteen minutes to make some calls and set someone else on the case.'

A quarter of an hour later, Sam checked out at the front desk and followed him to his car. It was already dark and the streets were deserted. Takeaway restaurants were getting ready for the evening trade but Gerry drove past them, out into the fringes of Edmonton, finally drawing to a halt outside a Victorian villa. A Volvo estate was parked in the driveway and the house looked like an oasis of domestic bliss. Two round tubs filled with blue winter hyacinths stood at the front door, the scent of the bulbs almost overpowering.

'Here we are,' said Gerry, putting his finger on the bell. It chimed in the hallway, and Sam heard a pair of high heels clicking towards them.

'Where are we?' she said.

'My ex-sister-in-law's,' he whispered.

'Are you sure we'll be welcome?' Sam hissed back, wondering why on earth she was there. Before he could answer, Sam heard the locks sliding back. Dana Black held the door wide open and ushered them in – Gerry must have placed a call before they got there and she seemed to be expecting them. They followed her along the original tiled floor, through a stripped pine wooden door that had been waxed until it glowed. A fire was blazing in the drawing room and a low oak table was set in front of it. Sam stared at the assortment of food in front of her amidst the perfect domestic scene, and Dana noted her hungry eyes. 'It's all out of a shop, I'm afraid, dear. I wasn't expecting guests, but I keep a few things in the freezer just in case.' She smiled at Sam and pointed to the food. 'Help yourself.'

Sam grabbed a slice of pizza before sitting down on the red velvet, overstuffed couch. Gerry widened his eyes; he flicked them towards the pile of side plates and napkins. Evidently Dana was house-proud. Sam picked up a plate and started piling the food high.

'Dana is head teacher of St Mary's Primary School,' Gerry said. 'Just go with me on this one – you gave me the idea, but I think you'll find we could get a lot from this.'

'I was very upset to hear the news about Matthew, obviously,' Dana interrupted. 'But when I saw the CCTV footage, I felt as if I'd been kicked in the stomach . . . it's enough to sicken anyone.' Sam had no idea what was going on – she and Gerry had worked well and quickly under immediately difficult circumstances, but why was he introducing her to his family – ex-family, to be precise – at a time like this?

Dana was continuing. 'Gerry, when you called and told me about the little boy breaking all the school windows, I did what you said and thought about how kids like that get through the system. What happens to them and what information do teachers have that never necessarily gets any attention. I thought the quickest way to find any problem children in the area would be to ask the teachers. I haven't had much time . . .' This was an understatement in Sam's mind. It had been just over an hour since she and Gerry had first spoken about that one little boy, and this woman was already working fast enough to put the task force to shame. '. . . But I called the teachers in my school as quickly as I could, made a shortlist, and then phoned the heads of the other schools for the names that kept coming up related to our boys and girls.' Dana pushed a piece of A4 paper across the table towards Sam and Gerry. 'It's not very PC,' she shrugged, and weakly smiled an apology.

It was obvious the woman felt she was betraying her charges. Sam leaned across the table and placed her hand over that of the teacher. 'I think we're past all of that. Thank you. Thank you so much.'

The list contained the names of thirteen children. The problem children. The police could have got to this information eventually, but Sam knew that one respected teacher asking others was much quicker. She was already indebted to Dana Black. She looked at the list intently. Two names were marked with a red asterisk. Sam held the paper up and pointed. 'Could you explain this? Why these two?'

Dana Black took the list from Sam. She pushed her glasses up onto her forehead to read the names.

'Kevin Milne and Renee Smith.' She pulled her glasses back down and placed the list on the table.

'I've already checked with their teacher, dear – they weren't at school on the day that poor little boy went missing.'

Chapter Twenty-Six

Sam paced back and forwards across the floor of the task-force room, gripping a lukewarm cup of black coffee, the sound of Yazz belting out somewhere in the background. She muttered as she walked. The clock on the wall showed it was ten o'clock. There was a TV mounted high up on the wall opposite her showing a trailer for a new daytime chat show that had started a few weeks ago – the hosts, Richard and Judy, were pictured, sounding and looking very concerned and saying that they would be discussing the Matthew Cook murder later that morning, so *do join them*. She felt that time was slipping away – she wanted this sorted before the media took over completely. DI Davies wanted to do as much background checking as he could before storming into Acacia Avenue, one of the most troubled areas in Edmonton. The avenue had the highest percentage of young adults living on benefits in the country. Single parents, suicides and state dependency were the norm. The residents were neurotic about police harassment – most of them had something to hide. If Davies was sanctioning a raid on the houses of these two kids, he wanted to be bloody sure it was watertight before he put a search warrant up to a judge. He was hunched over Sam's desk. A single light shone down on it, highlighting every line and old acne scar on his face, and a cigarette hung from his lips. Gerry Cornwell was at his shoulder, going through the reports that he and Sam had collated overnight on Kevin Milne and Renee Smith.

'Bloody hell,' Davies sighed and pushed his chair back from the desk. 'Tell me this is wrong.' He tapped the nicotine-stained forefinger of his right hand on the paper.

'No,' Gerry said, standing up and stretching. 'It's right, I'm afraid. The information is correct.'

DI Davies stood up and held on to the report, crushing it between his fingers as he went to refill his coffee cup.

'Kevin Milne actually asked social workers to take him into care? This says that he was in a foster home for three weeks and then sent back to his psychotic mother. The boy tried to commit suicide but the hospital pumped his stomach and sent him back to Acacia Avenue.' Davies threw the report down on the coffee table, where milk seeped into its pages and sugar stuck to the damp paper. 'What the hell is the British taxpayer paying these bloody social workers for?' he asked no one in particular, waving the report in the air. Social workers were DI Davies's whipping boys. They were either colluding with criminals to get them off or they were letting down children. Sometimes he accused them of both in the same case. It was anyone's guess which way this one would go. Sam joined him at the coffee table, took the report from his hand and read out loud a passage she had marked earlier.

'The social worker said Renee Smith's family is less chaotic, although her parents are also separated.' She turned over a page and continued to read. 'Renee is hyperactive and she has an older sister with learning difficulties so severe she cannot be educated in mainstream schooling. There's a younger girl, too, that Renee seems to dote on.'

DI Davies lifted an eyebrow at the last remark and lit another cigarette. 'Great. She's a caring little bastard, then, when it comes to family. Am I meant to feel sorry for her?' He offered his packet to Sam. She had given up six months before, but this case was straining her nerves beyond anything she had ever known. Sam Jones had escaped from somewhere very similar to Acacia Avenue when she was seventeen; none of her colleagues knew she had been raised in a viper's nest akin to that of Kevin Milne and Renee Smith. Every cell in her body was shouting 'there is no bloody excuse', but she also knew how hard it was to escape.

'Sam, read out the bit about Renee being abandoned,' shouted Gerry from across the room as he stood at a huge white board of information. She flicked through some pages at his request. 'The social work department was called in three years ago when the mother, Amanda Smith, went to Blackpool with a new boyfriend and left the children alone in the house for a week. Renee was seven.' DI Davies was back sitting at Sam's desk. He swore under his breath again and then put his head in his hands. He rubbed his palms up and down his face.

'Are you sure they are the only ones on Dana Black's list to have been absent from school the day Matthew Cook was taken?'

Sam nodded and DI Davies stared off into the distance. His eyes glazed over and he bit his bottom lip.

'Birmingham University did a study that proves a path between a violent home and offending,' said Gerry. He was trying to be helpful. Sam and the other officers in the vicinity all suddenly became interested in the papers on their desk, the stills from the CCTV footage, or their shoes – anything to avoid being sucked into DI Davies's next diatribe, which they could see coming a mile away. 'So Birmingham Uni did a study, did they?' he asked Gerry, his voice heavy with sarcasm. 'And they found out that crap homes breed crap adults? Bloody hell – how much did they get paid to do that? Christ, ask any cop or teacher and they'd have been able to tell you the same for free. Stupid bastards.'

Sam sought out Gerry's eyes, warning him to leave it alone, say nothing. Answering Davies back would be like pouring petrol on a bonfire. They'd be at the station all night as it was. The neighbourhood would be ready for a lynching as soon as the first arrest was made, and they all needed to save their energy and stick together when that happened.

'Williams, Brown, prepare the paperwork, and make sure there are no mistakes,' Davies shouted at two officers standing nearby. 'We need a search warrant for the homes of Kevin Milne and Renee Smith. We'll need a social worker. I want to be there at daybreak. If they get wind of it they'll scarper.'

A dawn raid seemed inflammatory, but it was the only way to enter Acacia Avenue, which for several years had been a no-go zone for the police. The residents of the avenue were not early risers, unless they had a court appearance or a benefits interview. The police team could get in and out without waking the neighbourhood.

It was the only way to avoid bloodshed – they hoped.

Chapter Twenty-Seven

The sirens were silent as they stole into Edmonton Green housing estate. The locals called it Shank Town. Three concrete tower blocks dominated the skyline. A stolen car abandoned in a patch of waste ground was still smouldering. It was the least of their problems. Many of the windows in the flats were boarded up. No matter how desperate families were, no one wanted to move there, and Sam didn't blame them. It was easier to get into Shank Town than get out.

Monday morning was refuse day and the only sign of life was from the bin men. A freezing fog had rolled in off the Thames and it clung to the concrete buildings, making everything look unfamiliar. The rain had finally been replaced with a fine drizzle and mist. At the 7 a.m. meeting in the task-force room, Sam was pushed to the front of the group of officers. She knew the inspector's reasoning – as a woman she was seen as less of a threat. Nonetheless, she felt like a sacrificial lamb. The boss decided on a two-pronged attack. Two groups of officers would go to the Milne and Smith households at the same time, Sam and her colleague for Milne, another two for the Smiths.

'This place fucking stinks.' Constable Williams took a deep breath as he stepped into the lift. The Milnes lived on the tenth floor and, unfortunately, the lift was working. Sam followed her colleague's lead and walked in on tiptoe, careful to avoid the pool of urine swilling around the floor. The lift was slow, clunky and jerky, and they were forced to take several more shallow breaths before they reached their stop. To Sam's relief the doors opened, and they staggered out. The air quality on the landing was a marginal improvement. Eight flats shared a landing. The tenants had their names on the door, and 'Milne' was written on lined paper and stuck with sticky tape to the outside. Kate Milne answered the door on the tenth ring. Nervously, Sam Jones held up her badge and identified herself.

'This is about that kid, right?' Kate Milne snapped. Her thin greasy hair was wound so tightly around some outsized rollers that the skin on her forehead was stretched, giving her a surprised expression. She wore a dirty, pale blue nightshirt with a teddy bear on it, hiding her bulk. Her pink furry slippers were discoloured round the edges, and she had a homemade ink tattoo on the back of her hand. The writing was poor but Sam assumed it was the name of some long-lost love. Maybe Kevin's dad.

'That's right, Mrs Milne,' said Sam. 'We want to ask a few questions about Matthew Cook. Can we come in?'

Kate Milne ignored Sam's request and hung on so

tightly to the front door it creaked. Her eyelashes were clogged with last night's mascara but Sam knew she had spotted PC Williams when she started fluttering them grotesquely in his direction. 'I heard you were going door-to-door round the flats,' Kate Milne smiled at Williams. 'Have you been at it all night?' she asked with a wink.

'I have, gorgeous . . . any chance of letting us in for a cuppa?' Williams winked back at the horrible woman; he knew they had to gain entry quickly, whatever it took. The instructions from the inspector were to get inside the houses and get the kids back to the station before any of the neighbours knew what was going on. If an arrest was made, they didn't have the manpower to protect the Milne and Smith families.

Finally, Kate Milne opened up the door. The stench was overpowering. Seven kids, one fat woman and an Alsatian dog in a three-bedroomed council flat. The paper in the hallway was ripped, dirty, and marked where a couple of the children had written their names on it in felt-tip pen. The sink in the kitchen was overflowing with dishes. The radio was blaring and the mangy-furred dog was sniffing Sam's crotch.

'My partner's not keen on dogs, darlin' – do you mind putting him in a bedroom while you and me have our chat?' PC Williams's voice was soft, low and surprisingly seductive, and Sam found herself impressed by his handling of the situation. The last thing she needed was an enormous dog sinking his teeth into her leg in an effort to protect his owner.

'Kevin, you little bugger! Get up! Start getting ready

for school. Get your arse down here and lock Rex in the back room,' she screamed, turning to smile again at PC Williams as the unseen boy did what he was asked. 'Everyone is affected by little Matthew's murder. Terrible thing. Kevin –' she nodded her head in the direction of the hallway – 'he stole fifty pence out of my purse yesterday morning. He bought a single rose and took it along to the yard where they found the little nipper. Heart of gold, that boy.' She smiled, seemingly proud of her son, while her neglected half-dressed brood ran around the flat unwashed and unfed.

'Mrs Milne,' Sam said, keen to move things along. 'We need to talk to you about Kevin actually.'

'What?' Kate Milne asked, looking at Sam as if she'd never seen her before. 'What could I tell you? Fucking shame, that's all. Sorry, bloody shame,' she corrected herself, looking back at Williams. 'Little bastards who did that – they should be hung up. Scum, that's what they are. Scum. Probably brought up like animals and then they kill a little kiddie like that – I know what I'd do to them.'

Sam waited a moment, almost willing the words 'hanging's too good for them' to come out of Kate Milne's mouth before she pulled out a search warrant. 'Please get dressed, Mrs Milne. We're taking Kevin into the station for questioning about the abduction and murder of Matthew Cook.'

'You're what?' she spluttered. 'Are you out of your fucking mind, you bitch?' asked the caring mother, squinting her eyes at the WPC and forgetting to watch her language now that the cards were on the table. 'Kevin?

My Kevin? What the fuck do you think he's got to do with that kid's death? He might be a little shit, but he's a good lad,' she said, ignoring the contradiction of her own words.

'Mrs Milne. I have a search warrant and I would like to take Kevin to the station.'

'Over my dead fucking body!' shouted Kate Milne, lunging for Sam, just as Williams moved in front of her.

'Now, now, Kate,' he said, 'there's no need for that. I'm sure you'd like this cleared up just as we would, so come along, love, let's get your son and we'll get things moving.'

Kevin's mother thought about the situation for a moment before turning round. 'Kevin! Get your arse in here, you little shit! What the fuck you been up to now? Did you nick something off that dead kid? Did you?' She didn't wait for him to appear before she started screaming the questions. Sam watched as a door slowly opened and a young boy stepped out. Kevin Milne stood in the doorway, his messy dark hair falling into his eyes, running his baseball cap through his hands and looking down. Sam had to check. On automatic pilot she took the cap from his hands and placed it on his head, and then with both hands she pulled his hood up over it.

PC Williams stepped back as the boy from the CCTV footage looked him in the eyes. It was a look that left no doubt.

Kevin Milne, aged ten, had taken Matthew Michael Cook.

Chapter Twenty-Eight

DI Davies was leaning against the car looking anxious, an ever-present cigarette hanging from his lips. Sam was relieved to see the boss there.

'Any luck?' he asked. She nodded and motioned her head back towards the high-rise entrance. PC Williams, Kate and Kevin Milne stood in the hallway waiting for the signal that it was all clear. Sam had come out first to check that the route was free of the press and that the bin men had finished their work and gone on to the next estate.

The fourth estate might have been missing, but the route was still far from clear. Mothers were now walking their children to school. The numbers of dutiful parents doing the school run had increased since Matthew's disappearance. Although a police car in Shank Town was not an unusual occurrence, it was still noted, and anxious glances passed between the car and the officer hanging back with the Milnes in the foyer. The family were well known in the estate – not the worst, but far from being respectable.

As he came out, Kevin Milne tried to look defiant,

but the mothers could smell something was up, even without the baseball cap and the hoody. Maybe they knew what he was. It was as if they had been waiting for a sign. Now it was here and everything fell into place. Whispers began to circulate as the boy and his mother moved over to enter the police car. Crowds seemed to gather within seconds, bending down to pick up the debris that was scattered all over Shank Town. An elderly woman dropped her granddaughter's hand and grabbed half a brick. Her aim was straight and true and if it hadn't been for the safety glass they would have been hit.

'Quickly!' shouted Sam. There was no point in placing the rough grey blanket over his head now; the neighbours knew who he was and what he had done. Fear ruled Kevin Milne's life – it always had, and this wouldn't change anything. He had an instinct for survival that Sam Jones had only ever seen in rats, and he took off like a sprinter the minute the first missile was thrown. In seconds he had outstripped his mother and PC Williams. Doubt flickered in the officer's eyes: was the little bastard going to try and leg it? Williams was no shirker. Instinct kicked in and he chased down the boy. His helmet flew off and the smooth operation descended into mayhem. The mist muffled the noise but Sam saw it all happen in slow motion. Someone shouted, 'Get her!' and Sam swivelled to check her back as DI Davies threw his cigarette away and readied himself.

In that instant the women of Shank Town saw their chance and headed for Kate – for years to come they would be bought drinks on the strength of this morning's

150

action. Years of pent-up emotion boiled over, children shrank into the background as their mothers turned into vicious baboons, spitting, scratching and hitting Kate Milne. She cowered and tried to protect herself. A stone cut her cheek, narrowly missing her eye, and a tear of blood ran down her face. An inch higher and she would have been blinded.

Sam radioed for backup. DI Davies waded in to break the women up, barging his way into their circle, his arms over his face and head for protection. He screamed that he was the police, over and over again, but in their blood frenzy they didn't hear – or they chose not to. Some started to back off but a hardened group of stragglers continued to kick Kate Milne. A couple of women punched DI Davies in the ribs as he passed and it wasn't a mistake. There was no need to show his badge to the crowd – they knew who he was. He'd arrested most of their husbands, and one or two of the women as well had been picked up for soliciting. The inspector thought it was a mercy Kate Milne was a fat cow, otherwise her internal organs would have been damaged from the force of the women's kicks. As it was, he gripped her arm and pulled her towards the car. She'd lost a shoe, her coat was torn and her hair was bedraggled. The mob parted for him, their lust temporarily sated, but Kate Milne was no fool. She knew this was only the start. And if it had been another child getting ready to sit in the back of the squad car, she would have done exactly the same thing. Blame the parents: everyone does.

She was thrown in the back of the squad car, where she landed heavily. Sam sat behind PC Williams and

Kevin was in the middle, dragged back from his pathetic attempt at escape. He slumped against his mother, both crying great, fat, heaving sobs. She was stroking his hair and telling him that she loved him. Kate wasn't much of a mother, but she was the only one he had, and she could go through the motions when she needed to. They had tried to cover him with a blanket, tried to keep his identity a secret, but they had failed. From the moment he left his mother's house, Kevin Milne was lost to the world, and Child X was born.

The rush-hour traffic was easing as they sped back to police headquarters, the sirens now blaring. The cat was out of the bag, and the papers would be laying siege to police headquarters before the morning was over. Fog still smothered Edmonton Green and the blue lights of the police car looked like a laser show. The newly planted trees along the roadside were doing poorly, and the occupants inside the squad car weren't doing much better. PC Williams screeched to a halt outside HQ. Renee Smith and her mother were already inside, but a couple of photographers who were quick off the mark were snapping furiously. Sam threw the blanket over the boy's head as they bundled him up the steps and through the doors.

A loud sigh escaped Sam's lips. The first stage was over, and the next would be played out under the glare of the world's media. But they had them – they had the little bastards.

Chapter Twenty-Nine

Sam joined the crowd behind the two-way mirror to watch the interview. She sucked in her breath as she jostled for a position where she could both see and hear. A quick glance to her left and right showed her fellow officers staring without blinking. The nation was horrified by children killing children – in this job, they got a front-row seat for the action and she hoped they could make sense of it. The wobbly brown Formica table held a box of Kleenex, a tape recorder and an untouched plastic beaker of Kia-Ora from the police canteen. The interview room was hot and stuffy. DI Davies had taken his jacket off and his tie was at half-mast.

Kevin Milne and his mother sat at the opposite side of the table to the inspector, and Kevin lay with his head in his mother's lap, whimpering and trembling. 'But I didn't do it, Mum.' Kate patted his back. 'Mum, tell them I didn't do nothing. What will they do to me? Will they hurt me? Will I get taken somewhere? Where will I get taken?' Rivers of snot, mingled with tears, ran down his face. Kate continued to stroke his back in a way she hadn't done since he was a baby.

'Everything will be all right.' She picked up a tissue and wiped his face. 'I'll always love you, Kevin. You're a good boy. I know you didn't do nothing.' Kate Milne's face had received some rudimentary help, a plaster covering the cut below her eye. In different circumstances she would have received medical treatment before this interview commenced.

'He's showing no remorse,' said Gerry Cornwell, looking at Kevin's tears, tapping the glass lightly. 'He's only sorry for himself . . . sorry he's been caught.'

'What about Kate?' Sam asked. She half turned to stare into his face. 'Will she stand by him when he admits he killed Matthew?' The officers in the viewing room had been silent, but they now held their breaths, anxious to know Gerry's opinion, asking themselves what they would do if their boy was a killer.

'The near-lynching at the flats this morning proved one thing to Kate. She's got no one but Kevin and her other children. No one will stand by her: they're all she's got left. She might kick in now with some motherly support – it might do her a bit of good if she feels she has to save face.'

Sam turned her head back to watch DI Davies through the glass, who was addressing the boy. 'We don't need a confession, Kevin.' He leaned over and took a sip from the boy's juice. 'We've got everything we need to put you away forever.'

Kate clearly didn't like the way he was turning nasty on her boy. 'What've you got then, smart arse? Show us what you've got.' She took a cigarette out of her packet and put it in her mouth. 'My Kevin wouldn't hurt a fly.

He's a good boy. He bought a rose for that kid. You've got nothing on my boy, he'd do nothing anyway.' She had a cruel expression as she spoke, and Sam didn't have to stretch her imagination too far to imagine where Kevin had inherited his tendencies.

'So you want to know what your little scumbag of a son has done? Fair enough.' The inspector pointed at Kevin. Sam wondered if he was going to punch the boy, but Davies banged his fist off the table and those in the front row of the viewing room took an involuntary step back. They had all been on the receiving end of the inspector's wrath at some point; most of them made sure the experience wasn't repeated.

'We have a shovel with Kevin's fingerprints on it and one of Matthew's eyelashes – how's that for starters?' Davies stopped to let the implication of that piece of information sink in. He turned his back on them and pushed a video into the wall-mounted TV. He sat down on the edge of the table, lit another cigarette and watched the CCTV footage of Kevin Milne holding Matthew's hand and leading him away from the toilets where Angie Bell was having a sly fag. The TV went blank and then more CCTV footage came up. The inspector walked up to the screen and pointed out a woman talking to the pair. He took his cigarette out to speak; he wanted to make sure they heard every word. 'Mrs Dexter is one of thirty-eight people who spoke to you, Kevin. Thirty-eight witnesses will say they saw you and Renee Smith leading the little boy away from different places that day. Some of them saw you hit him. Most of them say he was crying for his mummy. But Mrs Dexter will tell the

155

court that she stopped you and you said you'd found him, that you promised her you were taking him to the police station.' He took a draw on his cigarette again, and held it between his fingers as he pointed it at Kate Milne. 'Mrs Dexter is going to have to live with her actions for the rest of her life. Her GP has her sedated. She feels responsible because she believed your son and now Matthew is dead. It's no bloody wonder she can't sleep. You managing to get forty winks, Mrs Milne? How about you, Kevin?'

Kate Milne remained silent but defiant. She continued to stroke Kevin's head. 'He's a good boy, he's—'

'Shut up,' said Davies. 'He probably nicked that fucking rose as well. Have you any idea what your child is, Mrs Milne? Let me help you understand a little better.' Davies turned his attention back to the child. 'We have your fingerprints on the iron bar you used to batter the toddler with, Kevin. We have a witness who saw you torture him. We have a witness who can tell us every detail of how you planned this and orchestrated it. We even have a witness who saw you take Matthew's heart.' DI Davies stepped back. What would the little bastard say to that lot? A grim smile played across his thin lips.

Kevin sat up, lifted the corner of his hoody up, sniffed back the snot and wiped his face dry. 'I don't believe you,' he screamed. ''Cos I didn't do it! Who have you fucking got saying these things? Stupid Renee fucking Smith? She's so fucking thick she doesn't know what day it is, her and her retard family, so you can't believe a word she makes up. She's away with the fucking fairies.' He hawked back in his throat and spat a gob of phlegm full in the detective's face as Kate Milne looked proudly at him.

There was a sharp intake of breath in the viewing room. Sam had already decided that whatever Davies did now she wouldn't give evidence against him in a disciplinary hearing. Everything slowed down. Davies took a large, freshly laundered white handkerchief out of his pocket and wiped his face. 'Are you forgetting that witness there the whole time, Kevin? Renee Smith has already confessed to everything, and she's said you made her do it.' He crushed his cigarette in the ashtray. 'You're finished, boy,' said Davies.

Kevin stopped crying immediately. The tears were still there but he was eerily calm. 'You,' he said, pointing at Davies, 'you have nothing, mate.' The words made him sound like an adult, the tone even more so. 'You have a stupid girl from a stupid family who believes stupid things. She's making it all up – I took her with me that day when I wasn't going to school 'cos I felt fucking sorry for her. More fool me. She's a liar. You're all liars. She's heard stuff on the news and you've fed the rest to her.' He turned to his mother as the tears started to roll again. 'Mum, I didn't do nothing, I swear it. I'd never hurt a little kiddie.' Kate Milne looked warmly at him, possibly for the first time in years, as his eyes filled and he let her hug him. Kevin Milne looked back at Davies with a smirk on his face. 'I stole some sweets from the bus station. I admit it. Are you going to send me to prison for that? Sir?'

Sam prayed Davies was right, that this boy would go down for the murder he had undoubtedly committed and that the authorities would throw away the key. He was trying to play them all and she worried how far that might take him – he was smarter than she had expected. She glanced towards Gerry as he stood ashen-faced, looking at the scene in front of them. 'What's wrong?' she asked – foolishly, given all that was going on.

'In my professional opinion, I could write you a list of what that boy has probably experienced in his life. In my personal opinion? Jesus Christ – I think we may be looking at someone who was born to kill,' he whispered.

Chapter Thirty

Kevin Milne was deep in a dreamless sleep when the clanking of keys outside his room woke him. He jerked up in bed, flailing, and for a brief moment forgot where he was. The room in the secure unit was the nicest bedroom he'd ever slept in. It was clean – which was a novelty to him – and he had a bed to himself, which was unusual too. The staff had tried to make it homely. There were football posters on the wall and Ladybird books for age ten readers lined up neatly on the book-shelf. Of course, if they had really wanted him to feel at home, he would have slept on a urine-stained bare mattress on the floor with three other boys and a German shepherd dog lying on his feet. Enjoying the space and freedom of the bed, he turned over, pulling the covers with him. A shaft of moonlight illuminated the room, and he held his breath.

He waited.

The clock on the wall showed that it was 2 a.m., eight hours before the trial, eight hours in which to realize he had blown it. He screwed the bed covers up between his fingers and twisted them, hard. He should have been patient; patience certainly wasn't something that he found easy, but he would have to learn.

Learn to wait.

The hours, the wasted hours he'd spent with that idiot, Dr Cornwell, came into his mind. A tear ran down his cheek, soon followed by another one. He was crying for himself – the tears were always for himself. The boy sucked in his breath as he thought of the psychiatrist. The muscles in his jaw became tight and he could feel hot pain shooting up into his head. Cornwell had looked like a pushover. He smiled easily at Kevin, showing off his even white teeth, but his eyes were cold and, unlike the other members of staff, he never invited Kevin to call him by his first name.

Kevin had made many mistakes with Cornwell, but his first mistake of all was when he'd gobbed in DI Davies's face, and only seconds later realized that the psychiatrist would no doubt have witnessed it behind the two-way mirror. On reflection, Kevin realized he should have been subdued, frightened even, but he was just so furious when he realized that Renee had sold him out. The second mistake was when he took the IQ test a few weeks later. He should have flunked it, but he just couldn't resist showing off. The psychiatrist's eyes had widened – Kevin would have laid his pocket money down that his IQ was higher than the good doctor's. A slow smile crept across his face as he saw the books for children on the shelf again; he turned on his back, put his hands under his head and stared up at the ceiling. The light shade was navy blue with stars on it. The stars glowed dirty white in the dark. Gazing at the luminous blobs helped him think. He had read somewhere that intelligence was supposed to be inherited from your mother; he snorted out loud at the idea, then held his breath again. Every nerve was alive. The hairs on his neck stood to attention: was any 'carer' coming to investigate? Who'd been jangling those keys? What were they up to?

The minutes passed and there were no more footsteps. Kevin let the breath escape from his lips in a low whistle. Tonight, of all nights, the authorities had doubled the guards, and they were observing him closely, watching for suicidal tendencies. He swallowed another snort. Suicide wasn't in his plans. He had his whole life ahead of him.

Kevin Milne stared back at the stars and considered again the possibility that he could have inherited his genius (for that was what he considered it) from his mother. He shook his head silently. Not possible. His body shook. For months he'd seen only his family, the guards and Dr Gerry Cornwell, and he didn't really want to start thinking of anyone else now. Food had been plentiful for the first time in his life and he'd gorged himself on macaroni cheese, sausage and mash, ice cream, lots and lots of ice cream. Now he was paying the price; now he was getting fat and beginning to look like his mother. A great wail came from the pit of his stomach. This morning was his first entrance into the world as a killer.

A cold, hard realization hit him. His lawyer, an unremarkable grey man, had explained that the papers had been forbidden by the courts to mention his name. They would not say that Kevin Milne abducted and killed Matthew Michael Cook. Child X did these things. The television would not be allowed to show pictures of him, and the lawyer promised he was going to petition the courts to ask that Kevin Milne be given a new identity. The new identity would entitle him not only to a new name, but a background story with papers to back it up. A new passport, a new birth certificate and a new home. He would be given an education. With therapy, his lawyer assured him, he would be equipped to face the outside world. Kevin started to laugh; he laughed and laughed until his belly began to hurt. He would be prepared for society, but would society be prepared for him? He hoped not. He would do his time and then he would be safe.

Kevin Milne smiled. The naughtier you were, the better you were treated.

And the papers thought he was crazy.

Chapter Thirty-One

By the time the prison transit van arrived at Wood Green Crown Court, the world's media were ready, having been camped on its doorstep since before dawn. The reporters were wired on coffee, sugar and nicotine, and they were baying for blood. Journalists barged into one another jostling for position, notepads and pens held above heads because there was no space to keep them down by their sides. Photographers had long, fat lenses on their cameras, which made them look like offensive weapons. Television crews from every corner of the globe parked their vans in the car park. CNN had a satellite dish, and an impossibly glamorous, anorexic blonde anchor-woman who was trying to interview the onlookers. The parkland outside Wood Green Court might have been bare, but the angry mob and media frenzy covered the ground. The naked trees waved in the wet wind, and the sound of the prison transit van's wheels crunching on the fallen leaves was lost amongst the catcalls and swearing from the mob. The sky was grey and a fine drizzle landed on the crowds that had gathered, the reason for the large police presence. They looked ready to stamp out the first sign of trouble. A shield wall guarded the steps of the court; wearing riot gear, the officers linked arms and stood shoulder to shoulder behind Perspex screens. In clear view, a man bent down, picked up the biggest stone he could find and hurled it at the van. It bounced off the window, skittered along the side, and bounced harmlessly on the road.

Nine forty-five Tuesday morning, Kevin Milne stumbled out of the van, tired and frightened. The driver had pulled up at the back entrance to avoid the glare of the press. It hadn't been a good night for Kevin; he'd cried and felt sorry for himself. He wasn't sure whether the plan was going to work. What if he changed? He could keep his eye on the long view, but what if something about all of this changed him? He was the only person he could ever trust, ever rely on – if that went, he didn't know what he'd do.

Here he was, walking through a corridor. It was a private corridor, separating him from the other prisoners. A helpful prison guard had told him, with a smile on his face, that threats had been made on his life and the authorities doubted they could guarantee his safety if he was placed in the cells along with the other accused.

Kevin stared at his feet. He placed one foot after the other on the polished concrete floor, and felt eyes upon him. Civil servants were hiding in the rooms, staring out of half-opened doors, all desperate to boast in the pub after work that they had seen Child X. He felt sick; his stomach was churning and he wanted to vomit. He would have, too, if it would have helped, but he thought he would just want to throw up all over again, so what was the point in starting? The new clothes his mother had bought him for court were two sizes too small, even allowing for the fact that he'd piled on the pounds. The bottom of his trousers ended two inches above his ankle, and he thought that he looked stupid – or maybe his mother was smarter than he gave her credit for. She'd had her share of court experiences – perhaps she'd thought it would help if he looked pathetic. He was wearing an Argyll knitted sweater with a diamond pattern. No one had worn such a thing since the 1950s, but it was the furthest jumper Kate could get from a hoody.

Kevin was at this moment separated off from everyone he knew. Renee had travelled to court under a separate escort, and the authorities were determined they would never associate together again: except, of course, in the dock.

The guards led him into a large room. This was the holding area for prisoners in custody who were due to appear in court. It was empty except for a couple of grey plastic chairs placed against opposite walls. The vomit-green paintwork was badly damaged, names scratched into the plaster with knives, or gang names scrawled with felt-tip pen. It smelled of piss, unwashed bodies and industrial disinfectant. He was getting used to that smell.

A matronly woman with short, permed blonde hair asked him to sit down, and she pointed at the chair furthest from the door. Her name was Mrs Johnson and she'd come with the van and another two officers to collect him from the secure unit. She was a court-appointed social worker. Kevin thought she was a cow.

She pinched him when she thought no one could see. He knew, even if they could, no one would do anything about it. He was planning his revenge on Mrs Johnson when the door opened.

He was about to meet Renee for the first time since they'd been arrested and she'd grassed him up. He was looking forward to it. But he guessed she wouldn't be feeling the same.

Renee wasn't alone. She came in with her own social worker, a woman who seemed really young, with a posh voice and too much make-up. Her name was Michelle, she said. She smiled at Kevin and tried to chit-chat about the weather. Michelle stared at the two children; they were going to have to sit in this room until the jury was picked. The lawyers were having difficulties. No one wanted to sit through a three-week trial listening to the last hours of Matthew's life, and no one wanted to confront the 'Edmonton 38', people just like them who chose not to save the toddler's life. Michelle didn't care. She thought society was to blame.

Renee was smaller than Kevin remembered. He tried to catch her eye but the little bitch wouldn't look at him, except once when she puffed up her cheeks. It was the gesture they used to do to the fat kids at school. She would pay for that. Michelle turned on the radio. She was trying to be their friend. She was the only one. Mrs Johnson didn't approve of pop music. She switched the station to Radio Four and quickly turned it back again. *Woman's Hour* was discussing the danger faced by the Cook killers.

Kevin glanced at Renee out of the corner of his eye.

He understood what the announcer was saying. He had been threatened himself, although the 'carers' at the secure unit had tried to hide it from him. When he closed his eyes at night he still saw the mothers and grandmothers who tried to rip Kate apart – they weren't so different to him, whatever they might like to think. Renee sat on the edge of her seat, swinging her legs back and forward. His throat tightened until it was hard to breathe. She had grown; her body had lost the puppy fat and her hair was clean and shiny – custody agreed with Renee. He started to laugh. His coarse, harsh, hysterical laugh echoed round the room; he laughed until his belly hurt, tears rolling down his face; he had to grip the side of the chair to stop him falling off.

The adults stared in silence at one another, their eyes shifting from the giggling boy back to the faces of their colleagues, searching for an answer. Mrs Johnson closed the door of the witness room. It was disrespectful, that's what it was. What if Matthew Cook's family heard it? What would they think? They'd think that she was incapable of controlling a snot-nosed killer, that's what they'd think. Mrs Johnson straightened her back, the small muscles in her face tightening, twisting her mouth. She walked with a new purpose over to the door of the witness room and made sure it was closed. Breathing deeply, she walked towards the boy. Not for the first time did it cross her mind that the devil was at work within him. The palms of her hands were greasy with sweat; she rubbed them up and down her skirt. The social worker's flat shoes made no sound on the red linoleum floor. Even if they had, she doubted the boy would have heard or paid the slightest bit of attention. No one else noticed what she was doing. They stood mesmerized by Kevin Milne's performance. Only she could see it for what it was – an attempt to evade responsibility.

Mrs Johnson drew her hand back, and smacked her palm off the boy's cheek. The sound cracked round the room, rooting everyone to the spot.

He stopped laughing.

Renee clapped her hands over her mouth, shaking her head. She whispered, 'She shouldn't of done that.' Her hand went up to her hair and she pulled at the roots. 'She shouldn't of done that.' Michelle laid her hand over Renee's. It had taken months of patient counselling to get the girl to stop pulling her hair out. Renee was rocking back and forth repeating, 'She shouldn't of done that.'

Kevin's mouth fell open. Slack-jawed, he held his hand over his hot and swollen cheek. A slow smile of satisfaction crossed Mrs Johnson's face; she knew how to deal with unruly children. Her smile fell as she saw Kevin Milne smile too.

He was playing them all. Now he could go into court with a recent, red, shiny slap mark across his face.

Maybe things would work out after all.

Chapter Thirty-Two

The main entrance to Wood Green Crown Court resembled a medieval bishop's palace, the towers and turrets paying homage to justice. Lord Chief Justice Edward Hunter stared down at the media circus and the angry mob. He ran a tight ship. All the barristers and solicitors knew this, and over the course of the three-week trial the jury members and press were about to find out too.

Lord Hunter's heavy silk robes pressed against his legs and the long wig was hot on his head. At times like this he envied those of his brother judges who were bald. He longed to reach up with his forefinger and scratch the itch at the back of his head, but that would never do – the solemnity of the bench must be observed. He looked over at the dock where the two prisoners were sitting. It was like a scene from *Alice in Wonderland*. Just as in the Queen's court when Alice was on trial, everything was wrong. Little Renee Smith and Kevin Milne sat on their high chairs so that their faces were visible over the edge of the dock. The girl was white and tearful as she draped her hand over the edge of the box and her mother held it. Through the heavy silence of the courtroom her sniffles reverberated off the rafters. A chill ran up his back. All eyes in the court were upon Lord Edward Hunter, but he was only interested in one person – Kevin Milne.

The boy was dressed in clothes that did him no favours; the outfit was too small and he was too fat. His face was clean, his mouth down-turned; he caught the judge's eyes and he would not let go. The force of the small boy's personality stole his breath away. Lord Hunter's heart fluttered in distress at what he truly believed was evil sitting in his court; he would have to revise all his notions, regardless of criticism or the notion that an accused person is innocent until proven guilty. Lord Hunter knew, with a certainty he had seldom felt, that he was in the presence of something genuinely rare, even in the highest court in the land. He felt as if he was in the presence of evil.

Hunter narrowed his eyes until they became slits and stared back at the boy, refusing to be cowed. The corners of Kevin Milne's mouth slowly lifted, curling into a sadistic smile. The trial had hardly begun, but as Hunter stared at the snivelling boy, he made himself a promise. The boy would serve twenty-five years in correctional facilities and then be transferred to a secure mental hospital. He wasn't safe to be allowed to walk the streets again, and Hunter would do all he could to make sure that he never did.

Chapter Thirty-Three

The courtroom was hushed. It was after lunch, the air was stuffy, and almost everyone on the public benches was sleepy.

Dr Gerry Cornwell faltered. How do you look a mother in the eye and tell the world she produced a child so wrong that no drugs, no therapy, and no amount of love could fix him?

'Dr Cornwell, please answer the question,' bid Lord Justice Edward Hunter.

Gerry Cornwell scanned the court. Every seat seemed filled by a journalist ready to record and put a spin on whatever he said. Thankfully, Donna Cook was not in court. She attended most sessions, but on some days she was judged by her doctor as too fragile to attend. The sight of Renee Smith and Kevin Milne rendered her unpredictable, no matter how high her dosage of Valium. Gerry thought of his home visit to Donna Cook. 'Poor but proud' was how his own mother would have described her. The statistics didn't give her or Matthew a chance, but he thought differently after that visit. In his opinion, Matthew Cook and his mother had had a chance, a very good chance, of escaping Shank Town. But now, thanks to the work of Kevin Milne and Renee Smith, neither Matthew nor Donna would live again.

'Could you repeat the question, m'lord?' Gerry asked. His mouth tasted of the last cigarette he'd smoked in the witness room. When his name was called he'd rushed to finish it and now he felt sick. A hot fever was flushing through his body and he felt dizzy. Kevin Milne's eyes were on him. The boy was playing a game, a very clever game. He looked stupid; different in a harmless, village idiot kind of way – an image that Gerry knew from the shocking IQ results could not be further from the truth; he seemed totally different to the boy Gerry had got to know. Kevin was crying and simpering through the trial as the defence and prosecution teams questioned the witnesses. His blue eyes were glazed. He turned to stare at the world's press as if he didn't know where he was. He'd worn the same stained trousers and jumper for fourteen days, and he'd chewed a hole in the jumper sleeve.

The jury were buying into his act. Kate Milne stood up in her seat and reached into the box to stroke his greasy, lank hair and give him drinks of water. Tears ran down her face, but Gerry wasn't fooled. He had been to the house. He'd seen the holes she'd punched in the partition walls in drunken fits, witnessed first hand the barbaric cruelty between the siblings, who were allowed to bite and torture one another while Kate ignored them.

Sir John Limington QC, barrister for the prosecution, coughed. 'Dr Cornwell, in your professional opinion, is there any condition which would explain the behaviour of the two accused?' The queen's counsel half turned and waved his forefinger in the direction of the dock, as if anyone could be in any doubt about whom he was speaking.

Renee Smith, or child Y, as she was now known, was playing with her hair as her involvement in the killing was discussed. Gerry Cornwell turned and faced the jury box. He made sure his eyes connected with every single juror.

'Child Y has a mental age of seven or eight at best. She has an elder sister who attends a special-needs school. At present her doctor has her on a dosage of behaviour-modification drugs that is at the upper end of the scale for a child of her weight and age. In my professional opinion, Renee Smith is easily led and eager to please.' Gerry turned and faced the other accused, daring Kevin Milne to break his act. But Kevin met his eyes, lifted his arm to his mouth and started to chew the end of his sleeve. A wool ball formed in his teeth, saliva ran from the sides of his mouth, and the jurors recoiled back into their seats.

'And Child X? From what you have uncovered, what is your assessment of Child X?' asked Limington. His half-moon steel glasses were perched on the end of his nose, one hand was resting on a large pile of leather-bound law books and his free hand was on his kidneys. There was a pained expression on his thin, lined face. He already knew the answer: Sir John did not ask any question to which he did not know the answer.

Gerry didn't really want to talk about what had made Kevin Milne into the monster he was. It was totally unprofessional, but he disliked the boy intensely. He knew that his background was horrendous, but he also felt that there was something about Milne that would have made him act the way he had, irrespective of whether he had been brought up by nuns. Still, he was here for a reason, and the real Kevin would be revealed soon enough.

'In the course of my sessions with Kevin, and in conjunction with social work, educational and police reports, there is no doubt that Kevin Milne comes from a dysfunctional background. His mother has had eight children, six of whom have been in care at one time or another. She claims that there are five different fathers involved, but none is mentioned on the birth certificates and we have no way of knowing the paternity of any of the children. There have been no father figures of a positive note in Kevin's life at any point.'

Gerry reflected on his own words. The picture wasn't an unusual one but it was pitiful. A series of one-night stands when Kate Milne was out of her head on one thing or another had led to too many pregnancies – sometimes she could be bothered to terminate, sometimes not. None of the men stuck around, and she often brought in others to her life who stayed but who had nothing to do with the children in the household. The actions of these men bordered on abuse of various types, and the children who had been in care at times were generally sent back to the same sort of hell. It was no wonder that Kevin had asked to be taken into care permanently at one point. Donna Cook wasn't the only one who would be wishing he'd had his wishes granted.

Limington grabbed his attention back.

'What else have you discovered about Child X?'

'He has been a victim of physical and mental abuse throughout his life. There are medical records of unresolved injuries since he was nine months old. This is a feature that runs through the histories of his siblings as well. He has been neglected, underfed, lived in dirty, unhygienic surroundings and allowed to miss out on a great deal of education. Through speaking to neighbours, the police uncovered a number of occasions on which Kate Milne left her children for days on end to fend for themselves. They were often seen running wild, and would knock on neighbours' doors asking for food.' The entire courtroom seemed to look at Kate Milne, who sat with her head held high as her life was laid out in front of the world. If they were waiting for her to cry, to apologize, they'd have a long wait.

'And this situation was allowed to go . . . unchecked?' asked Limington.

'To a degree,' answered Gerry. 'As I've said, some of the children were taken into care at different times, and the mother has been charged on a number of occasions, but this isn't my area of professional expertise, so I can only summarize what I have read in reports.'

'Yes, quite,' sniffed Limington. 'I believe that there will be a number of questions raised from this case. However, to return to the matter in hand,' he said, as if he hadn't been the one to digress in the first place, 'what did you uncover that is of direct relevance to Kevin Milne's alleged crime?'

'With all due respect, his background is relevant,' said

Cornwell, 'because Kevin isn't necessarily the product we would expect from such a situation. Yes, his neglect and abuse have contributed to his liking of violence, but he is actually an incredibly intelligent boy. One normally associates his type of childhood with low intellect and ability, but the opposite is true with Kevin Milne. I have never met such a clever child – and he far exceeds what many, in fact what most, adults are intellectually capable of.'

'So,' asked Limington, smiling despite himself, 'in your professional opinion, is Kevin Milne capable of rationally deciding to murder another human being?'

Gerry Cornwell didn't have to pause.

'Without a shadow of a doubt – yes.'

Chapter Thirty-Four

'Is there any evidence you can bring to the case to support your answer, Dr Cornwell?' asked Hunter.

'Yes,' said Gerry, as the other man looked at him blankly. Dr Gerry Cornwell widened his eyes, staring at the production table then back at Limington. Cornwell repeated this process three or four times until the QC remembered. 'Ah, yes, quite,' said the prosecutor, taking the hint about what was to be displayed next.

'Prosecution production number three-four-three,' he said, turning to the court usher. 'Could you show it to the witness, please?' The old usher limped to the table and lifted up a plastic evidence bag with a white label on it. He carried it across to the witness box and handed it to Gerry Cornwell. He then picked up a pile of copies and handed them out to the jurors.

'Can I take it out?' asked Gerry. Limington nodded, and the psychiatrist fumbled with the plastic bag. It was a plain, sky-blue, school notebook. The notebook was anally neat, the type of book that belongs to the class swot; every letter was drawn using a newly sharpened pencil.

There was no graffiti on the front of the book. The drawings in the book were excellent, indicating that the owner of the book had a talent, a rare talent beyond a schoolchild's years.

'How did you hear about the existence of this notebook?' Limington asked.

Dr Gerry Cornwell placed the book face down on the witness box – it always made him feel sick. 'I have been seeing Child X and Child Y at least once a week since their arrest. Whilst Child Y –' he nodded at Renee – 'has shown remorse during our sessions, Child X has never admitted the murder or expressed any sorrow or regret over his actions. In all my time as a clinical psychiatrist, I have never met a more cold and calculating personality.' Dr Cornwell swallowed and tried to moisten his dry mouth. 'In an attempt to make progress, I asked for permission to hypnotize him.'

Limington let the word 'hypnotize' sink in. 'Is this a perfectly acceptable practice in a court of law?' he asked, knowing the answer.

'Yes,' answered Gerry. 'I needed to relax Kevin so that I could get at the truth of some of his answers. This was difficult to do. He always seemed to be on his guard, never in the state of relaxation that was necessary. Permission was asked from his mother.'

'And she granted it readily?' asked the QC.

'Erm,' said Gerry, 'I'd have to check my notes.' He knew what was in them.

'Yes?' asked Limington again. 'She willingly agreed?'

'Her words were, and I quote, "Do what you like to the little fucking bastard – he's wrecked my life, so you can hypnotize him into thinking he's Myra fucking Hindley if you like."'

'Can we take that as parental consent?'

'We did clarify it in stronger legal terms,' confirmed Cornwell, stealing a glance at Kate Milne, who had found this was the best time to be looking in her handbag.

'Turn to page eight,' commanded Limington. The jury opened their copies of the production as he nodded at the witness to continue. 'What happened next?'

'Child X proved an excellent subject for hypnotism. Whilst in a deep state, he started to boast about what he called his manual. This took some time, but when I asked him to explain, he told me that for the last three years he had kept a manual of murder, a diary of a would-be killer. I asked him where he hid the manual, as it hadn't been discovered in the police search. He told me it was in a graveyard in a tin box.' Dr Cornwell held the manual up. 'As you can see, Child X told the truth.'

'Would you describe the drawing on page eight to the court?'

Gerry Cornwell picked up the hateful manual and flicked over the pages. He held the book aloft. 'This drawing, and the explanation, details exactly how a toddler would be stolen from a busy bus or railway station and then tortured and killed. It's dated three months before Matthew was abducted.'

There was a gasp from the public benches of the court.

'But that is not what shocked you, is it, Doctor?' Limington stared at his expert witness.

Dr Gerry Cornwell was hanging his head and shaking it from side to side. 'No, sir,' he said, 'that was not what shocked me.' He held the book up again. 'You see, the drawing you asked me to look at is on page eight. But there are four other murders detailed before this, and sixteen after.' He placed the book down. Defence counsel was on his feet shouting objections, but Dr Gerry Cornwell wanted the jury to hear this so he shouted even louder. 'Every time Child X kills, he puts a big red tick.' He showed page eight and the murder of the toddler. He then held the pages aloft so the jury could see the murder of *pensioner*, the murder of *perverts*, the murder of *black girl* and the murder of *retard*.

It was Kevin's wish list.

Chapter Thirty-Five

On the twenty-first day after the trial of Child X and Child Y for the murder of Matthew Cook began, the jury returned a verdict. The pair sat in the dock and stared straight ahead at Lord Justice Edward Hunter. Even Kevin Milne had stopped crying and chewing his jumper. There was no point in acting any more: the verdict was now out of his hands.

Lord Hunter stared as the foreman of the jury stood up and handed the usher a folded white piece of paper. It had been an unsettling trial for all involved; the evidence of the children's teachers about their pupils' home circumstances, and the attitude of the 'Edmonton 38' had shocked the world. If only one of those adults had intervened, there would have been no case, no trial and no murder. Matthew Cook was two years of age and by no stretch of the imagination was it his time to die. Some had said that, perhaps in the long run, it would be a good thing. Lessons would be learned that would save other children, other families. Nonsense, he thought. There was no extra funding to be put into the desperate environment in Shank

Town that had spawned this tragedy. Nothing would change. All he could do was try to ensure that Kevin Milne would never be free again, and if that meant Renee Smith would have to suffer the same fate, then so be it.

'Have the jury reached a verdict?' Lord Hunter asked.

The foreman nodded and the other eleven members of the jury stared at the judge. Experienced members of the press pack knew Lord Hunter would give nothing away as he read the verdict over, so they in turn stared at the individual members of the jury. The long and harrowing trial had taken its toll. The unnatural pallor and the shadowy bags under the eyes of most of the jurors told their own story.

'Would the accused please stand up?'

Child X and Child Y jumped down out of their built-up chairs and disappeared inside the adult-sized dock. His Lordship cleared his throat. He held the white piece of paper flat on the wooden bench in front of him, not trusting himself to hold it aloft, as his hands were trembling like someone in the latter stages of Parkinson's disease.

'We, the jury, find the accused not guilty of charge one in relation to the abduction of Matthew Michael Cook.'

Donna Cook screamed, 'Noooooo!' A relative tried to escort her from the court, but she fought like a wild animal for her right to stay, her right to hear justice for her child. After several long seconds, the noise subsided, and Lord Justice Edward Hunter looked up from the piece of paper and continued with the verdict.

'In relation to charge two, we the jury find Child X and Child Y guilty of murder in the first degree.'

Renee Smith covered her face with her hands. Her nails were bitten down to the quick, and some were covered by plasters, just like Donna's. Tears rolled down her face and her shoulders slumped. Her mother couldn't get into the dock to comfort her, and the two police officers charged with guarding Child X and Child Y stood impassively. Kevin Milne didn't weep, but he did start to chew and pick at the hole in his sleeve.

Donna Cook lay prostrate across the benches. Her chest was heaving with dry sobs that racked her body. The jury had done their best, but even they could not bear to witness this mother's pain.

'Order, order!' the judge's clerk called.

Lord Hunter was forced to bang his gavel on the bench. The police moved into the public benches, forcing people to sit down and, slowly, the noise subsided. The judge took a deep breath.

'Taking account of the fact that the jury has found you both guilty of the second charge, namely the murder of Matthew Michael Cook, I hereby sentence you to twenty-five years' imprisonment.'

It was now Kate Milne's time to cry. Her child, her little Kevin, would be thirty-five before he was allowed to walk the streets again. What would he be like when he came out? He'd be institutionalized. He'd never hold down a job, never have a chance at marriage. Reaching out, she tried to grab his hand in a long-overdue stab at parental concern, but Kevin moved out of her reach. Kevin was probably going to be the lucky one. Kate and the rest of the kids were going to have to deal with this on their own. There would be no forgiveness for Kate Milne or her family.

There was no going back for any of them.

PART THREE

Edinburgh
November 2008

Chapter Thirty-Six

Bancho finished reading the documents and clippings on the case and looked up at Sam Jones. Her green eyes were burrowing into his, begging for some sign he would support her. After twenty years, why was this case still so important to her? An unsolved murder, well, he could understand how that would eat away at an officer's soul. But this one was solved. He narrowed his eyes as he searched her face for the truth of her story. The canteen was still full of officers who had lingered long after their dinner had gone cold and the football was over.

'I'm a wee bit confused here. Maybe I'm missing something. I remember the Matthew Cook case, everyone does. God, do I remember it?' He put both his elbows on the table and leaned in close, so close he could smell her perfume. 'What you've told me so far would mean that they were still in jail, so if they're in jail, how come I've got a madman on my patch cutting out punters' hearts?' He scratched his head again. 'Unless you're saying those kids *didn't* kill Matthew Cook twenty years ago?'

Sam picked up her empty coffee cup and stared into

the bottom of it. She was tired and this was harder than she'd thought it would be. 'We didn't get the wrong killers. Kevin Milne and Renee Smith murdered Matthew Cook at a scrap yard at Edmonton Green and they were put away for twenty-five years. Lord Justice Edward Hunter intended at the end of that period to make life really mean life.'

Bancho didn't believe in coincidences, but he'd never heard of that particular English judge until a couple of days ago, when he'd seen his face on the *News at Six* coming out of 10 Downing Street with the prime minister. 'Lord Justice Edward Hunter who just happens to now be the new Lord Chancellor of England?' he asked.

Sam Jones nodded. 'The very one. He was the trial judge, as you know. Hunter was a hard sentencer, hard on crime. Not a man that kowtowed to political correctness.' Her eyes glazed over in memory. 'He saw what an evil little shit Kevin Milne was but . . .' Her voice trailed off.

'What happened?'

'Human rights.' The London cop spat the words out, but she was singing to the converted. Bancho gave her his full attention. DI Sam Jones was exhausted. The hot, tarry coffee was disgusting, but it was filled with caffeine and she would take anything to stay awake and hunt down the bastard who had haunted her dreams for two decades.

'Milne's lawyers took the case to the European Court of Human Rights. The verdict was that we had violated their rights, and Kevin Milne and Renee Smith were given compensation. The exact amount was kept secret. For eight years they were housed and cared for, given the best education. It would have been cheaper to send them to Eton. Then, when they were eighteen, they were released back into society. Newspapers and Internet groups have been searching for them for years, but there's a lifetime media ban on the British press ever revealing their new identities.'

Sam lifted her coffee cup to her lips and finished the dregs. 'For the first time in twelve years, I know for sure where Kevin Milne is. He's on your patch, Duncan.' Her eyes were cloaked. It seemed as if she still held on to a secret, and Bancho wondered what it was, as well as how the hell she had made the leap from this notorious child killer to the adult maniac stalking the city. 'Kevin Milne is in Edinburgh, and he's killing again.' She handed him a card. 'I've jotted down the hotel I'm staying at on the back and my mobile's always on. Let's meet here tomorrow morning at nine.

'He's your killer. Kevin Milne is your killer. You just have to pick him up – then maybe both of us can sleep easier.'

Chapter Thirty-Seven

I followed the maître d' through the lunchtime crowd, searching each table for a lone woman. Almost every seat was filled at The Tower, the rooftop restaurant on top of the new Museum of Scotland. Seated at a table next to the window, I spotted an attractive, athletic woman, wearing a black Prada dress with matching shoes, a large designer handbag at her feet. As I approached she stood up and held out her hand. It was professionally manicured. 'Patsy Barnes, I presume?' I said as I shook it. Patsy's face was tanned, and her eyes were dark blue and lustrous. I detected coloured contacts. This was a woman who spent serious money on her appearance. She wore her chestnut hair loose around her shoulders.

'It's good to finally meet you. I appreciate you giving up your time, Ms McLennan.'

'It's Brodie, and you have my secretary to thank.' It sounded harsher than I had intended. Lavender had finally succumbed to what seemed like twenty-four-hour vomiting, and I was in the clutches of a temp. The new girl, Lois, who I hoped wouldn't be around much longer, hadn't seen anything wrong with the approach from Patsy Barnes. To be fair on her, she was probably right, but it made me realize how much I was missing Lav. Lois was the one who'd agreed, without consulting me, that I should speak to this journalist. She got all defensive when I told her to cancel the interview, and said that she thought it would be good for my profile, I'd be getting a free lunch; and then she looked a bit weepy. I gave in – and hoped Lavender wouldn't hear about how soft I'd been.

'Well, I'm delighted that you're here anyway,' Patsy Barnes replied.

'And you? You're from London?' I asked.

'Is it that obvious?' she grinned as she sipped her wine. 'Essex, actually. I followed my latest squeeze up the M1. He dragged me here, then he left practically before we'd unpacked, and went back down. I stayed – I guess I must have fallen in love with the cold nights and wet days . . .' She smiled ruefully, then went on, quickly getting back to business. 'Brodie, I've read some of the articles about you in the press and, feel free to correct me if I'm wrong, but you seem to have become a bit of a whipping girl for the powers that be,' she said. No doubt she knew that we were singing from the same hymn sheet. I had taken to Patsy Barnes. Maybe that girl Lois was right and it would be good for me to get some positive publicity. 'I got the idea for an article when I heard you on the radio after the Kenny Cameron murder trial. Since I moved up here, I've been freelancing. I've still got plenty of contacts from when I was in London, but it can some-times be hard finding something that needs a Scottish angle. I'm sure I don't have to tell you how London-centric the nationals can be.' She was good, I'd give her that. Letting me know how professional she was, how much work she could still get, laying it on a bit with the Scots-against-the-world angle.

'So, what do you want from me?' I asked, wondering what she had heard.

'Well, I've run this past a few editors and they're all quite interested, if I can get the right person. There's a new drama series starting in a couple of months, with a glamorous, sexy, female lawyer at the centre – always wins her cases against the odds and all of that type of thing.' She laughed as I raised my eyebrows. 'I know – it all sounds a bit dated, doesn't it? But I thought that's where you could come in. What's it really like? I'd use you as the main focus of the piece, hopefully you'd let me shadow you for a while, then have the usual couple of other case studies down the side. To be honest, I need someone photogenic. It doesn't matter what the story's like if you look rotten on a full-page portrait in a glossy.'

'I really wouldn't be comfortable with you building me up, or making too much of anything I've achieved.' Or digging too deep into my private life, I thought to myself.

'Strange, I've heard a lot of things about you: some good, some bad. But no one told me you were publicity shy.' Patsy smiled.

'What would you want me to do?' I asked.

'Not much. Mostly it will involve just talking to me about cases like the Kenny Cameron one, angles that have something a bit different about them. Some days I might want to watch you in court.'

'I think I could do that,' I said cautiously, wondering how much time it would take against how much income it might generate for the firm. 'Do you want to go over anything today?' I asked, and she nodded immediately. I had no cases calling in court in the afternoon, and Lois had cleared my diary for the lure of the glossy magazine woman, possibly hoping she'd get her pic in there too. I gave in and ordered a double malt. 'Well, let's start on the personal stuff . . .' she began.

'Let's not. Let's start with the Kenny Cameron case, given that you claimed to be interested in that,' I snapped.

Patsy Barnes pushed her chair back from the table a little and took another sip of brandy. She forced a smile, no doubt thinking she'd worm other things out of me at a later date. 'Right, well . . . why did you agree to take on the Kenny Cameron case to begin with?' she asked, continuing to smile. The woman was a professional; no doubt she'd been thwarted many times in her professional career, but I would remain on my guard.

'I received a call on a Friday night that Kenny Cameron was in custody and about to be charged with the murder of his wife. Mr Cameron had no previous convictions, which was surprising because he'd hooked up with Senga Boyle. The Boyles are one of the top three criminal families of Edinburgh. There isn't an illegal racket they don't have their fingers in.'

'Did you decide right away to run the battered husband defence?'

'I didn't know very much about it at that stage. I'd seen

an expert on the syndrome talk on TV, and read a few articles that cropped up, but that was the extent of my knowledge.'

'What was your first impression of him?' she asked.

'When I looked at that weak, downtrodden little man and at the pictures of what he had done to his wife, I knew that, given the right circumstances . . . anyone could kill.'

Patsy's eyes lit up. 'I like that,' she said, 'I can use that, definitely! Thanks,' she smiled. 'See – you're practically writing this for me already. Are there other cases you've taken on that have been causes célèbres? Anything that has taken on a life of its own, perhaps?'

Christ, where would I start? Actually, I wouldn't. I didn't want this to be about my personal life, and so many of my recent cases had linked exactly that. I needed to make sure that Patsy would keep on the path I chose for her. 'I'll get my secretary to look out some material for you, some case summaries.' I was already wondering what Lois was capable of – Lav would have done what I wanted in about five minutes and she would have protected me at the same time. 'Lois will get in touch with you and I'll clear it with past clients that they're fine about any identification.'

'Will that be a problem?' Patsy asked.

'I doubt it – although they'll probably want some cash for it. I don't necessarily deal with the salubrious legal clientele your TV character might be involved with,' I smiled. 'Now – shall we get another drink?'

Chapter Thirty-Eight

Did it ever stop raining in this city? As she walked along the cobbles, she felt different; not much, but there was a difference. She had hoped that it would get better. As it moved towards the end, she had thought there would be a feeling of either peace or success. She had done this, she had won – and, even if she was not there yet, she was almost at the end-point. That feeling hadn't kicked in yet. Would it? It had to; she had to believe it would – otherwise what would all of this have been for?

It was the weather. It was the uncertainty. It was the downright incompetence of Edinburgh's police force. There should have been an arrest by now – she shouldn't have to do it again, but they were so slow. Why hadn't they made an arrest? Why hadn't they played their part?

She knew that there were other women watching her as she walked on. Her high heels keep sneaking down the cracks in the cobbles as she made the precarious journey, balancing handbag, umbrella and some degree of dignity. She was surprised in one way that they hadn't tried to get her off their patch – she thought that prostitutes or their pimps were territorial. Maybe they didn't care, or maybe there was enough to go round. There was also the fact that she was about a hundred times better and cleaner looking than any of them. Maybe word had also got round that she was new. She laughed quietly to herself as she realized there wasn't any chance that she was getting known by reputation – ex-customers were hardly likely to be recommending her.

The lack of safety around here horrified her. She knew none of these women or their stories, but they must have known what was going on – if punters were being killed, didn't that make these working girls fear for their own lives too? Perhaps not – perhaps they thought there was some justice in the men finally being the victims.

She could feel a rising panic in her chest as she stopped in a doorway to look around. There was a narrow road running straight in front of her and a number of similar doorways in which women slumped or stood. She had no idea how many times she would have to do this, but she felt uncomfortable tonight. What if the car she chose had a cop in it? What if she wasn't strong enough? What if she picked the wrong guy?

Stop it, she told herself. There's no time for this. Be careful and be quick. A few cars had crawled past her but, without her initiating any contact, they'd gone past. She knew there must be police officers somewhere – or were there? From what she could tell, and from what she'd heard, this part of Edinburgh was pretty much left to its own devices, and there was a thin line between the police turning a blind eye and actually colluding. Maybe there was pressure on them to solve the murders, but there could also be pressure on them to leave the business alone given that the customers could never be fully identified. That was what she was counting on. The lowlifes who walked down to the Shore and paid a fiver for a quick blow job from some poor tart who didn't know what day it was were not her target audience anyway.

A Merc drove past so slowly he would have been quicker walking. There was a sticker in the passenger rear window – *Taxi for Little Miss Perfect*, it read. She let it pass. She didn't see the driver well; if he knew what he was doing he'd drive past again. If he knew what he was doing, he'd put the light on so that she could see him. She slipped her hand into her bag to check that everything was there. She hated all of this; there was nothing she needed to get out of it except the final part. Once it was over, she would rest easy. Wouldn't she?

The Merc was back. She'd had quite the hit-rate with those, she thought to herself. Maybe they were her good-luck charm. The light was on. He looked – he actually looked good. Early thirties, clean cut. Suit. Laptop bag on the seat next to him. He smiled at her and she smiled back. Cop? She'd soon find out.

'Hi,' he said, almost shyly as he pressed the window down. 'How are you?'

Better than you could imagine, she thought. Nice manners. Nice guy. No doubt a good father and husband.

What a shame.

Chapter Thirty-Nine

DI Sam Jones was booked in at the Travelodge at Tollcross. 'I've been trying her mobile all bloody morning,' Bancho said agitatedly to his companion, PC Sheehy, trying to disguise the concern he felt as he walked in through the electronic glass doors.

Her failure to turn up at St Leonards had at first been an inconvenience. He gave her a couple of hours, assuming she was sleeping off her exhaustion. But, as his attempts to rouse her failed, he became increasingly worried. It was now after twelve, and all the business guests had checked out for the day, leaving the place almost deserted. Their feet clacked noisily across the shiny black marble tiles. The receptionist's head was bent over the computer, checking the availability of rooms for a telephone caller – their arrival went unnoticed. Years of practice meant that Bancho could fish the warrant card out of his pocket without a second glance; he was flipping it open for presentation to the receptionist when he was still ten feet from the desk. Bancho was moving at quite a pace, and PC Sheehy was having difficulty keeping up with him. They stopped in front of the desk; the receptionist was still engaged on her call so she nodded at them and mouthed that she would be one minute. She held up her index finger to confirm it would indeed be just that one minute.

DI Bancho stared at his watch, tapped his feet, and then flashed his warrant card in front of the receptionist again.

She hung up, but still maintained her receptionist's cool. 'Can I help you, sir?' she said, just managing to curb the irritation in her voice.

'You have a guest, Sam Jones. I need to see her immediately.'

'I'll try her room, sir, if you'll just take a seat—'

'What's her room number?'

'Well, I can't just let you—'

'What is her room number?' Bancho spoke slowly, emphasizing each word before adding, 'Or would you rather we discussed obstructing a police inquiry?'

The receptionist struggled to reclaim her aplomb and said, 'Two four three.' She handed Bancho the key-card and added helpfully, as she had no doubt done a thousand times, 'It's on the second floor.'

The 'Do Not Disturb' sign hung on the handle of room 243. Bancho knocked and, as expected, there was no answer. He inserted the electronic card into the lock, but the light stayed red; he jiggled it in and out of the slot agitatedly before PC Sheehy took over. Turning the handle she opened the door and held it open. 'After you, sir,' she said smugly.

Everything was in its place, and the bed was made. Sam's mobile was even charging on the bedside table.

But there was no sign of her. Bancho picked up the mobile and checked the missed calls. All of his own attempts to contact her were listed there. He used the hotel phone and called reception as he checked her inbox to see if there were any new texts. 'Give me a record of any phone calls Ms Jones made last night.'

The room phone rang within seconds. The receptionist was delighted to report that they had no record of the guest in room 243 making or receiving any phone calls. Bancho put the phone down and turned to PC Sheehy, who was on the mobile ringing the last number dialled. She put the phone on loudspeaker.

'Royal College of Psychiatrists. Dr Gerry Cornwell's office. Can I help you?' PC Sheehy didn't want to show their hand, so she hung up. 'Why would the inspector be calling a psychiatrist?' she asked.

Bancho said nothing, recognizing the name from his read-through the evening before of the Cook case papers. Yesterday, when he had first seen Sam Jones, she had been carrying a briefcase. Where was it now? He got down on his hands and knees, searching under the bed, desk and couch for the bag. Sheehy had Sam's mobile in her hand as he looked. 'You check the other numbers on the mobile and I'll search for the case,' he told her.

It didn't take long but his search was fruitless. He stood up and brushed down his trousers before walking over to the closet. Sam Jones had unpacked. He ran his fingers through the work-friendly blouses and tailored dark trouser suits. This could all be stupid – if the briefcase was gone and she was gone, she could very well be on her way to find him. But he had a feeling that wasn't the case; there was something about Sam Jones that had bothered him. She seemed obsessed by that one case and she appeared to be the sort who would keep to her word and her plans. So where was she?

'You're never going to believe who she contacted last night?' From the awe in PC Tricia Sheehy's voice it was all too easy for Bancho to guess. He sat down on the bed. Leaning forward, he placed his head in his hands and said, 'At a wild guess I'd say . . . the Lord Chancellor of England.' Sheehy looked at him as if he was Sherlock Holmes. 'That's right!' She looked again, suspicion dawning in her eyes. 'What's he got to do with this?'

Bancho stayed silent. He stretched out his foot and kicked away the blouse that had fallen from its hanger – concealing the very thing he was looking for. At the same time his heart sank. A detective like Sam wouldn't leave her mobile and a briefcase full of sensitive information in a Travelodge, protected only by a 'Do Not Disturb' sign, in a hotel teeming with housekeeping staff with pass keys.

'Open it,' he said.

PC Sheehy's lips pursed as she focused on the combination lock.

'It was too easy,' she said, shaking her head as it popped. 'If this is important she would never have let it out of her sight.' She handed the open briefcase to Bancho who laid it flat on his lap. He opened the lid fully. The tan leather interior was obscured by papers, reports and photographs, black-and-white photographs taken by what seemed like a surveillance photographer.

'Do you recognize him?' DI Bancho asked. They both

stared at the variety of shots of the same man: some were pornographic in nature, and others were more domestic shots of him getting into his car and going to an office.

Sheehy shook her head. 'The quality's not great and whoever took the photographs . . . I'd guess they don't do it for a living. The number plate? I'll get that run through the computer. I recognize the hotel, though.'

'So do I,' said Bancho. 'It's this place.'

'It's hard to tell if it's the same room.' PC Sheehy looked around Room 243. 'They're all designed the same but, if I was a betting woman, I'd lay good money down that she asked specifically for the same room if these pictures were of such interest.'

Bancho nodded his head in agreement.

'Get the fiscal on the phone – we need to contact the Lord Chancellor . . . and it might be best if the request comes through them. This isn't going to be straightforward.'

Chapter Forty

The procurator fiscal for the sheriffdom of Lothian and Borders was Agnes Sampson; the archaic title simply meant she was the chief prosecutor for the Edinburgh area. A pear-shaped woman with mousy brown curly hair, she had achieved her promotion through a razor-like intellect, which was hidden behind an extremely plain facade. DI Bancho had the utmost respect for her, as did anyone with half a brain who came into contact with her.

Agnes Sampson's career had started out in the typing pool of the fiscal's office. She quickly realized that the prosecuting lawyers, who were earning at least three times her salary, were useless. Agnes thought she could do better, so she went to night school, sat her exams, and worked her way through law school. After law school Agnes had gone back into the fiscal service because she realized that, in the legal profession, contacts are everything. And she didn't have any. Sadly, she was still in the same position, which was why, when she received the phone call from DI Bancho, she decided to enlist the help of the dean of the Faculty of Advocates. She was sure that someone in his social circle would have gone to school with Lord Edward Hunter, the newly appointed Lord Chancellor of England.

DI Bancho was again impressed with the wise decision of the senior fiscal. She didn't let her ego get in the way, she just wanted the job done, which was why he was standing in front of a blazing fire in the Great Hall of the Scottish legal establishment's Parliament House. He could see into the Faculty of Advocates Library. The advocates were dressed in their striped trousers, black waistcoats and jackets, much like those of any good hotel manager, but their suits were bespoke and cost more than most managers make in two months. An old man in a blue wool suit with silver buttons, a white wing-tipped shirt, and a white bow tie approached the inspector. He bowed very slightly.

'Detective Inspector Bancho?' he asked.

'Aye, that's me,' said Bancho. The old man led him through the Corridor, as the Library of the Faculty of Advocates was known. First editions of all major books lined its shelves. He hoped they had a good sprinkler system in case this lot ever went up in flames. He craned his neck, staring at the floor-to-ceiling bookshelves filled with priceless leather-bound volumes. The old man opened a heavy Georgian door, which led into a circular room where Agnes Sampson was sitting down having tea with a man of diminutive stature. His black hair was slicked back with handmade gentleman's pomade, the smell of pine and amber scenting the room. He wore large, dark-rimmed circular glasses – hardly a style statement, but they did add to his air of immense intelligence.

DI Bancho suspected that David Menteith, Dean of Faculty, knew exactly what he was doing when he purchased them. The dean smiled and stretched out his hand. Bancho bent in the middle to shake it.

'I've asked a senior member of Faculty to join us ... Ranald Hughes QC. Have you come across him before?'

Disappointment flooded through Bancho. 'I haven't met Mr Hughes personally, but I'm aware that he prosecuted the Senga Cameron murder trial against the defence team led by Brodie McLennan.'

The dean's nose wrinkled. 'Ah, the redoubtable Ms McLennan; a formidable opponent, I fear.'

There was a knock at the door and Ranald Hughes QC walked in. 'Did I hear someone mention Brodie McLennan? What's she been up to now?' he asked.

'Nothing. We were just discussing acquaintances,' said the dean, changing the subject; perhaps the Senga Cameron case was still a sore point. 'I wanted to call you in at the start. We have a tricky situation on our hands and it needs to be handled delicately from the word go.'

Ranald Hughes nodded, walked over to the silver tea tray and poured himself Earl Grey into a fine bone-china cup, added a slice of lemon and sat down. Bancho stared at pretty much everything in the room, his inferiority bubbling.

On the desk were the contents of Detective Inspector Sam Jones's briefcase. The dean held up a photograph of a naked man in bed with an attractive dark-haired woman.

'Is it a blackmail case?' asked Ranald Hughes, looking about him at the other people in the room.

All eyes in the room turned to DI Bancho. 'We're not sure quite what we have. These photographs were found in the possession of Detective Inspector Sam Jones. She travelled up from London to see me about the spate of recent murders here. We have, as you probably know, three victims. The killer is removing the heart.'

'Ah. I didn't know he was a trophy-taker,' said Ranald Hughes, raising an eyebrow.

'No, we've managed to keep it out of the papers so far. Quite a few favours we'll have to pay back there. But DI Jones has disappeared and I'm worried for her safety. In fact, I believe her life could be at risk.'

Hughes was a caring man. Unsuited to criminal work, he was only doing his stint prosecuting in the Crown Office so that he could be elevated to the bench. He lost some of his colour as Bancho spoke. 'The endangerment or murder of a serving police officer is always a matter of concern,' he said. Bancho nodded. When they heard the rest of what he had to say, they'd know the case could have a higher profile than any they had experienced before. Any mistakes would be criticized in the press and the Crown Office had made a number of widely publicized gaffes recently. The prospect of one more was enough to make Hughes feel his judicial appointment slipping away. Bancho didn't want to heap more shit upon the man, but that's what they were here for.

'DI Jones had a theory,' Bancho said. He looked around at the assembled bigwigs, wanting to make sure he had their attention. 'She thought that our serial killer was one of the children convicted of the Matthew Cook murder twenty years ago. In fact, she thought that Kevin Milne, under his new identity, murdered these men. She told me she knew that he was here in Edinburgh. Since she was here to get him, it seems likely these are surveillance photographs of Milne.'

A stunned silence filled the room. Bancho ploughed on. 'One of the last calls she made was to the Lord Chancellor of England,' he said.

'Eddie Hunter?' Hughes asked. 'What's old Eddie got to do with it?'

The dean answered for Bancho. 'The Lord Chancellor was the original trial judge, and then an appeal judge in the House of Lords when the appeal against sentence was heard. Although he couldn't sit on the bench, I heard he lobbied behind the scenes to have his earlier decision reversed.'

There was only one question on everyone's mind. Why would Lord Edward Hunter flout public opinion and campaign to release these killers early?

Chapter Forty-One

The dean's office remained in silence. Bancho stared around the walls. Behind the dean's desk there was an oil painting of Lord President MacGregor, presiding in the Court of Session in the mid-nineteenth century. He had no doubt the man was a relative of Brodie's. Brodie's father, grandfather and most of her male lineage had been judges in the highest courts in Scotland. As he looked into the smoke-damaged painting, he fancied he could see a family resemblance. This particular Lord MacGregor, dressed in the traditional ermine and red silk robes, looked like a hard man. There was a fixed, determined set to his mouth that Bancho had come across several times in his many encounters with Brodie. He cleared his throat. He was tired of losing, and he didn't care if he stood on toes here.

'I was thinking, if this goes the way I think it will, it's going to be a case where no one wins. Whoever takes it on has a poisoned chalice, because these killers should never have been released.' He paused to let his words sink in. 'It might be best for the prosecution services if we had an outsider.'

Agnes Sampson glared at him out of the corner of her eye. She knew exactly what he was thinking, and, in her opinion, Ranald Hughes wasn't up to the job. Maybe he was thinking along similar lines himself, for Hughes jumped for the bait. 'Did you have anyone in mind, Detective Inspector Bancho?' Bancho tried not to smile. 'The picture behind your desk, Dean – I take it he's one of Ms McLennan's ancestors?'

The dean turned round in his chair. Craning his neck upwards, he stared at the portrait. After a long moment he said, 'Yes, he is.' He nodded and turned to Ranald Hughes. 'I keep forgetting she's Arbuthnot's bastard.' Brodie's father, Lord Arbuthnot, had been Scotland's highest judge before he had been dispatched by Kailash, Brodie's birth mother. The manner of his death had been covered up at the highest level and most people, including these fools, thought he had died a hero's death. For a second, just a second, Bancho felt sorry for Brodie having to put up with these pompous arseholes. No wonder she only did defence work. 'I'll speak to her grandfather tonight,' the dean said, throwing the pictures across to DI Bancho. 'I believe he is abroad, but I'm sure I will be able to make contact. Have you any idea who the porn star is?' He smiled at his own pale joke. Bancho had decided not to be polite. He had what he wanted and he stared coldly at the dean. 'The photographer caught the registration number of his car . . . we're running it just now. When we have a name we'll make an arrest. He should be in custody, for questioning at least, this evening.'

Agnes Sampson got up and poured herself a fresh

cup of tea. 'So Kevin Milne could be appearing in Edinburgh Sheriff Court any day now? It will be interesting to see what kind of monster the taxpayer's money has created.'

The dean sat up to his full height, and cleared his throat. 'No one outside these four walls must know that he is Kevin Milne – if that is who he proves to be. There is the media order that bans any mention of his former identity.'

Bancho rankled at the words. His priority was not Kevin Milne at this point: it was Sam Jones. Her safety was paramount, even though he feared, if her theory was correct, she could already be beyond help. 'DI Bancho?' the dean went on. 'I take it you will speak direct to the Lord Chancellor at this stage? Find out what she said in her last conversation with him?' There was a threat, an edge to his voice. If they didn't get the information he wanted from the Lord Chancellor, then he would bloody well go down and feel Lord Hunter's collar himself, Lord Chancellor or not.

'I assure you, I will make every effort to contact him immediately.'

Bancho's phone vibrated with a text from PC Sheehy. *Suspect 3 Crowley Lane Morningside meet there asap*

'I have to go,' he told the assembled group. 'We have a lead on the man in the photographs – well, his car at least.' He wasn't quite sure how to leave – this bunch would have the ears and the attention of his superiors, he knew that. 'I'm sure that you'll all get the information you need when you need it,' was all he could think of to say as he left.

As he made his way out of Parliament House, Bancho was already returning Sheehy's call. 'What do we know about the car owner?' he demanded as soon as she picked up.

'Are you anywhere near a seat? You're going to need it,' said Sheehy.

'Go on,' urged Bancho. How much more complicated could this get? He was about to find out, as Sheehy gave him the name.

'Graham Marshall?' Bancho breathed out slowly. 'Do you mean *the* Dr Graham Marshall? Plastic surgeon to the rich and famous and generally needy? It's him? Jesus Christ. My life is about to get even fucking worse . . .'

It wasn't possible. Could Sam have been wrong? Otherwise, in less than twenty-four hours they might have pulled off what various Internet groups, vigilantes and 'friends' of the Cooks had been unable to do in two decades – found Kevin Milne.

Chapter Forty-Two

Crowley Lane in Morningside was a prestigious address, and most of the houses were substantial sandstone villas. Number three was different. The owner had bought a house, demolished the period property, and erected in its place an edifice of modern architecture that was all angles and glass.

DI Bancho drew up outside the black, wrought-iron electric gates. By Christ, he thought, there must be a hell of a load of money involved in making women's fronts look like flotation devices these days. The fact that some guy, barely in his thirties, had managed to accumulate all of this rankled a lot. PC Sheehy and PC Alex Lodge were already there, waiting. It wasn't often that the police had occasion to patrol these quiet, moneyed streets, and their arrival was attracting a lot of interest. The inspector pressed the button on the intercom system; it buzzed and then a woman answered. Her voice was cultured and aloof, an archetypal Edinburgh accent.

'Evening, ma'am,' Bancho said. He coughed, wondering how to phrase his request as to whether they could talk to her other half about his naked pictures. 'Detective

212

Inspector Bancho from St Leonards police station here . . . erm, is your husband in?' There was a crackling silence, then another buzz and the gates swung open. Bancho flicked his hand and beckoned PC Sheehy and PC Lodge to follow him. It was a pitch-black night but the solar lights lit the driveway to the house. An outside lamp came on next to the outsize maple front door. It all looked very welcoming. Bancho wondered how long that would last.

Alison Marshall's black dress clung to every curve. She was in terrific shape and she knew it – she had, after all, had the best of cosmetic surgery on tap, given her husband's profession. 'About time you showed up,' she said, throwing a half-finished cigarette down onto the pathway. 'What took you so bloody long? I reported the break-in weeks ago. Just because nothing was taken, doesn't mean you can just ignore me. And why does my husband need to be here? Scared of dealing with a woman?' Alison Marshall was squaring up to DI Bancho and, from what he could tell, there was an accent behind the words that wasn't all Morningside.

'I think there's been some mistake, ma'am,' piped up Sheehy. 'We're not here about the break-in.'

'It's been nearly two months! I've called the police station four times and left God knows how many messages and you tell me it's not about the break-in?' Her eyes widened. 'Well, what the hell is it about, then?'

'I think it would be best if we discussed this in comfort.' Bancho nodded and put his hands out in front of him in an effort to shoo Mrs Marshall inside, but she wasn't for shifting. 'The neighbours,' Bancho whispered, and flicked his eyes up to the next-door neighbour's curtains which were already twitching. 'I don't think you'll want the neighbours to hear what we have to say.' Alison Marshall followed his eyes up to the offending window, did an about-turn and said, 'You'd better come in then.'

The floor in the hallway was reclaimed oak planks. They covered the whole of the bottom floor and gave the property a seamless flow. PC Sheehy tripped over her own feet as she struggled to take it all in: the suspended glass staircase, the original art on the wall and the handmade Italian furniture. Everything in this house was paid for by face-lifts, boob jobs and pec implants courtesy of Dr Graham Marshall, cosmetic surgeon to the celebrities and rich locals alike. His wife's face and body was his calling card, and Bancho had to admit that the doctor seemed pretty talented.

Alison Marshall opened the door at the end of the hallway. 'Wait in here,' she said. 'I'll go and get him.' The police officers were still staring at each other when the door opened and Graham Marshall walked in.

'I take it this isn't a social call,' he said. Bancho didn't answer him. He took a moment to consider whether this could be one of the most famous killers of the twentieth century. The inspector had seen the court artist's impressions and the photographs taken when Kevin Milne and Renee Smith were first arrested. But no later photograph or representation had been allowed out into the wider world. The official reason for this media ban was public protection, in case a vigilante mistook an innocent teenager or youth for Smith or Milne and ripped them limb from limb. Bancho stared at the tall, physically fit, potential suspect before him. The inspector sucked in his gut and tried to see the boy in the man. Where had the pudgy ten-year-old gone? Dr Marshall's face had definitely been worked on. Bancho suspected a chin implant at the very least. For now, at least, he had to tread carefully. Whatever this man was suspected of, they had no proof. But Sam's surveillance of him had to mean something, and it tied him to her disappearance.

Bancho took a deep breath. 'Dr Marshall, a colleague of mine has disappeared under suspicious circumstances. DI Sam Jones? Your name has come up in connection with our inquiries. I'm afraid I'll have to ask you to accompany us to St Leonards police station for questioning and—'

Marshall held up his hand and interrupted the inspector. 'I have no idea why you think this is anything to do with me, but I know my rights – and yours. Let's get this over and done with.' He turned to Alison and handed her a card. 'Call Brodie McLennan and tell her to get down to St Leonards immediately.'

Bancho sighed at the words – and prayed that the dean contacted Brodie before Alison Marshall did.

Chapter Forty-Three

The phone call from Alison Marshall came through at seven thirty. I was still in the office trying to catch up on a backlog of accounts. I'd roped Eddie Gibb in because he was terrible at writing down his court attendances on file notes. As a result we lost hundreds, sometimes thousands of pounds' worth of billing hours on each of his cases. I wished Lavender had been with us – she would have been much more efficient and she would also have seen, yet again, what a financial disaster her husband was. There was no way he could make partner unless he improved. I might actually have been glad of an excuse to bail out of the whole tedious process but, as I explained to Alison Marshall, that wasn't the way Scots law worked. 'There isn't much I can do at this stage apart from letting the desk sergeant know that he's my client,' I told her. 'The police are completely entitled to hold him for questioning for six hours without any legal representation at all.'

She seemed to take it surprisingly well. Most clients or their spouses are outraged, having gained most of their legal knowledge from TV shows where the suspect is always backed up by a lawyer who stays permanently by his side and usually tries to obstruct the police as much as possible. The only frustration at the six-hour rule was mine. What could an eminent cosmetic surgeon possibly have to do with the disappearance of a London police officer? As that was the only information Alison had been able to give me as grounds for Bancho taking him in, it was all I had to go on.

Eventually Lois, Eddie and I called it a day, and I trudged home, longing for a bath. I'd only got halfway through pouring it and some wine when the phone rang. Swearing in irritation, I grabbed it and snapped, 'Yes?' A defence lawyer's relationship with the police is complex. With certain detectives it can be ropey at best. They want to secure a conviction; I want to avoid it. Desk sergeants are a different breed. Their job is to keep everything moving smoothly, and for that they often need our cooperation and understanding. Sergeant Murphy and I had a good working relationship. I'd phoned him only an hour earlier to declare my interest in Dr Marshall. His call now wasn't exactly by the book, but we'd indulged in mutual backscratching before so I wasn't surprised by it. 'Word to the wise, Brodie,' he said. 'There's been some kind of tip-off about a search for a London DI who's been visiting our fair city. Rumour has it your man Marshall's involved. The whole squad's crawling over Brown's scrap yard with sniffer dogs. Don't know much more at this stage.'

I thanked him and went to pull the plug out of the bath, counting the cost of my wasted bubble bath and time, and then dressed in my leathers. I left the flat and mulled over what was happening on my way to the scrap yard. What the hell was going on? Had Marshall known exactly what was going to happen when he contacted me? Who was this DI Jones anyway?

The scrap yard was filled with car wrecks, tyre mountains and old fridges. It was pitch black. I was glad I was wearing my bike gear. The leather trousers protected my legs from the stinging nettles and I'd had the foresight to bring an industrial-sized torch that marked out the territory before me and showed just how steep the terrain was. I flicked the torch over to my right and caught Duncan Bancho in its full beam.

He stumbled, squinted through the glare, and bore an expression of both surprise and anger when he recognized who was on the other end of the torch. 'What in hell's name are you doing here?' he growled. Bancho being one of those detectives with whom I was often at loggerheads. Actually, chief adversary would be more like it. We hadn't so much crossed swords as buried them in each other up to the hilt. Clearly Sergeant Murphy hadn't mentioned my involvement, and I was about to try and justify my presence when a shout came from a female officer that drove any questions about why I was there from Bancho's mind. 'Sir! The dog's on to something!' She was up ahead with the handler and Bancho pressed forward to join them, leaving me in their wake. They were heading down into the centre of the scrap yard where the going was easier – there was a definite, albeit narrow path between the fridges and exhaust pipes. The night was quiet. There was no traffic on Bernard Street and the sound of the other folk breathing behind me carried easily in the air. So did their voices – not that they made much sense.

'Christ, what a godforsaken place,' said one of them. 'Why do we think the DI's here?'

'She left a voicemail from a public phone just before she went off the radar. Said if she went incommunicado, these coordinates should be searched,' said another, adding to my confusion.

'Why did Bancho wait so long then?' asked the first voice. 'He's been looking for her since first thing this morning.'

'It wasn't Bancho she rang. It was the bloody Lord Chancellor of England.'

I didn't have time to get my head around the involvement of the Lord Chancellor because I was suddenly assailed by the smell of decaying flesh. It was overpowering, and coming from up ahead. I caught up with the female officer who had shouted and whose torch was spotlighting a bare leg. The skin was white and the toenails were painted red.

'Oh, Jesus Christ,' said Bancho.

It was a bloodbath. Her chest was gaping and she'd been butchered. Her Burberry raincoat lay sideways beneath her like a blanket. The left side draped down over her head and the right tucked up between her legs.

'Are you sure it's her? The woman you're looking for?' I asked Bancho.

'I recognize the coat,' he said dully.

I shone my torch on the body as he donned latex gloves and peeled the coat away, bottom flap first, to see if she had been stripped or violated. Then, much more quickly, he flipped back the fabric covering her head and let out a relieved groan. Whoever had once lived and breathed in this body, it was clear from his reaction that it wasn't DI Sam Jones.

'I'll speak to you in a minute,' he snarled at me before moving off into an urgent huddle with the other officers.

No, he wouldn't. It would be much later. I looked at my watch and realized Marshall's six hours were up.

Bancho would have to wait.

Chapter Forty-Four

I slipped away and made my way back to the bike, intending to head straight to St Leonards, but there were two messages and two missed calls, all from Agnes Sampson, the procurator fiscal, on my mobile. The messages demanded a reply, regardless of the hour. I took her at her word, and was amazed when she picked up straight away. 'This is quite a surprise,' I said. In nearly ten years at the bar, a head fiscal had never phoned me out of hours.

'The dean wanted to call you, but I thought it might sound better coming from me.' How odd, I thought. The dean of the Faculty of Advocates hated me; he wasn't ever polite or even civil to me, and he thought I didn't know he referred to me as 'Arbuthnot's bastard'. My back was up at the mere mention of his name. 'This suggestion might have been best coming from your grandfather, but he is unavailable,' she said. I nodded. It was well known he could emotionally blackmail me into doing almost anything he wanted, so I said a prayer of gratitude that he was on his cruise.

'I know it's the middle of the night, but I'm rather busy, Agnes. Just spit it out.'

'Do you recall the Matthew Cook case?' she asked.

It was before my time, really, though I'd picked up vague snatches on TV news programmes; but the legal implications had been such that we'd studied it in detail at university. I said I did. She continued, 'We think Kevin Milne is responsible for the murder of the three men in Edinburgh and we'd like you to take a sabbatical from your practice and lead the prosecution team.'

I said nothing.

I needed to think. If I took this high-profile case I would be doing them a favour and, if I so chose, I would be elevated to the bench. Working for Crown Office was a civic duty. The pay was shit and the only reason for good court lawyers to do it was to become a judge. Agnes Sampson's request wasn't unusual. At any one time in Crown Office there was never more than one competent prosecutor – that's why the one guy had to do all the work. Sometimes, like now, they had no one who could be trusted not to make a right royal fuck-up of a case. Kevin Milne's second murder trial, if he was indeed the killer, would make worldwide news. 'Let me think about it for a moment,' I lied. To be honest, I was fed up defending monsters, and prosecuting a particular monster of the calibre of Kevin Milne appealed to me very much.

'Okay,' I said, not sure whether or not I sounded too desperate. 'I'll do it.'

'Good,' replied Agnes Sampson. 'Well, he's in St Leonards and you'll be pleased to know that this little arrangement was DI Bancho's idea. I know you two have had your disagreements in the past, but perhaps that's all behind you now.'

A smile crossed my lips. Duncan Bancho. Well, well, wonders never ceased. 'Is there anything else I should know?' I asked.

'Well, the alleged killer is, of course, known by another name now, in accordance with an English legal judgement . . . The name he's living under is Graham Marshall. Dr Graham Marshall.'

Kevin Milne and Graham Marshall were one and the same.

Shit shit shit.

'I can't do it,' I burbled. 'I can't do it. I've already been instructed by Dr Marshall.'

Agnes Sampson was, for once, lost for words. After what seemed like an eternity she said, 'He hasn't been formally charged, only held for questioning. You can't have seen him yet. Just withdraw from acting, Brodie.'

I had never taken a retainer from a client before. Greed led me into it; an easy way to solve my financial problems. And now I was stuck with it. I knew nothing about the case yet, but if Marshall was Kevin Milne, I couldn't believe he was innocent.

'He gave me a retainer.'

'That's very unusual in Scots criminal legal practice, Brodie. Didn't it strike you as odd? Do you usually do this? Ah,' she sighed, as if a thought had just occurred to her, 'do the Dark Angels have you on a retainer?'

I didn't answer her. I didn't need to. I knew that I could poll my colleagues in the Edinburgh Bar Association and none of them would have a retainer from a criminal client. I put the phone down and rested my head on my arms. Would I never learn? I had to think. The rules had changed. For once in my legal life I hadn't a clue what to do, and indecision paralysed me. I needed space, and that space wasn't in the wee small hours in St Leonards police station with the client from hell.

Chapter Forty-Five

I found myself being drawn back to the Grassmarket. I couldn't work Graham Marshall out. There was no doubt that he had been providing a free clinic there and there was no doubt that he was well thought of. Who was this man? What was he up to, if anything? Even although I had spent barely any time at the Mission on my last visit, I had enjoyed it, so I could reason to myself that I might find out more if I went again.

As I drove there, I couldn't get what I had read in the files out of my mind. What had happened to little Matthew Cook had been horrific, and the children who had murdered him had revealed a lot about our society and our legal system. But was Graham Marshall really that boy? It was incredible to imagine, but the reports had said that he was prodigiously intelligent and cunning. He had been taken away from the environment that had spawned him and given shelter, food, education. Was it really such a stretch to wonder whether that had been the making of him? Added to that, if it was true, then he had chosen a perfect profession. He could work on himself, or get colleagues to do so, thus changing his appearance. He could make lots of money quickly and live in a world where secrecy and discretion were of the essence. I assumed that, if he was Kevin Milne, he had chosen Edinburgh to get as far away as possible from his original life, whilst remaining in the UK, which was probably part of the conditions. There was certainly no shortage of vain money and easy cash in the capital.

I parked the bike and walked past the bodies at the door of the Mission, none of whom I recognized. As soon as I got into the main hall, Ina was there. 'Back already, hen? I'll need to get you a name tag made up at this rate!' She laughed and grabbed my elbow, steering me through to the kitchen. 'You know the drill.'

I did. I started chopping a huge pile of vegetables that were lying on the worktop as Ina washed more beside me. 'I like to get well ahead of myself with the cooking,' she explained, studying me. 'But I don't think you're here for recipes, are you? The doctor's not here just now; neither's Wee Elvis.'

'That's fine,' I said, 'I'm not sure why I came anyway.'

She studied me some more. 'Is that right? Well, you're not like your mother then. Mary McLennan always knew exactly what she was doing. I've been thinking about her a lot since you were here. I hardly recognized you. All grown up, all successful. She'd have been proud of you. She sent you to a posh school, didn't she?'

I smiled. Typical Scottish approach – a bit of a compliment but make sure there was no chance of you getting above yourself. 'Yes, yes she did.'

'Aye, we all had a laugh about that. Local one wasn't

good enough for her wee darling. Your mother worked her fingers to the bone for you, Brodie. I hope you appreciate it.'

I was chopping onions anyway, but the tears started to flow.

'Aw, what is it hen, what is it?' asked Ina.

'I miss her. I just miss her so much,' I sobbed. 'I thought it would get easier but it was always just me and her, really, against the world, and I'd do anything to get her back. Just to talk to her, just to have her tell me everything will be all right.'

'And would she? Would she tell you that?'

'What do you mean?' I asked.

'Well – I don't mean to rain on your parade, hen, but Mary McLennan wasn't exactly a soft woman. She might tell you that everything would be all right – but there would be conditions.'

I laughed. Ina was right. 'I know, she would. She'd tell me that if I worked hard and I did right by people and I kept myself to myself, then, maybe then, it would be okay.'

'So, what's bothering you?' asked the older woman. 'You know what she'd say; I bet you can still hear her voice all the time. What's happened?'

I wasn't one to confide in people – and this woman *was* a stranger, even if she did remember me as a little girl. But she was also a link to my past, she'd known my mother; she even reminded me of her, and so I was tempted. I kept thinking of that child, Matthew, and his mum, too. The parallels between my mother and Donna Cook were obvious. Both of them had only children

227

whom they adored, and both of them had been willing to do all they could to get them out of poverty. Neither woman had been prepared to accept the fate that should have been reserved for their babies – but what Matthew's fate had truly been was beyond anything I could relate to. Donna would have fought for him had he lived – I felt that from what I had read, and the experts in the reports seemed to agree. What would he have been? What would he have achieved? Ina couldn't say anything to stop images of that poor child rushing through my head, so I kept chopping while she washed, thanking God that Mary McLennan had been there for me.

Chapter Forty-Six

The next morning I was still in shock. I grunted rather than spoke to Lois and Eddie on the way into my office; once there I slammed the door and slumped with my head in my hands. I was curious that I hadn't heard anything further about my client, when the other call I had been expecting all night came in.

'Brodie? Duncan Bancho here. The girl we found last night? She was an air hostess. Kelly Adams. Your client's late girlfriend, bit on the side, as it happens.'

'I take it you've confirmed that,' I said, knowing it was a useless question.

'Didn't have to. We already had photographs of them together. Very together.'

When people say things can only get better, I know for a fact they get worse. This was proof. I was now so far behind in the developments of this case that I didn't know which end was up. 'And how did you come by these photographs?'

'I'll fill you in when you get here,' he said. 'I'm just ringing to tell you we've just charged him with four counts of murder . . . the Cupid murders, as the wags round here are calling them, so named because the bastard takes their hearts. Won't be long before the papers pick up on that – we can only keep it quiet for so long; we're going on goodwill more than anything. And, in case you're interested, we still haven't found DI Jones.' He hung up.

'Sorry to interrupt . . .' Eddie popped his head round the door of my office, 'but there's a Mrs Marshall in reception. She says you're representing her husband. Will I show her in?' he asked.

I lifted my head up and shouted to the outer office. 'Put the kettle on, Lav.' I banged my head back down onto the desk. 'It's Lois. Again,' said the disconnected voice. 'Do you want sugar in your coffee?' she asked, and the fact that she had to ask made me miss Lavender even more.

Alison Marshall wiggled her way into my office. There were no tear stains on her immaculately made-up face. I gestured wearily to her to take a seat. Mrs Marshall sat down and allowed her coat to fall to her waist, revealing an incredible figure. She saw me staring, forced a smile and said, 'It's the only advantage of being married to a top cosmetic surgeon.'

Lois placed two cups of coffee on the desk. I don't know if she heard Alison Marshall's next words to me – at first, I wasn't sure if I had either.

'Whatever they're saying . . . he did it.'

I think that my mouth was probably more open than it should have been at that point. Alison Marshall went on. 'Don't look so shocked, Ms McLennan. Surely, I'm not the first wife to think her husband capable of murder?' She flipped her hand at me as though she would dismiss anything I had to say to the contrary.

230

A wife cannot be compelled to give evidence against her husband in a criminal trial but, in this case, if Alison Marshall was ever in the witness box, I would have to treat her as a hostile witness. I also had to be careful; it was likely that Alison didn't know her husband's true identity. The public hatred stirred up by Matthew Cook's murder was incalculable. When Renee Smith and Kevin Milne were granted new identities, they were advised never to divulge their secret to anyone. Someone in authority had leaked this to the press, and periodically they would run a story. The venom in Alison's eyes assured me that if she knew she was married to Kevin Milne, it would have been all over the Internet and she would have been waiting outside the insurance company offices to collect on the sum assured on death.

Part of me wasn't yet convinced that Dr Graham Marshall was indeed Kevin Milne. The main reason for my doubt sprang from my own background. I had been raised by a loving single parent in the high-rise slums of Leith. Mary McLennan had worked two jobs and arranged for me to sit the scholarship exam for Gordonstoun. The school favoured by royals offers nine free places to children from villages in the northeast of Scotland, so Mary used her sister's address and got me in the back door – without that shove up the social ladder I would be sticking on labels in the whisky bonds. I knew how hard it was to make that move: but as I had already contemplated, prison must have provided all sorts of opportunities that Milne's natural environment could never have done.

'Aren't you going to ask me why I think my husband is guilty?' Alison asked.

Not trusting myself to speak, I nodded.

'He's a cruel man.' A bitter laugh escaped from her lips. 'He thinks I don't know that he dreams of strangling me. Sometimes I pretend to be asleep and I can feel his eyes on me. He's considered many different ways of killing me. I found his little notebook,' she laughed again. 'Of course, I couldn't let him know I'd found it. I put it right back where it was.'

'You could have left him,' I said. I have never understood why people stay in abusive relationships, even after defending Kenny Cameron.

'Do you think he would have let me?' she said. She shook her head, 'No, no. He'd never let me leave. I'm all he has.'

'Perhaps lots of men dream of killing their wives.' I was playing devil's advocate, something that I felt was going to prove to be extremely difficult in this case.

'He doesn't just dream of killing me. He draws it and describes it.' Her eyes were cold and hard. She took a deep breath and continued. 'I can always tell when he has been studying his little book – it's the only time he comes to bed wanting me.' I sat still and listened. I'd learned enough over the years in practice to know that no words would bring her any comfort; she just needed to talk. After all, it wasn't the kind of topic she could bring up at a New Town coffee morning. Alison paced up and down the floor of my office. Unlike her husband, she did not stop to stare at herself in the gigantic mirror: perhaps staring at her reflection brought her no sense of comfort.

'It's not just me he dreams of murdering.' She placed

her index finger in her mouth and bit the skin at the sides of her nail. 'In the notebook, I only read one page, it's filled with people I don't even know. Maybe he'll put you in it.' She glanced over her shoulder and smiled, her lips forming a thin white line.

'Your husband does a lot of charity work,' I said, standing up and joining her at the window. I wanted her out of my office as quickly as possible. For better or worse, I had to see my client and, given her views on him, the necessity to be polite was rapidly receding. She turned on me. It was the first time I had noticed how tall she was. In her bare, perfectly manicured feet she would be at least four inches taller than me; in those killer heels I had to strain my neck just to look into her face. Alison Marshall was used to making people feel small. 'You're mistaken.' Her eyes held nothing but contempt. 'Graham has never done anything to help another person in his life.'

The Marshalls didn't strike me as the type of couple who lived out of one another's pockets, but even so it struck me as strange – she obviously had no idea that her husband ran a free clinic for down-and-outs at the Mission in the Grassmarket, and yet that was the one thing that was making me question whether he actually had some good in him – whoever he was.

Chapter Forty-Seven

It was almost 11 a.m. when I drew up outside St Leonards police station on the bike. The first thing that struck me was . . . no press pack. That was good. Bancho was managing to keep a tight lid on the identity of my client. It was more than I had expected.

The desk sergeant shifts had changed. This morning's specimen leaned on his elbow and flicked through the *Daily Record*. He looked up at me, knowing that I wanted Bancho. Sighing, he closed the paper, pressed a button under the desk and came round to the public side. Lifting the heavy bunch that hung from a steel chain on his black leather belt, he selected one large brass key, inserted it into the lock and opened the door. We were into the inner sanctum. The atmosphere changed almost instantly. The reception in the police station was sterile and abandoned, giving the public no clue as to the secret hive of activity going on behind its closed doors.

St Leonards is like a rabbit warren. We walked down the stairs towards the cells. Offices and interview rooms led off to the side and, behind venetian blinds, I could see movement of police officers and civilians. I knew this route so well, I could have walked it blindfolded, but – even if I had never been in this corridor before – my sense of smell would have let me know that behind the door in front of me were the police cells. There is something peculiar about the odour: hopelessness, unwashed bodies and desperation. I stood at the door to the cells, shifting from foot to foot, whilst my escort wandered on ahead without me. He turned and glanced over his shoulder. 'You're not getting in there until you've spoken to Bancho.' He turned his back on me and walked on. The length of his stride meant I had to scrabble to catch up with him; I finally managed it when he was almost outside an open door.

'Don't hold back on *me*,' Bancho shouted, 'I don't button up the back.' I'd heard him use that tone with me too often for there to be any doubt that he was genuinely angry, not playing at it.

'There's not much else to tell . . . I need to see Dr Graham Marshall to convince myself it's really him.' The unseen Irishman talking had a soft cultured voice; in my opinion he was no match for Bancho.

'Christ . . . now is not the time for doubts.' Bancho sounded worried. 'The assistant chief constable is pissed that the suspect I arrested on the say-so of your missing friend is one of Edinburgh's most eminent citizens.' Bancho stopped for a moment and then he continued, his tone even more frustrated. 'I've got a bitch of a defence lawyer winging her way here as we speak and if you're wrong—' We didn't hear whatever threat DI Bancho was going to issue to his unknown visitor because the desk sergeant coughed and knocked on the door.

'Sorry, boss,' he shrugged his shoulders. Bancho jacked up his eyebrows, lifted his hand and, curling his fingers, welcomed me in. To be fair to him he raised an apologetic smile and said, 'Nothing you didn't already know,' before adding, 'No offence and all that.'

'So you would be the bitch of a defence lawyer DI Bancho was referring to.' A thin man smiled. The smell of stale fags and whisky from his breath made me gag almost as soon as I entered the task-force room. I took his hand and shook it; his palm was firm and dry. 'Dr Gerry Cornwell,' he nodded.

'Brodie McLennan,' I answered him. There was something likeable about him I thought – the poor man had been crying for hours, his nose was red, and my instinct told me he was not merely a crying drunk.

'I could murder a coffee, Duncan,' I said. Bancho appeared to be too preoccupied with his troubles with the ACC to have noticed that Dr Gerry Cornwell was two sheets to the wind. 'I'll see to that right away,' said PC Tricia Sheehy. She caught my eye and in the silent glance an understanding passed – she had been thinking the same thing. Cornwell's elbows were resting on his knees as he held his face in his hands and rubbed his eyes.

The task-force room was large, with rough grey carpet tiles on the floor. A fluorescent strip light in the middle of the room buzzed and flickered. Large cork boards dominated the room. Before-and-after shots of the victims were pinned up using Blu-Tack. A large map of Edinburgh dominated another cork board and showed where the murders had taken place, each murder spot marked by a coloured tack and the whole area delineated by a red piece of thread joined to the tacks. The area made an uneven circle, roughly a mile in diameter, circling the Docks and the red-light area of Leith.

'If I were to hazard a guess,' I said, tapping the board, 'I'd say you should be looking for a whore as your murderer, not a plastic surgeon.'

Bancho said nothing. His crumpled jacket hung across the back of a chair, his shirtsleeves were rolled up and his tie was at half mast. Dr Cornwell's head remained in his hands. I doubted we'd get much sense out of him until we'd poured at least a gallon of coffee down his throat.

'Alan Pearson, aged thirty-six, married with two boys . . .' I glanced at the photograph of the financial consultant. I was drawn to touch the picture, the one given to the police by his family, the one where he was fully clothed, and in which he still had a heart. 'Alan Pearson, what's his connection with my client?' I turned and asked Bancho: 'What's the connection between my client and Alan Pearson, or any of the victims apart from Kelly Adams? Did they belong to the same tennis club, amateur dramatic society, or gym?' I tapped my finger off Alan Pearson's face. 'What is Dr Marshall's motive for killing this man?' PC Tricia Sheehy joined me at the board as I drummed my fingers.

'As far as we can tell, there is no known link between Dr Marshall and Alan Pearson. In fact, Mr Pearson lived in Newcastle. He was only up on business when he fell into Cupid's clutches,' said Sheehy. Bancho was right. The Cupid monicker was already embedded. Sheehy handed me a cup, which I placed down on a desk to cool as she continued. 'There's no link between Dr Marshall and any of the victims except the one you know about, the one he was sleeping with. The others – Grant Lindsay and Jeff Connors – had no links with each other. There's nothing there. They don't live near each other, nothing. All they had was that they were all in Edinburgh on business at different times and they all used prostitutes. There's not a single other thing.'

'There's Sam.'

Dr Gerry Cornwell lifted his head and fumbled in his inside pocket to pull out a brown leather wallet. 'DI Sam Jones is still missing and, if your client is who I think he is, she has a definite connection with him apart from the recent photographs in her possession. It goes way back. Way back.'

He handed me a battered, dog-eared photograph. The hairstyles told me it had been taken in the Eighties, and a much younger and more sober Dr Gerry Cornwell was standing with a pretty young policewoman.

'Sam Jones, I presume?' I handed him the photograph back.

'We haven't found a body, so there is still hope,' said PC Sheehy, handing him his cup. Tears rolled from Cornwell's eyes. He wiped them away with the back of his hand. 'If he's taken her, she's dead.'

'Are you sure you're strong enough to identify him?' Bancho asked Cornwell. Bancho's upbringing meant he didn't cry and he distrusted men who did.

'Are you having an identity parade?' I asked, trying to deflect his question. Where the hell they were going to find a bunch of people who resembled Graham Marshall was beyond me. He was a professional man, too old to fit into the same line-up as students, too affluent and well fed not to stand out like a sore thumb in a parade of the usual suspects. 'Button your lip and save your objections till later,' said Bancho, straightening up his tie. A red sore patch covered his hand. 'We're not having an ID parade. Dr Cornwell is not a witness to any of the incidents in Edinburgh. We merely want to see if he recognizes Dr Marshall from past dealings.' He was halfway out the door when he turned to me and said, 'Now, do you want to come or not?' I nodded at Bancho as PC Sheehy walked in front of me. An air of trepidation followed our little party. It seemed too much for the law enforcement officers to hope for that they had caught Cupid so easily.

Graham Marshall was behind the third cell door as we entered. The door was painted grey, six inches of steel with a tiny peephole in the centre. Bancho went up to the door and waved Gerry Cornwell forward. 'Have a gander, he can't bite, and he can't see you.'

Cornwell stepped up to the door and peered through. We waited, holding our breath. He turned to face us. 'I can't tell through that little hole.' He pointed to his glasses. 'They're getting in the way . . . you'll need to open up the door.'

Bancho turned and shouted, 'Ruby!' When there was no answer, he stepped out into the middle of the corridor in front of the cells and shouted again. 'Ruby!' It was louder this time, and Ruby the turnkey came out from her side office, muttering under her breath and flipping through her keys. 'Out the way, out the way.' Although she was a civilian, she ruled the cells, and in her domain she was queen. Bancho scurried back; she unlocked the cell door and waited. There was no sound of feet. I wondered if Marshall was alive, or if by chance he had somehow managed to commit suicide. The door swung open. Gerry Cornwell stood in the crack and said nothing. Several long moments passed, then he leapt at Graham Marshall with a speed and ferocity that belied his years, drunkenness, and profession.

By the time Bancho got into the cell, Cornwell was straddling my client, sitting on his chest pinning him to the floor. He had his two hands in Graham Marshall's hair and was banging his head up and down off the concrete like a basketball. A small pool of blood was forming underneath Marshall's head. There was no doubt in my mind that he knew the psychiatrist. It was only the shock of seeing Gerry Cornwell that prevented him fighting back. Bancho pulled the psychiatrist off his prisoner, but Gerry Cornwell got one last kick in.

'You little fucker . . . you tell me where Sam is!' he shouted as his shoe connected with Marshall's face.

'I don't know!' he screamed back, spitting out blood. In a flash he was calm again. 'I don't know. Why? Is it important?'

Chapter Forty-Eight

We were back in the task-force room; Ruby had called out the police doctor and she was waiting with Graham Marshall until medical help arrived. From the grim smile on his face, I sensed Dr Cornwell had waited for a very long time to give my client a good kicking; surprising behaviour for a psychiatrist, I thought, but what did I really know? There were a few clients I would have liked to have slapped in my time, but I hadn't enjoyed what I had seen. My mobile chirped in my pocket as I sat down. The screen told me it was Kailash, so I pressed 'reject' without a second's thought. No sooner had I put it back in my bag this time than it rang again.

'Put it off or answer it,' growled Bancho, as if I was a teenager, as I rejected it again.

'It's Kailash,' I said, 'she can always sense the worst time to call.'

'Christ, if I had a mother like that, I'd have her working here,' he answered. 'That woman knows more about crime in Edinburgh than I do. Do us all a favour, Brodie, and answer it. She won't give up, and she'll probably start phoning here if she knows where you are. Tell her

241

you'll be round the whorehouse later for a nice cup of tea.'

Just as he finished, and just as I was about to get started on him, it rang again. Bancho was right though, so I pressed 'accept'.

'Thanks so much for deigning to pick up,' came my mother's cultured voice immediately. 'Get round here now.'

'Kailash! I'm working,' I protested.

'That's why you need to get round here now. I know what's going on, and, trust me, you'll want to know this – so do as you're told for once and get here.'

I looked at Gerry Cornwell and knew that I still had a bit of time before he sobered up. Kailash was generally right, even if I hated to admit it. 'Duncan, I'm going to pop out for a bit. I take it there's nothing going to happen for a while?'

'Nope. We'll get this guy sorted, then we'll see what state your one is in, then I might just let them stew for a bit. Off to Mummy, are you? She got some new knocking-shop gossip she needs to share?'

'You might be surprised,' I said, walking out. I hailed a taxi outside the station, reckoning it would put Kailash in a better mood. Even the sound of the Fat Boy pulling up seemed to piss her off, and I didn't want to waste time finding a parking space – the day was going to be busy enough. I was at the brothel quickly, and the door was opened by Malcolm as soon as I stepped out of the car. He hugged me warmly, as always, and indicated towards the kitchen. 'In there, Brodie – she's got her back up . . . but you're in the clear this time.'

My mother was sitting at the big wooden table nursing a huge mug of cappuccino – she probably wouldn't drink any of it, too many calories, but she seemed to be getting some comfort from the warmth. She even smiled at me when I walked in. 'Sit down,' she said. 'Are you well?'

'Erm, yes – why wouldn't I be?' What was she getting at?

'I worry about you, Brodie,' she said. 'I do. You don't see what's staring you in the face. You have so many people ready to love you, wanting to love you – you should let them.'

'Where's this going? I thought you had something to tell me about Graham Marshall?'

Kailash looked at me as if I hadn't even spoken. 'I'm not talking about myself. I don't need your permission to love you.' She paused. 'Where's Joe?'

'I don't know – why would I know that? He'll be doing . . . something I guess. Now, why did you drag me down here?'

'Malcolm?' she sighed as he sat down beside her. 'Last night – something happened. I'm still angry about it, and there will be repercussions, but Malcolm will tell you what you need to know.'

'One of the girls came to get me up this morning,' he began. 'Rochelle? Do you know her?' I did. She was the Amazonian American that I had found friendly. 'She doesn't know all of the rules yet . . .'

Kailash cut in with, 'That's no excuse. She should learn them. Quickly. She's damn lucky to be working somewhere like this.'

'Well, anyway – she'd let a punter stay over. He was still asleep, and when she saw him in the morning she was worried. She asked me to take a look at him.'

'Look at what?' I asked Malcolm. 'Had he hurt her?'

'No, no – someone had hurt him, though. When she saw him in the light, she saw that he had been attacked.' Malcolm was the one the girls went to with cuts, scratches, bites and everything else. He always knew the right lotion or potion, and he could keep secrets – or so they thought. He actually only managed to keep them from anyone not called Kailash Coutts.

'Get her in here,' commanded Kailash, as Dina, the little Irish redhead, wandered into the kitchen. 'Get Rochelle, and make sure everyone else keeps out until I say so.' Rochelle must have been hanging outside the door anyway as she came in immediately; she'd probably sent Dina in to see how Kailash's mood was in the first place.

'Right,' said my mother. 'From the start.'

Rochelle sighed theatrically, looked at the three of us, then began. 'I was waiting last night to see if anyone would come in; it was pretty quiet and after midnight but my shift was a long way from over. I was in the waiting room with another three of the girls when this guy came in. Pretty good looking, tall, clean – but he seemed nervous. That was odd, because he didn't seem the type who would be unsure at all; he wasn't nervous about being here exactly, and he'd paid upfront of course – but there was something. Anyway, he came over to me, we chatted then went to my room. He was straight-forward, didn't want anything weird, just sex. He took

244

a while, he seemed kind of worked up, but it was fine – then he asked if I would hold him while he fell asleep.'

'Is that odd?' I asked.

She shrugged. 'It's his dollar. He'd paid for the night, Claire said.' Claire was one of the managers who took the money and she had a system of signs when she introduced punters to the girls to let them know what the state of play was, and whether she'd picked up on anything. 'They can do what they like.'

I could feel Kailash fuming. 'We're not a dosshouse. He's not here to sleep.'

Only my mother would come out with something like that. If Rochelle had wanted to get on her good side, she'd have woken the bloke up, made sure he had a new fantasy involving someone else he'd have to pay again for, then got him out to another girl or out of the building so everything could start all over again.

'What else?' I asked, wondering what this had to do with me.

'He kept his shirt on when we were having sex, which is fine I guess, but when I looked at him this morning, it had come off. He was covered in scratches, really bad ones, and what looked like knife cuts. That's when I went to get Malcolm.'

I raised my eyes at him, needing to hear something relevant, or more nonsense that would convince me to cut my losses and get back to the station. 'I cleaned him up as best I could – and he told me a few things. He was in Edinburgh for business and he'd gone down to the Shore to find a girl.' Kailash snorted. 'He'd looked around, saw someone he liked the look of and picked her up in his car. They'd gone to a business park nearby and got started. He said she moved over to her bag to get a condom and brought out a knife instead. The guy was still terrified, Brodie. He said she was possessed; she was slashing away, scratching him, trying to cut him, until he finally managed to push her out of the car and get away. He's not going to make a complaint to the police, is he? In fact, he's probably well on his way home. I just thought you need to know this stuff – it might help you.'

'What?' I snorted, just like my mother a few moments earlier, ignoring the fact that she seemed to be trying to give me information that might aid my case – even though it would harm her reputation if it got out that she wasn't as discreet as she needed to be about all punters. 'He's so bloody traumatized that he still needs to get laid a couple of hours later? If he had the money, why didn't he come here in the first place?'

'You'd be surprised,' said Kailash. 'Or maybe you wouldn't. They come here claiming to be upset about their wives dying, or their kids being ill, or their businesses folding – they can always find the money and the inclination for a pretty girl lying on her back. Sounds like this guy – my new lodger – didn't get what he wanted from the psycho down the Docks, and he realized that later when he'd calmed down, so decided to stop being such a cheapskate.'

'Why do I need to know all of this?' I asked her.

'Because there is someone out there killing punters. Wealthy punters who are in the city for business. Now I'm telling you that someone has tried again. It's the

246

same pattern, from what I can tell, from what . . . sources have told me. Now, go put two and two together and see if you can come up with four.'

'Kailash, you're always so far ahead of everyone else that half of the time we don't even know what you're going on about,' I told her.

'You'll see. Now, it's time for you to go. I have house-keeping to deal with.' She fixed a steely glare on Rochelle as Malcolm and I got up. Good luck to the girl, I thought.

Chapter Forty-Nine

'How long have you known Dr Marshall?' I asked Cornwell. I was back at the station after my mother's cryptic conversation, and he had sobered up a lot since my last view of him, but adrenalin was still pumping round his system. His hand shook as he dabbed the blood from his face, a reminder of his earlier violent encounter; most of it belonged to my client. 'How long have you known Graham Marshall?' I asked again. I turned to Bancho for some assistance. It could be argued that the police had stood back and allowed my client to be assaulted in the police cells. Unless you had been there, you would never have believed the mild-mannered psychologist could move so fast or so viciously.

'I don't know any Graham Marshall,' he smiled, his lips forming a hard, obstinate line. To be truthful, after the first consultation with my client, I'd felt like punching him myself. But I did object to being taken for a fool. Years of dealing with unstable patients probably helped Dr Cornwell make his next decision. He sat down next to me; the smell of drink was overpowered by the scent of fresh perspiration and blood. 'I'm telling you the truth when I say that, when I say that I don't know Graham Marshall. The man in that cell is Kevin Milne, and it doesn't matter what the courts allow him to call himself, that's what he will always be to me.'

Kevin Milne.

Dr Graham Marshall had boxed me into a corner. I'd taken his retainer and now I was forced to defend . . . whatever he was. The anger building up inside was bringing acidic bile to my throat. I had to blame someone. The only person I could think of in the whole sorry saga to heap it on was sitting right next to me, staring at his bloodied hands. I walked over to the victim board and, with great care, peeled the photographs given by the families away from the Blu-Tack. I carried three of them over to Gerry Cornwell. The picture of Alan Pearson was uppermost. I laid the other two down on the desk and handed him the one of the Newcastle man. 'At one time you must have written a report stating that . . .' One glance at Cornwell out of the corner of my eye told me he would never permit Graham Marshall to be called anything other than Kevin Milne. I started again. 'At some time in the past you told a court that Kevin Milne was not a danger to the public.'

The blood drained from his face and the pupils in his burning blue eyes became pinpoints of darkness. He shook his head for a long time before he spoke. 'From the first instant I met Kevin, I knew he was evil. I don't say that lightly. In fact, until I met him, I didn't think such a thing really existed. It's the cop-out of newspapers and stupid people who can't properly think things through.'

He breathed deeply, staring straight ahead at an unknown point. In the heavy silence, he ran the photograph of Alan Pearson, the third victim, through his fingertips, and he seemed to draw strength from it. 'People are always fascinated by murders. It makes their normal problems seem diminished.' He looked me straight in the eye. 'But when a child kills, it threatens the fabric of society . . . what have we become if a child is capable of torturing and killing another child? When I knew that we were looking for children twenty years ago, I wrote reports, hypothesized about what they might be. I was right to some extent, but there was something else – something about Kevin Milne that wasn't in any book or lecture.'

He stared down at the photograph of Alan Pearson.

'We cannot accept that some people are just born *bad* . . . of course, it's easy to say an abused child becomes an abuser, but I can assure you that the vast majority of abused children go on to be good people.'

Cornwell was hiding something. I wasn't in court so I broke the golden rule. I asked a question to which I did not know the answer.

'What did Kevin Milne have over you?' I asked. He gripped the corners of the photograph so tightly it bent in the middle. 'Kevin was very good at a lot of things. One of them was finding out secrets.'

He fell into silence and I couldn't allow that. 'If you don't tell us everything, I will insist DI Bancho charges you with assault,' I told him.

Cornwell looked into my eyes. His gaze was dark and I saw he was in a place where no threat I made could hurt him. A tinge of shame came over me. Cornwell started to speak. It was like rapid gunfire; now he had opened up, nothing could stop him, the deep creases on his forehead eased, even his breathing seemed less laboured. 'After the initial trial,' he said slowly, 'Renee and Kevin were sentenced to twenty-five years. Once the lynching mob mentality died down, there was a back-swing. Some lawyers argued the children had been unfairly treated. They took a case to the European Court of Human Rights. They were awarded compensation, but their sentences remained intact.'

'What was your recommendation?' I asked.

A thin grimace twisted his lips and he jerked his head backwards, still holding on to the photograph of the third victim. 'I . . . me . . . I . . .' he stuttered. 'I wasn't in the liberal vanguard. My report stated they should serve twenty-five years and then Kevin Milne should be remitted to a secure mental hospital. Renee was safe to be released.'

'What changed your mind?' I asked.

And this time a bitter laugh escaped his lips. 'Kevin Milne changed my mind, of course!'

'Because he knew your secret, he blackmailed you? Simple as that?' I asked. Cornwell became angry. 'Do you really think I would be so callous as to release a fiend like Milne just to save my own skin?' He didn't wait for me to answer. 'When Kevin and Renee reached eighteen, they were due to be transferred to the adult penal system to serve out the rest of their sentence. Kevin's lawyers appealed against the sentence. I'd spoken to the Home Secretary months earlier, and he had publicly stated they would never be released.'

'A lot of people seem to have changed their minds,' Bancho muttered, and I nudged him in the back to shut up.

'As I said, Kevin was good at guessing people's secrets.' He took a deep breath and spoke very quickly, without any unnecessary explanations. 'I attended a Catholic seminary in Cork. I was abused by the master of the novitiates. It wasn't something I broadcast – but he guessed. In fact, until that point, I hadn't told a living soul. He got little bits out of me, little bits of my life, and, because I thought that I could . . . I could trade him, I suppose, I foolishly told him. He only needed a few bits of background information and he knew.'

'Did Kevin try to blackmail you?'

'I never gave him the chance. I knew he was about to say that I'd touched him inappropriately, so I made sure all our sessions were videotaped and that I had someone with me at all times but . . .' He looked down at the photograph of Alan Pearson again.

'But?' I urged.

'But I should have warned the staff in the young offenders' institution. One guard had indeed taken to abusing the boys.' He shook his head from side to side. 'The night before the guard was due to go to a disciplinary hearing, he hung himself.'

Bancho snorted, 'Good. He did our bloody job for us.'

Gerry Cornwell continued to shake his head. 'The death of the pervert did not solve the problem . . . his habit was to take the boys out of the institution for days out to get them ready for release. Instead, he took them to a safe house where he abused them. One vulnerable young boy was missing, and the only person who knew where the safe house was located was Kevin.'

I stood up. 'And he wouldn't tell you where it was unless you changed your report.'

Gerry Cornwell nodded. He continued, 'I couldn't let the young boy die, and I knew Milne wouldn't tell us unless he got his own way. Milne was an expert at manipulating people, including me. I enlisted the help of Lord Edward Hunter and Sam Jones. The police could not track down the boy. He had been missing for over a week and we had to take action. I changed the report, and Lord Hunter spoke to the Court of Appeal judges off the bench. He didn't tell them the truth – he couldn't be seen to be giving in to blackmail.'

'You thought you could control Kevin Milne,' I said quietly.

He nodded. 'Kevin's IQ is remarkably high. His exam results were exceptional, and the Appeal Court had no difficulty in believing he had changed. They couldn't believe a boy from Kevin's background could be so intelligent. They knew nothing.'

'You were wrong,' I said.

He nodded in agreement. 'We were all wrong, and now . . . ? Now he's got Sam.'

Chapter Fifty

Tired, exhausted and sick to death, I decided I'd better stop off at the hospital to see my client. The car park at the Edinburgh Royal Infirmary is always busy, but miraculously I found a space near A&E. Rumour had it that they had moved the hospital away from the centre of town to keep the hypochondriacs and time-wasters away – it didn't seem to have worked if the queue for medical attention was anything to go by. A nurse with an armful of files managed to raise a smile in my direction when I walked in the door. I looked like trouble. I carried my battered black helmet under my arm. My scuffed boots were trailing mud through the A&E and she still smiled: maybe they were angels after all.

'I'm here to see Dr Graham Marshall,' I said. She was tired, her eyes flicked up to the right going through the duty roster of junior doctors. She was about to tell me there was no such doctor on call when I explained, 'Police brought him in earlier.'

She rolled her eyes. 'Ah, him. Are you family?'

'No,' I continued to whisper. 'I'm his lawyer.' Her eyes

flicked over me and her mouth curved into a smile. I could tell she didn't believe me, and it was a testament to his temperament that she led me to his cubicle, although her eyes told me she hoped I was an assassin. I was just pleased to be moving out of the main concourse. The fact is that a number of my clients hang out in the Accident and Emergency, usually after drunken brawls, knife fights, or spousal abuse. I didn't want to talk to any of them. Marshall was enough to contend with. The nurse stopped outside a blue-curtained cubicle. She pulled the drapes back.

'Thank you,' I said.

'You're welcome.' She threw a disdainful look at the battered man on the trolley.

'About time you showed up,' he snarled. His ribs were bandaged but his teeth all seemed to be in place. He caught me staring at them. 'They were porcelain veneers; I superglued them back – it's a temporary measure.' He glanced at me, then down at the pink cotton blanket that covered him. 'I suppose you've guessed by now my background was not one where oral hygiene was of primary importance.'

I stared at Kevin Milne aka Dr Graham Marshall and tried to ignore the cold running through me. 'I met Kelly Adams,' I said.

He nodded his head, sucked in his cheeks and smiled slowly. 'Is she the one who's been blackmailing me?' He laughed out loud. 'I didn't think she had the guts.'

I put my helmet down heavily on his stomach and he winced. It was my turn to smile. I started to clap. I didn't care what the nurses or doctors thought, although

I suspect none of them heard. If they were wise, they were giving this cubicle a wide berth.

'Bravo,' I nodded my head and clapped louder. 'Bravo, first-class performance.'

Every muscle in his face tightened. I watched his micro-movements, searching for the telltale signs of a liar: there were none.

'You listen to me, and you listen to me well, because I have bought you, Ms McLennan. Just because I made a mistake when I was a child, a small innocent child, a mistake I regret every day of my life and try to make amends for—'

I interrupted him. 'Let's be clear on this. When you killed Matthew Cook, it was not a mistake, it was premeditated murder.' I stared into the canvas of his face again. He breathed deeply, trying to control his temper, and he winced in pain as his chest moved up and down. I was tempted to remove my helmet but I resisted the urge.

'If Renee and I had carried out "the act"—'

I interrupted him again. 'It wasn't an "act". A two-year-old boy died a brutal, painful death at your hands.'

'If it had happened in Scotland, would I have been tried in an adult court?' he asked. The answer to that was no, but every instinct I had would not let me agree with him so I remained silent. As soon as you start agreeing with someone, they can persuade you round to their way of thinking. Marshall's demeanour changed again. It was like stripping away layers of old wallpaper. I wanted to get as near as possible to the real Kevin.

'Whatever I am, and whatever you think I did, one

thing we will all agree on is that I am not stupid.' He raised his left eyebrow and stared straight through me before he continued. 'I didn't want to get caught when I was ten and I sure as hell don't want to get caught now.' He took my helmet and threw it on the floor.

'Nurse!' he screamed. 'Nurse, get me some fucking painkillers now!'

'Charming,' I smiled.

'I paid you to get me out of here. It must be obvious that I'm being set up. Find out who hates me and work backwards.' His eyes were screwed shut and he held his torso, giving himself a cuddle.

'People who hate you? I bet that's a fucking long list,' I said as I bent down to pick my helmet up off the floor. 'Add me to it.'

Chapter Fifty-One

'You look like shit,' Lois said, handing me a photocopy of the court diary for the day. I glared at her. She wasn't Lavender and she never would be, but had she got a manual from her somehow on how to treat me? Shouldn't temps be lovely in the vain hope that you'll keep them on? On second thoughts, she probably wanted out as quickly as possible – I wasn't in the running for any Boss of the Year awards. My eyes were burning from lack of sleep and I still hadn't forgiven Lois for introducing me to the journalist Patsy Barnes. Ms Barnes was sitting in reception, pen at the ready, gearing herself up to shadow me in court. Lois had assured her this would be fine. That was before I'd found out Marshall's true identity. In journalistic terms, Ms Barnes had just won the lottery and she didn't even know it yet.

'We've got a problem,' I said. Lois raised her eyebrows; even temps knew that, in court work, we were always fire-fighting.

'I guessed as much. St Leonards have been on the phone. Dr Marshall wasn't arrested until after midnight, so he's not appearing in court until tomorrow. Desk

Sergeant Anderson said something about Dr Marshall being kept in hospital overnight. What's that all about?' I flapped my hand dismissively; Lois dropped the subject.

The case against Marshall looked open and shut, and I just didn't have the energy for going through the motions, especially with a journalist reporting on my every move. It wouldn't be good for business: the public would have no sympathy for Kevin Milne, Graham Marshall, or his lawyer. My head fell into my hands. 'We are fucked, totally fucked,' I said. I was careful not to pin any blame on Lois verbally, but my head was screaming. It would have been just a bit easier not to have invited a member of the press pack into our office meetings at the present moment.

Glasgow Joe strode into the office. For once he wasn't wearing a kilt. He meant business. He often carries out investigative work for us, so he's part of the team, but today he had on his leathers. He too looked as if he had been up all night. He placed his gloves down on the desk and took my chin in his hands. Staring directly into my eyes he said, 'Where the hell have you been? I've been up all night waiting on you to come in. Half an hour ago I went up to the Royal to see if you'd been checked in. I thought you'd had an accident, Brodie.'

His anger was disappearing now that he knew I was safe. He yanked me up out of my chair and held me close to his chest. His leather jacket was cold and hard, but the emotion in his moss-green eyes was raw. One quick glance down at Glasgow Joe's hands told me everything I didn't want to know. The Celtic gold band I had given him when we married in Vegas eleven years ago was back on the third finger of his left hand. My fault. I'd thrown a drowning man a rope and he was hauling himself in. Joe had let me go once and his every move told me he wouldn't make the same mistake twice.

I didn't have time for this. I pushed him away just as a knock on my office door made us all look up. Patsy Barnes stood in the entrance. Her shoulder-length chestnut hair was glossy, and the full-fringe style made her look years younger than she had in The Tower. She was clean and presentable – everything I wasn't. I tried to straighten out my hair by finger-combing it, but my hands became snarled up in the bird's nest on my head almost immediately. I tried to pat the wild curls down, but I didn't stand a chance.

'I'm not interrupting anything, am I?' The journalist smiled a practised winning smile, her teeth dazzling me with their unnatural whiteness. I ran my tongue over my own teeth, alarmed at what I felt; I reached down into the bottom drawer to see if I had any disposable toothbrushes left.

'No,' said Lois, a trifle too quickly, still staring at Joe. 'We were just discussing what cases we have on in court. Take a seat outside in reception and then we'll call you back in five minutes when we're sure we are not breaching client confidentiality.'

'Okay.' Patsy Barnes smiled at Glasgow Joe and held his eyes as she said, 'I'll see you in five minutes.'

The office door closed. I turned to Joe and said, 'She's after you.'

He grinned. 'Tell me something new, Brodie. When are you going to realize you've won first prize? Go on, admit it – you can't believe your luck.' He tried to grab me but I got away.

'You like it, don't you? All these women throwing themselves at you – the girls in Suzie Wong's the other night and now her.' I threw my head in the direction of the reception area.

A great belly laugh escaped from Joe's lips. 'If I didn't know better, I'd say you were jealous.'

I was trying to find a way to burst his bubble when Lois poked me in the shoulder. 'I don't think there is any way we can get rid of her. She'll realize there's a big story if we try.' She sighed and pursed her lips as though she was swallowing a bitter pill. 'Sorry, but I think the only way is to invite her in, tell her everything is off the record until you give her the nod, and you get to review any written material before it's published. What do you say?' This girl was actually quite good, I thought, but before I could tell her, Patsy Barnes spoke from the doorway.

'The five minutes is up and I agree to your terms. It's going to be a pleasure doing business with you, Brodie.'

Chapter Fifty-Two

I had an hour before I had to leave for court. The work for the day was organized, so I decided to spend the last hour going over the case against Marshall. I couldn't reveal his true identity to Patsy Barnes. The information was too explosive. Lois set the white board up in my office, I had a black dry marker pen and I wrote up the name GRAHAM MARSHALL in capital letters.

'Is that *the* Dr Graham Marshall, the plastic surgeon?' asked Patsy. I nodded and I wondered if he'd done any work for her; if so, he deserved his reputation.

'Last night I didn't get any sleep,' I moaned. 'St Leonards called saying they had arrested him and he asked for me. They were arresting him in connection with the Cupid murders. A police officer from London is missing and they believe he is responsible for her disappearance. They are also investigating allegations following the discovery of a female body in the scrap yard off Bernard Street.' I reached onto my desk and picked up copies of the photographs Bancho had given me, stuck Blu-Tack on them and attached them to the board.

'Kelly Adams, deceased air hostess, aged twenty-four. The naked man on top of her, for those of you who haven't met him, is our client. I don't have the post-mortem photographs, but the cause of death looks as if it was a massive overdose and, before you ask, the needle was still in her neck.' I paused. 'Then her heart was removed.'

Joe sat impassively in the front. He had irritated me by reminding me of how much he meant to me, and the only way I knew how to deal with that was by being a cow to him and giving him chores to do – he could bloody well help out by keeping Patsy Barnes busy and off my back. If he wanted female adulation, then I would make sure he got it in spades – just from someone else.

'There's something about this case that's bothering you,' Joe said. 'What is it?'

Patsy Barnes picked up her pen, and stared at me. I stared back at her pen. She laid it down again. I looked down at my scuffed bike boots and prayed I had clean clothes for court in the office. Joe knew me too well. Maybe I should have let him in on the identity of Marshall. I had to box clever, and I did what I always do in those situations. I let my mouth run away with me. I nodded at him to let him know he was right, other-wise he would have been like a dog after a bone, and he wouldn't have given up. 'The case against Marshall is almost overwhelming. No DNA evidence on any of the bodies except one stray hair of his. These photographs of Marshall and Kelly Adams look to me as if they were taken by a surveillance camera. They were found in DI Sam Jones's briefcase after she disappeared. But I don't think she took the photographs. I think they were sent to her and my gut tells me someone is trying to frame Graham Marshall.'

'Why?' asked Joe. He always had to ask the question I didn't want to answer. I widened my eyes at him and smiled. Every brain cell I had telepathically shouted at him, 'Shut up Joe!', but it made no difference. Patsy Barnes stared at me, pen at the ready again, eager to jot down the pearls of wisdom that flowed from my mouth for her article. She smiled and nodded at Joe, fluttering her eyelids at him. 'Joe's right. Why would anyone go to the bother of trying to frame Dr Marshall?' she asked.

'Revenge?' I offered.

'It's easier to kill him than set up an elaborate ploy like this. Maybe you'll just have to accept, Brodie, that the bastard is guilty and you don't have a hope in hell of getting him off.' Joe's comment didn't help. Patsy was shadowing me to find out how I thought and it was embarrassing that I couldn't be the perfect case study she expected. My mind tended to jump from subject to subject, and when I was in court I listened to my gut more than my head.

I'd asked Eddie Gibb to track down Renee Smith. If she wasn't blackmailing Marshall, or Milne, or whatever I should call him, she might know who was. It was a condition imposed at the first trial, when they were ten, that Kevin and Renee had no further contact for the rest of their lives. I doubted that either of them had stuck to that. Eddie now came in smiling and waving a piece of paper with an address on it. I was surprised at what it revealed, but it was an area Renee knew. Her family had moved and the thirty-year-old Renee Smith would bear no resemblance to the little girl. It was clever of Renee to hide out in the last place the vigilantes would think of looking for her, but she hadn't come across anyone quite like Eddie, who was learning tricks from his wife by the day. 'How did you do it?' I asked. Just like Lavender, Eddie tapped the side of his nose. Lavender kept her methods and contacts very close to her chest, and I knew that was probably the safest way for Eddie to work as well.

I held the paper up. 'Eddie,' I said, and turned to face the journalist with an enormous smile on my face, 'and Patsy . . . you can go with him to court. I need to check out this witness in London. Lois? Book me on the next shuttle – I should be back tonight.' Patsy's face had tightened into thin lines. She was no doubt furious at being sidestepped by me, and then Eddie slapped her on the back, adding insult to injury. 'We'll have a great time, hen,' said Eddie.

I couldn't afford to alienate her completely; I tried to come up with a reason that was more than simply getting her out of my hair. 'A criminal case isn't won or lost on the day, Patsy, as I'm sure you know. Thousands of hours go into preparing a murder trial. The better we prepare, the more chance we have of getting our client out of jail.' Prosecutors are overworked and underpaid; they have hundreds of cases to deal with. When a big case like that of Graham Marshall comes along, I can drop everything and focus on winning. The fiscal's case is like a house of cards, and if I dig deep enough I can make it all come tumbling down. 'Dr Marshall will appear on petition in Edinburgh Sheriff Court tomorrow. He will make no plea or declaration and the case will be continued for seven days.'

Patsy Barnes was puzzled. She had been brought up in the English legal system, and even then she wouldn't have fully understood it. 'So, if you get evidence, he could be released next week?' she asked.

It was highly unlikely, but the boastful part of me came into play. 'Yes,' I said. 'I fully expect that Graham Marshall will be a free man this time next week.'

I may have said the words, but my heart shivered at the thought.

Chapter Fifty-Three

Glasgow Joe insisted on accompanying me down to London. I was glad of his company and relieved he was wearing his biker gear. Joe in a kilt attracted enough attention in Edinburgh – in Edmonton Green he would have stood out like a sore thumb. By the time we arrived we decided to go straight to Renee Smith's workplace. She had gone through several incarnations before ending up back where she had started; Renee had been unable to keep as low a profile as Milne because she blabbed. The name and identity we had for her was a long shot, but Eddie had information to suggest that Renee was now a member of some group that rejected the media's views of what was beautiful in a woman. Jesus Christ, I thought to myself as Eddie read from a page he'd printed full of Internet information. As if I didn't have enough to put up with. In America they were known as the Suicide Girls, but we were scouring the streets of Soho looking for some stripper known as Lola d'Amour – aka Renee Smith.

We stood outside some shit stripper bar just before six as the dirty-mac brigade was heading home for dinner. I had checked with Kailash. Of course she knew the owners of every strip joint and sex shop in London. My darling mother assured me that all I had to do was mention her name and the underbelly of the East End would crawl out of its way to help me. Joe marched in and paid for two. The interior was dim. Uplighters shone out of the red carpet, showing us the way to the bar and to booth seats centred round the stage. I settled down on the upholstered leather, and Joe went to the bar. The man in the next booth, with his anorak across his lap, leered at me before turning his eyes back to the stage as the next act came on. I leaned back against the leather and stared up at the ornate crystal chandelier, waiting for Joe.

Some rip-off Peggy Lee was singing and her smoky voice actually relaxed me a bit. I started to think about Joe. Was he the love of my life? Lavender maintained he was and that you only got one chance. Joe and I had our chance and he blew it by loving me too much. The pain of losing him was so bad I couldn't go through it again, so I had always treated him badly in the hope that he would get the message. Maybe it was my turn to listen to him. Joe placed a bucket of ice with champagne chilling in it on the small table; he had two flutes between his fingers.

'You mentioned Kailash's name didn't you?' I accused him.

'Too bloody right I did! I don't mind paying their rip-off prices – you'll let me claim it back on expenses, I suppose – but I do object to drinking watered-down booze.' Joe filled my glass and handed it to me before taking off his jacket. His T-shirt was muscle fit, tight across his chest. He kissed my nose and pulled me close; his body was lean and hard, and I felt myself go weak. My hormones stirred against my better judgement – but God, he was gorgeous.

A small thin man in a blue Lurex tuxedo, white shirt and country-and-western tie came onto the stage, breaking my thoughts. His black hair was slicked straight back from his forehead into a shiny cap, and a pencil-thin moustache graced his top lip. It was cliché city here tonight.

'Ladies and gentlemen . . .' There was a drum roll. I sat up and he continued, 'Put your hands together for the star of our show, the lovely Lola d'Amour!'

The red silk curtains were closed but, as a single spot-light lit the stage, they opened up: a five-foot martini glass complete with an outsized stuffed olive occupied centre stage. Dita von Teese had a lot to answer for. Every stripper in the world now thought they were in a classy profession that required them to climb out of or onto things every night. A girl reminiscent of Rita Hayworth strolled on dragging a simple wooden chair behind her. Renee Smith had aged well. Joe sat up straight and I kicked him. The silver lamé evening gown was held together with Velcro and, in no time at all it was ripped off and lying round her feet. Six-inch silver plat-form shoes, a nude-coloured satin basque and stockings were all she wore as climbed onto the chair. In one deft move she climbed into the martini glass, which had a chair as well as an olive in it. Joe wore a frown, which I assumed was for my benefit.

'Let's go round the back to see her when she gets off stage,' I said, trying to distract him as much as trying to find Renee. A bouncer stood at the stage with the precise purpose of stopping punters jumping up on the girls, but he took one look at Joe's size and backed off as we pushed through the curtain. We had to traverse the wings, which were a small corridor of curtains. The next artiste stood waiting to go on, and I could hear that she was on her mobile to her mother while she passed the time. She was a vision in ostrich feathers. I assumed she would be doing a fan dance. Backstage proper was dingy. There was a battered brown door with a star on it, and I knocked and walked in. A long mirror with lights round it dominated the room; women's clothes hung everywhere and the stench of hairspray was so intense it activated my gagging reflex.

'Does Lola d'Amour change here?' I asked a girl with red shiny tassels on her nipples. 'No,' she shook her head and the tassels swung. I turned round to find Joe who was waiting outside the door. 'Lola's dressing room is along here.' He pointed up the corridor. 'Are you sure that's her, Brodie? She looked awful young. Isn't she meant to be loads older – like thirty or something?' Joe realized his faux pas just as my foot made its way to his shin again. 'Thirty isn't quite the ancient age you might think,' I told him. 'You didn't seem to be complaining last time you were close to it. Anyway, it fits in with what I've been thinking – not only has Renee been in contact with Graham Marshall, it looks like he may have done some work on her. Old pals stick together, after all.'

I didn't bother to knock on the door. As soon as I

walked in, I realized that this really wasn't my day – Joe was right. Lola d'Amour was far too young to be who I was looking for. But sitting next to her was a woman who was clearly her older sister – we'd found Renee Smith and that was all that mattered.

She had aged badly. Her collar-length black hair was in pigtails. I'm always suspicious of grown women who wear their hair in bunches. Her body was slim but her teeth were rotten and suggested to me she had a life-long problem with bulimia. She cast her eyes over each shoulder. Like a cornered animal she was looking to run. Glasgow Joe stood up to his full height and blocked the doorway.

'There's nowhere to go, Renee,' I said. 'Don't worry, I'm not from the papers, I'm not going to harm you. I'm an Edinburgh lawyer.' I paused before I said the next sentence. 'I represent Kevin Milne.' I took a card out of my pocket and handed it to Renee. She spat in my face. Glasgow Joe took a step forward; I pushed him back to the door. 'I can take care of myself,' I said, reaching forward for the box of tissues on the dressing-room shelf.

'So? I'm guessing you don't like Kevin Milne?' I asked.

Renee turned her head away from me like a sullen teenager and started to swing her leg up and down. She wore ripped black fishnet tights, a crotch-gripping denim miniskirt and a white blouse tied underneath her bust to reveal her extensive tattoos. On her chest was a large red heart with black pins sticking out of it; one pin was larger than all the others – it was more of a nail really. I pointed to it. 'Does that represent him?' I asked.

271

'No, you stupid bitch!' she said, shaking her head with such fury it was almost like an epileptic fit. Her chin fell onto her chest, and then her index finger went up to the red heart and fingered the black nail. I could see it was a gesture she performed so often it was almost reflexive.

'Who is it?' asked Joe from the doorway. From her past, he assumed that she didn't like lawyers and remembered her low intelligence from the file notes I'd summarized. Renee looked up. Surprise was in her eyes. We knew her story. Couldn't we guess? 'Is it for Matthew?' he said. Renee nodded. 'Kevin Milne ruined your life, didn't he?' Joe said, and his voice was tender for such a big man. Renee gasped for air and opened and shut her mouth like an angelfish.

'He ruined everybody's life,' she answered, 'except his own.' She twirled her fingers in the hem of her skirt; she looked as though she had been trapped emotionally at ten years of age.

'So you kept tabs on Kevin?' I asked. Her mouth turned down at the corners; she shuddered and recoiled backwards. I guessed the answer was no.

'The courts said we weren't allowed to contact one another. I stuck by it. I did.' She took a deep breath in and clasped her hands together. 'I sometimes had the feeling he was watching me though.' She glanced over her shoulder. 'He was furious that I'd grassed him up, he didn't understand I had no choice.' Renee gazed off into space, and then she said, 'Is he still fat? When he was in custody, he became a right podgy little shit.' I sensed Renee had drawn comfort from that fact. I didn't want to burst her bubble by telling her what a success he had made of his life. 'You said that you're his lawyer. Is he in trouble again?'

'Yes,' I nodded. 'That's what I wanted to see you about. Someone is killing – and . . . Kevin is convinced he's being framed.' It sounded so weak. There was silence for a while, then Renee started to laugh. 'And you believe him?' She chuckled, slapped her knee. She looked at my business card for the first time. 'If hearts are going missing from the bodies in Edinburgh, Kevin Milne is your murderer.' She tried to hand me back my card. 'See, they never put that in the papers . . . it was too grue-some, but it was what Kevin liked to do.'

'Is there anyone you can think of who would frame him?' I asked, not wanting to dwell on what truly made me feel ill.

'I take it you have met Kevin?' she asked. I nodded. 'Well, in my opinion they would be queuing up – starting off with his mother. Kate Milne was never up to much but she stood by Kevin. The whole family moved north and then, as soon as he got out of the detention centre, I heard he fucked off and never as much as gave her a by-your-leave.'

Renee had chosen a different course, she told us. She'd kept her family close and her mother had sobered up, tried to make amends. 'Do I have to move, change my name and leave Lola?' she asked.

Glasgow Joe spoke up, soft as always. 'No, you're safe, you're safe.' When he said it, she believed him. A sigh escaped from her lips. I hadn't realized she'd been holding her breath. 'If Kevin really thinks he's being set up, perhaps he is. If he is, then there's only one person who has the patience to wait all these years.'

I moved a step closer to her. 'Who is it?' I asked.

Renee rubbed her fingers over her face. 'Swear to me you'll never say where you heard this.' I nodded but it wasn't good enough. Renee held out her pinkie. 'You are joking,' I said. But she wasn't, so I entwined my pinkie round Renee's and made a promise to keep her secrets. Once it was done she looked satisfied. 'Have you heard of a police officer named Sam Jones? She was a constable when we were arrested, but she's been promoted since then, I've heard.'

'Yes, Renee, I've heard of Sam – but she's missing, and they suspect Kevin has murdered her too.' Renee started to laugh, a long, hysterical belly-aching laugh. 'She's a sly cow that one.' She bit her bottom lip. 'No one has found Sam's body? You found all the other bodies, didn't you? So, where's hers?' She tapped the side of her nose and it pained me with a thought of Lavender – I wanted to be home, away from all of this.

'Listen to me, lady lawyer – find Sam Jones and you'll find your murderer.'

Chapter Fifty-Four

As we flew into Edinburgh Airport, the city and its lights sparkled below me like a fairy town welcoming me home. All I wanted was bed. As we turned left over the River Forth I was too sleep-deprived to notice the cantilevered grandeur of the rail bridge or the snake of traffic still making its way across the Forth Road Bridge. Glasgow Joe had wrapped his arms around me, and asked the stewardess for a pillow. He didn't mind that I snored or dribbled on his jacket. I woke up feeling hellish, my mouth dry and sour. I knew my breath wouldn't pass the sniff test, but Joe still looked at me as if he had won the prize draw. We had walked on the plane without bags, so we were able to walk off and hit the taxi queue first.

Glasgow Joe was anxious to discuss the case. He loved the chance to interfere and do investigative work. He had a talent for it because of his contacts in the crim-inal fraternity but, at least this time, he was on *my* side.

The cabbie was unnaturally silent and seemed un-concerned when Joe closed the glass partition to give us privacy. 'So, what do you think?' He sat forward on the edge of his seat and looked into my eyes. 'Is Sam Jones setting up Marshall because of the hatred she still has for Kevin Milne?' I leaned my head against the cold taxi window and stared out. Maybe if I feigned disinterest he would let me sleep. We drove towards Princes Street, past the private hospital where Marshall sometimes worked. 'They're the same person, Joe. Kevin Milne's crimes are Graham Marshall's – but everyone is entitled to a second chance. Aren't they?'

'Shit – you getting at me?' he said. 'I admit I'm a sinner, Brodie. I haven't found God, and I have killed a man.'

'Or two,' I said.

'I'm not proud of it. I did what I had to . . . to survive.'

I laid my hand on his heart. It was beating strong and steady. 'When you were ten, I seem to recall you had a habit of saving people, rescuing damsels you thought were in distress.' He smiled, recalling how we had first met. Some boys from the Protestant primary school had picked on me for being a Catholic and Joe had jumped in.

'You could have taken them yourself . . . you were a feisty, bad-tempered little madam,' he said. I nodded. 'I can guess the punch line,' I told him, smiling before getting back to business. 'Renee Smith was Kevin's stooge . . . I don't believe she touched that child, look at how she was. It was all him.' Leaning against the glass was giving me a pain in my neck. I shifted round to look into Joe's face. 'You know what my mother Mary McLennan always used to say . . .' He interrupted me. He had heard her say it time and again, usually when she was trying to stop me hanging out with him. 'You fly with the crows, you get shot with the crows.'

He smiled at me and it melted every bit of ice I had put in place of emotions. 'I don't do so good flying solo, Brodie.'

The taxi had pulled up outside the house in Cumberland Street. Joe leaned forward to pay the driver. It was obvious that he had no intention of going back to his flat. The Georgian panelled front door was in need of a fresh coat of black paint, the large brass knocker was a lion like the one Scrooge saw in *A Christmas Carol*. I stared into its face, half expecting it to morph into the head of Mary McLennan warning me to start living my life, time was passing by. In spite of Joe's bad-boy traits, she had seen the good in him.

For once the house was tidy. The long corridor had been cleaned by my flatmate and trainee Louisa, and I hadn't been home to untidy it. It was late but she was still up, the kitchen light was on and the house smelled of roast chicken. Louisa must have been entertaining one of her men friends. I said a silent prayer that he was not a big eater and that there was some left for me.

It turned out that Louisa was alone, leaning against the kitchen cabinets with her arms folded across her chest. The rare brittle-bone condition that stunted Louisa's growth and twisted her skeleton rarely holds her back from anything. I was forced to give her a position in my firm by her father who is a judge, when she graduated summa cum laude from the Edinburgh Faculty of Law. She is a genius and sex maniac rolled into one little package.

'Where's the man?' I asked. She always had men. Louisa made no bones about the fact that she had economic power over male lawyers. She had this leverage because part of her job was to see that we had enough bodies to cover our very busy court workload. This meant she had to instruct lawyers who did not work for us on a full-time basis, so if Louisa liked you and you were nice to her, which usually involved sexual favours, she gave you work. There had been numerous complaints about her, but she said men had been doing it for years. I tolerated her foibles because she was very good at her job, and was also a magnificent cook and a neat freak who kept the house habitable. I went up to the stove and opened up the tin-foil parcel. The chicken had been soaking in its own juices for at least a couple of hours and it smelled delicious. I reached my hand out to take a piece.

She slapped my fingers.

Joe pulled off a leg. She ignored him.

'When were you going to tell me?' she asked, arms still folded angrily across her chest. Her foot had now begun to tap and I knew she was seriously pissed off.

'I am an integral member of the team, Brodie. I deserve to know that we are acting for Kevin Milne or Graham Marshall . . . I shouldn't have to find out from somebody called Lola something-or-other.' My heart stuttered. How did Lola get this number and why was she calling? Louisa didn't allow me to open my mouth. She held her hand up, she hadn't finished with me. 'She was hysterical.'

My heart missed another beat.

'Someone called Renee Smith – as if I don't recognize that name – was found dead half an hour after you left.' Louisa took a deep breath. 'And guess what? Her heart was missing.'

Chapter Fifty-Five

At nine forty-five, Edinburgh Sheriff Court was teeming with life, and all of it, especially the lawyers, looked like creatures found in the slime at the bottom of a pond. The big Mercedes sports cars had taken up all the parking spots in Chambers Street when I arrived, but I managed to find a space for the Fat Boy in a solo motorcycle bay further up the road. As usual when I roared up outside the court on the Harley we attracted attention. I knew I was in trouble when I saw the CNN van with the satellite dish on top. I had never seen such media interest before and it could only mean one thing – the papers had discovered Marshall's true identity.

A woman from *Sky News* was racing down the street towards me; her hair and make-up was media ready, which was more than could be said for mine. I tried to remember if I had even brushed my teeth that morning.

I'd had very little sleep, even with Joe holding me tight all night. Our bodies had fallen together in a way that we both recognized and, even although there had been no sex, we both knew that we were slowly moving towards what had always been inevitable. After the shock of Renee's murder, I needed to be close to him. There was no doubt in my mind or in Lola's that I had led the killer straight to Renee's door. And we had promised her she would be safe. The murderer had made me break my promise, and I didn't like that, I didn't like it at all. I tried to act nonchalant and carried on removing the files from the bike. The reporter stuck a hairy microphone in my face. '*Sky News*,' she said in a perfect accent. I held the files closely and started to march up the street towards the court. She ran after me and, out of breath, began to speak. 'I understand from a source inside Lothian and Borders police that Kevin Milne, the killer of Matthew Cook, is appearing in court today.'

I reached the glass entrance to the court and half turned, looking over my shoulder. I smiled and said, 'I think you'll find if you check the rolls of court today that there is no one called Kevin Milne appearing.' I stopped smiling and pushed in through the revolving doors, grateful she could not follow to clarify my answer. I made my way to the agents' room. Eddie was already there and he had warned them to back off. The other lawyers in their black gowns huddled in small groups and whispered about me behind my back. I was used to that. I pulled an expensive navy blue suit out of my locker. It was bought for me by Kailash – it had cost thousands of pounds but was now crushed and reminiscent of a dishtowel. The only kind of office wear that worked for my lifestyle was drip-dry polyester, but Kailash would not hear of such a thing. I tried to smooth some of the creases out with my hand but it just wasn't happening. I shoved my feet into the heels I kept at court. I'd forgotten tights, so my legs were bare. I could pull this look off – just.

The cells were busy with custodies; inmates had been brought in for deferred sentences, trials and probation hearings. There were also a number of new custody cases. The punters who had asked for Lothian and St Clair were being seen by Louisa and Eddie; they were already seated at tables with clients in front of them. I stepped up to the desk. Before I had said the name 'Graham Marshall', the desk sergeant had shouted, 'Marshall for Brodie McLennan, Table Three.' The desk sergeant winked at me. There was no doubt he knew Marshall's true identity. My day was getting worse by the minute. Kevin Milne's original trial lawyer twenty years ago received death threats. I hoped history would not repeat itself, but suspected it would.

Marshall stumbled out of the cells. He had lost some of his edge, his navy pinstriped suit was not freshly pressed, and his Oxford cotton white shirt had been worn before. It seemed Alison Marshall was not standing by her man. If that was the case, then Lothian and St Clair would have to take over, ensuring he had suitable clothes for court, especially if he appeared before a jury. The fifteen jurors definitely judged a book by its cover. Marshall sat down opposite me. His face was a mess, bearing the after-effects of Gerry Cornwell's fists. It seemed more and more likely that DI Sam Jones was involved; the original prosecuting team had already proved that they were not afraid to get their hands dirty. I leaned in towards Marshall. I didn't want anyone to overhear. 'I saw Renee yesterday,' I whispered. His eyes widened. I heard his breath catch in his throat. He crushed his teeth together and the sound grated on my nerves. After a moment he asked, 'How is she?'

'Dead.'

'Dead?' he repeated and grabbed my hand. 'Was she murdered?'

I nodded at him.

'Was her heart taken?'

I nodded again.

'Don't you see? It just proves what I've been saying. Someone is setting me up.' He smiled, then squeezed the back of my hand to make sure I was paying attention. 'Do you have any idea who?' he asked.

'Sam Jones,' I said with authority.

He pushed his chair back from the table and nodded. His hand went up to his face and rubbed his cheek. 'It makes sense. That bitch has always hated me; she's even faked her own death, hasn't she? Well, she's totally screwed up – how could I have killed Renee if I was in jail? Stupid, stupid, stupid.' He was lost in thought; I studied the tic throbbing on the side of his neck and his white, bloodless knuckles. I didn't need to be psychic to see his eyes had moved up to the right, probably whilst he fantasized about strangling Sam Jones. If he had moved his eyes to the left, he would have been recalling her murder. However, his point was bang on – in which case I was dealing with an innocent man and ethics demanded I do my utmost to have him set free.

The case of HMA v. Graham Marshall was being heard in chambers, which meant no member of the press or public was allowed in. Agnes Sampson had prepared the complaint herself. She was trying to limit access to the file papers in a vain attempt to keep Marshall's notorious past a secret. Agnes was going to these lengths not for his sake but her own. She knew I would appeal any mistake she or her office made and hang them with it. Agnes Sampson was determined to give me no rope.

Court Seven was almost empty when I walked in. Directly underneath the judge's bench is known as the well of the court. In the well, there is a large table. The clerk sits at the top of it, the prosecutor sits on the judge's right-hand side and the defence team sit on the left. The clerk was Alex Grant, a guy I'd always thought I might have a sneaky wee go at – if it wasn't for Joe. His body was thin but muscular, his face was thin but chiselled; everything was aesthetically pleasing, actually, which was a rarity in the Scottish legal world. The clerk was already in position, sorting through his papers from the morning court, and Agnes Sampson was appearing alone without the aid of a trainee. I couldn't recall the last time I'd seen her in a courtroom.

The door of the court opened and in walked Dr Cornwell and Bancho. I had been expecting Bancho, but the presence of the psychiatrist surprised me. Bancho walked towards the well of the court. Cornwell hung around at the doorway, looking as tired and worried as I felt.

'What's he doing here?' I asked Bancho, jerking my thumb towards the psychiatrist.

'I wasn't taking any chances. I thought you might ask for bail. Dr Cornwell will be able to give a report on Marshall's mental state.'

I glanced over my shoulder at him. His glasses were taped together. They must have been broken in the scuffle with my client, and his knuckles were skinned. Graham Marshall looked in better shape than Gerry Cornwell.

'It's a murder charge, Bancho, it's highly unlikely I would get bail. And in any event, I can't ask for it at the first hearing.' I poked his shoulder. 'You should know that.'

He sighed. 'The Met contacted me about Renee Smith's death; in view of the circumstances I thought you might push it. I understand you and Glasgow Joe paid Renee a visit yesterday?' I nodded. 'The Met wants me to take a statement then . . . one of their officers will fly up to interview you.'

'Am I a suspect?' I asked.

'They don't have any leads, so what do you think?'

'I think we should find Sam Jones. All the evidence is pointing to her,' I said.

Bancho screwed up his face and looked as though he wanted to tell me to go and boil my head. 'I met Sam Jones, don't forget. There's no way she's crooked.'

'Someone is setting up my client,' I said.

'Says who? Graham Marshall? No one is going to believe him. The official line is the murder of Renee Smith is unrelated to the Cupid murders in Edinburgh.'

'Except Renee's heart was removed.'

'Not my problem. I've got enough on my plate with your bloody Dr Marshall. There's more than enough evidence to tie him to the victims in the morgue.'

'But it's too convenient, Duncan, even you must see that?' I said.

'You're not going to hear me complaining that I've got a cast-iron case. You're just sore because this time you're going to lose.' He smirked and took a seat in the back of the court.

Alex Grant shouted out, 'Court!' I pushed the heavy chair back and stood up. Marshall was led into the dock by two burly police officers. His eyes widened when he saw Gerry Cornwell seated in the back row of the public gallery, but he exercised the utmost control. No emotion played on his face and he turned to face the front of the court.

I kept my eyes on the psychiatrist. It was personal with him; his face reddened and he was sweating. The swollen vein on his temple throbbed and told me he still believed my client had murdered Sam Jones. I was guessing, but I felt that there was more to his feelings than friendship or professional concern. Did he love her? Had they met again over the years? The vendetta against Kevin Milne and Renee Smith had started twenty years ago with the murder of Matthew Cook. Venom had not cooled over the years, and it wasn't beyond the realms of possibility that Dr Gerry Cornwell had found out Renee's address and murdered her. He might even be biding his time to take out my client. In my work and in my life, I had seen too many people blinded by emotions, blinded beyond all sense, and capable of more than they would ever have thought themselves capable of as a result. Was Cornwell a killer? Had he set Milne, or Marshall or whatever he was called, up?

The judge came onto the bench and smiled at me, a rare occurrence with other judges, but not this one.

It was Louisa's father, Sheriff Harrison, and we both always acknowledged that he owed me a favour for taking his daughter off his hands. Alex Grant called out the accused's name. 'Are you Dr Graham Marshall?' he asked. I made no plea or declaration of guilt or innocence on behalf of my client once his identity was confirmed. He was led away to be taken back to prison. He was due to appear in this court in one week. His true identity would be known to the prison population within minutes, I would guess. I doubted that he would last much longer than a week.

If I was to save the man who I knew had been a monster, I had to prove him innocent of these recent crimes before it was others who passed judgement of their own kind.

Chapter Fifty-Six

A thin sliver of moonlight poked through the blackout curtains I had hanging in my bedroom. I found it hard to sleep most nights. Once upon a time, long ago, Duncan Bancho had said it was my conscience that made me an insomniac. Then I had dismissed him with a derisive laugh. Now, in the dark hours of the early morning, his words seemed quite accurate to me. Joe lay beside me. His breath was even and deep, every muscle in his body was relaxed and, as I stared into his sleeping face, the years rolled back. His heavy fringed eyelids were closed and he looked divine. I couldn't resist reaching out to touch his cheek; he wrinkled his face and moved away. A vague noise outside my window made the fine hairs on the back of my neck stand up. Cumberland Street isn't frequented by vandals, louts, or drunks – unless you count the retired advocate who lives across from me, and he's usually staggered back from the pub before midnight.

I threw my legs over the side of the bed. The soles of my feet hit the carpet and it still surprised me that the floor wasn't littered with dirty clothes and half-eaten pizzas.

I was naked, so I grabbed his T-shirt and threw it on. The soft blue shirt smelled of fresh air and motorbikes. It reached my knees and my modesty and backside were preserved. I blinked several times to get my eyes used to the darkness; they were sore and gritty from lack of sleep and wearing contact lenses too long. I didn't know if what I saw was actually happening. I pulled the curtain back just in time to see a large man pour a can of petrol over the Fat Boy. With great care he stepped back and threw a lit match onto the seat. I rocked backwards as the bike went up in a whoosh of flames. I heard a scream – it took a second to realize I was making the noise and that what I was watching was real.

'You bastard!' I hollered, and I ran towards the front door, stopping just a moment to pick up my old hockey stick. Yelling and shrieking like a banshee, I opened the door and ran out into the street. The icy-cold cobbles on my feet meant nothing to me as I ran towards the squarely built man. He stood his ground, not running as I charged towards him. He was huge and I recognized him as Ma Boyle's eldest son Billy. It crossed my mind as the distance between us narrowed that I didn't have the faintest idea what I would do when I reached him. Billy Boyle was a street fighter of some renown; the damage I could inflict upon him was minimal compared to what he could do to me. Fuck it, I thought, he'd taken my bike from me. At least I could get in a few good whacks before he rendered me unconscious. I was close enough to smell his aftershave when he flipped me the finger, turned on his heels and ran. I continued to give chase, shouting after him, 'Come back and face me, you bastard!' But Billy Boyle's head was down and he was running home to his ma.

I could feel the heat from the flames on my back. I turned round. By the light of the fire that engulfed the bike, I saw Joe, wearing nothing but a towel, leaning against the doorjamb. The mystery of Billy Boyle was solved. He wasn't scared of me after all, but of Joe, who had the fire-extinguisher from the kitchen in his hand. He turned it on the bike and, within minutes, the blaze was under control. I was glad it was dark, I couldn't see how bad the damage was, but, from the heat of the flames I had felt, I was pretty sure the bike couldn't be saved. A stupid tear ran down my face. Over Joe's shoulder, I saw that arson wasn't the only thing that had kept Billy Boyle busy that night. Written in red spray paint across my front door was the memorial: **Senga Boyle RIP**

'Let's get inside,' said Joe. He didn't suggest calling Bancho and I knew why – he would take care of this matter himself. My reunion with Joe obviously hadn't hit the streets of Muirhouse, otherwise the Boyles wouldn't have been so careless with their health. I ran inside and pushed my feet into some trousers. Then I started thinking straight. The Boyles knew that even if Joe wasn't occupying my bed, he'd protect me no matter what. I took one backward glance at the burned skeleton that had been my bike. I was protected and it hadn't been enough. There was someone I still felt some responsibility for who didn't have Joe looking out for him. I had to see if he was all right, if he was still safe. Joe didn't question me when I told him we needed to go.

In two minutes he was out there, starting up his trike. The noise must have woken the neighbours, but not so much as a curtain twitched – no one wanted to get caught up in my business on any level.

As we drove into Muirhouse, I felt like a Valkyrie riding into hell. The flames shooting out of the windows were the first thing I saw, just before I smelled the petrol fumes.

I was too late.

The neighbours in pyjamas, nighties and tracksuits were out in force, staring in disbelief at the inferno burning down the eight-in-a-block council flat. The light from the flames highlighted the faces in the crowd. I stared at each and every one; some of them were my clients or their mothers. Excitement showed in their eyes. I knew one of the throng was a Boyle who had put a petrol bomb through the letterbox. The arsonist always stayed around to enjoy their handiwork but, try as I might, I couldn't spot who it was. The fire-fighters were throwing everything at the inferno. Water gushed from their hoses up to the second-floor window, and I was pleased to note that the youths of the area had their arms crossed. For once, no one was throwing stones at the firemen.

I ran into the crowd shouting, 'Kenny! Kenny Cameron!'

A boy of about eight pointed to a figure silhouetted against the flames in the darkness, his shoulders slumped. He didn't look like a man who had been saved.

Chapter Fifty-Seven

I stood at the entrance to Edinburgh Sheriff Court; as the November winds belted me in the face, spring seemed a very long way off. The Fat Boy was gone, Kenny Cameron would have been safer being found guilty of the murder of his wife, and I felt responsible for the death of Renee Smith. I'd finished in court. I hadn't the heart to do any of the trials, so I passed the cases to Eddie and Louisa; given the mood that I was in, the clients were better off in their hands. I turned right along Chambers Street and walked into the wind towards George IV Bridge. Joe had offered me another motorbike, but I didn't want it.

Lost in my own thoughts, I didn't hear the footsteps until they were upon me; a hand on my shoulder jerked me back to full awareness. Patsy Barnes stood at my shoulder, smiling ingratiatingly. She now knew who Graham Marshall was and she had no intention of letting the scoop of the century slip through her fingers. No doubt she saw a true crime book in it; this was her ticket to a bit of fast cash.

'Can you spare five minutes?' she said, her eyes

pleading with me. I stuck my chin down into my black wool coat to protect my face, eyeing her suspiciously. 'Quick coffee? Please?'

The café was busy and I wondered about the other people around us, what their stories were. To an outsider my life was wonderful. I was successful and earned good money, but no one seemed to notice that I worked 24/7 for my salary. My working conditions were the dives of Edinburgh, there wasn't a skanky high-rise flat in the city that I hadn't been in, or a drug addict or dealer I didn't know by name. I took out my BlackBerry and scrolled down for messages while Patsy ordered. There were twenty-four pleas for help. If Patsy Barnes wanted a view inside my life then I was just in the mood to give it to her, but only after the caffeine and calories.

'You seem tense, Brodie – is anything wrong in Dr Marshall's case?' she asked, obviously leading straight to what she was interested in. Of course she would only be interested in the headline grabber, but my job meant that sometimes I felt more like a social worker than a lawyer. 'No, the Marshall case is going according to plan, better than I could have hoped actually.' I stared down at the messages again. 'Remember when we met I had just got a not-guilty verdict for Kenny Cameron?'

Her face lit up as she recalled the landmark case. 'It was a great result,' she said.

'Was it?' I took a deep breath in. 'Last night his house was fire-bombed, and this morning he has been told by the District Council they can't rehouse him because he doesn't have any dependent children living with him. He'll have to find his own accommodation until his house is repaired.'

Patsy picked up her large white cup of swirling hot chocolate. 'That doesn't seem too bad – at least he's alive. Wouldn't anyone be grateful for that?' I shook my head. 'No landlord will give him a room – who would take the risk of a flaming bottle of petrol landing on the doormat?' I asked. I bit into the flourless chocolate tart; delicious though it was, it couldn't remove the bitter taste from my mouth. 'At least with a guilty verdict, Kenny Cameron would have had a roof over his head and three square meals a day.'

'You can't mean that,' she said.

'Of course I do,' I nodded, pushing another bit of chocolate goo into my mouth. 'In prison, guards would have watched out for his safety, but who'll take care of him now?'

She wiped her mouth delicately with a white linen napkin. 'Surely that's not your problem?'

'If it's not my problem, then whose is it?'

Patsy Barnes stared into my eyes, noting luggage under them. 'You don't sleep well, do you?' she asked.

I laughed and shook my head.

She placed her hand over mine. 'Get me a face-to-face interview with Graham Marshall.' She paused to make sure she had eye contact, than went on earnestly, '. . . or Kevin Milne. I'll see what I can do for Kenny Cameron, Brodie. An article in the local paper might put pressure on the District Council to rehouse him.'

'That would be great, Patsy, I'll take you up on that.'

I smiled. 'But there's no way *Dr Graham Marshall*,' I emphasized his name, 'will agree to meet with you. He maintains he's innocent and he has every faith that I will get him off these murder charges.'

Patsy Barnes's face fell. Her reaction was greater than I would have expected from a professional who knows you can't win them all. Perhaps she had money worries and had built her hopes up that the Marshall trial would bankroll her out of them. I was too soft. 'I'll try, I'll see what I can do,' I said. 'But the murder of Renee Smith has made him jumpy. When he's released, he's going to have to build another new life for himself, and I doubt he'll get much help this time.'

'There's always someone willing to help out,' she replied. 'Always someone willing to get people what they deserve.'

Despite being a writer, I wondered whether Patsy Barnes's experiences of life had been anywhere near mine. Maybe I had been landed with the world's only soft journalist.

Chapter Fifty-Eight

Joe was supposed to be meeting me for dinner in Suzie Wong's. The illuminated clock shining on the wall opposite the bar showed the time as nine fifteen. He was over half an hour late, and even Moses was running his black enamelled nails through his peroxide white hair. It was a sure sign that the leader of the Dark Angels was worried – he didn't mess with his look lightly.

'Run this past me again,' he said. 'Glasgow Joe went after the Boyle clan on his own, over a motorbike?' I nodded. 'Who does he think he is? He's hard, but . . . I mean – the Boyles? There's fucking hundreds of them,' he spat the words out. 'And you? You should have known better.' Moses turned on his heels, his floor-length black leather coat swirling out behind him like a cape. His eyes were blazing; he hated the Boyles but he wasn't stupid enough to take them on himself.

I ran after him, just in case Joe going after them on his own had given him any ideas. His words suggested otherwise, but you never could tell anything where Moses was concerned. He had gone to his office; it was a grand name for a small room next to the gents' toilets. Moses kept all his space for earning money, not wasting anything on niceties. He took a small bunch of keys out of his pocket and unlocked a long walnut cabinet that I had simply never noticed before. He pulled out a sawn-off shotgun, tucking it under his armpit, covering it with his coat. He marched out into the public areas again with me trailing, dumb, after him. Customers nodded at him, but Moses didn't look to his left or his right, he simply marched. I finally opened my mouth to speak. He placed his finger over my lips. 'Sssh,' he said. 'Glasgow Joe and Kailash would kill me if I got you involved. Stay behind and pretend you haven't seen me.' He tapped the package he was discreetly carrying and asked, 'I take it this is covered by client confidentiality?'

He didn't wait for an answer. If he thought I was just going to wait by the phone for news, he had another think coming. Moses was right. I should have known Glasgow Joe would do something stupid, and I felt a need to help out now. Christ, what would the Boyles be planning for him? I ran after him. 'Wait!' I shouted as he climbed into the passenger side of a rusty Ford Escort. 'I'm coming.' He opened the door for me and I slid into the messy back seat. 'You don't mind?' I asked. After his speech moments earlier, I'd expected to have to fight him to go along. He shook his head. 'Actually, I'd have been disappointed in you if you hadn't come – it's Joe we're talking about.'

The driver of the car, which was probably stolen, looked too young to have a licence, but I figured joyriding was going to be the least serious offence I would be involved in that night. I could tell myself that I was going along to make sure Moses's violence didn't get out of hand, but it wasn't true. If Billy Boyle had harmed Joe I'd pull the trigger myself and to hell with the consequences.

The Boyles lived in Pilton. They were council flats, but the family had taken over the whole landing of one high rise. The exterior of the houses looked like any other and, in spite of the fact that the Boyles' gross earnings were over a million quid a year, they still claimed incapacity and housing benefit and anything else that was going. The battered Ford Escort screeched to a halt outside the stair where Ma Boyle lived. Lookouts were posted on every landing; they weren't scanning for us particularly, it was just a general precaution against the drug squad or the vice squad. Not many rival gangs walked into the Boyles' heartland, and the appearance of Moses Tierney caused quite a stir.

I craned my neck upwards as the doors and windows opened. Unlike in Cumberland Street, these neighbours liked nothing better than to watch a good fight. Moses kicked the car door shut with his boot; he pulled the shotgun out from under his coat and the driver stayed in the car with the engine running. I ran out after Moses and followed him. Gun crime isn't a huge problem in Edinburgh, and whilst the guards were carrying blades, they bowed to Moses's superior weaponry and melted back into the shadows. No one doubted that the leader of the Dark Angels was just the kind of crazy bastard to use what he was carrying.

Ma Boyle lived on the third floor. Her kitchen window faced onto the landing and the net curtains that hung on her windows offering a modicum of privacy were spotlessly white. The door to the flat was open; news of our arrival had spread fast. Moses wiped his feet on the doormat and walked in.

The hall was laid with a new carpet. The living-room door was open and Ma Boyle sat royally in her chair. She was fat, with a face like a toad, warts and all. On top of her head was a startling mop of bright yellow permed hair that was more suitable for Shirley Temple than the leader of one of Scotland's biggest criminal families. Ma Boyle stared up at Moses and a smile cracked her face. 'It's good to see you, son . . . take a seat.' She pointed to the chair opposite her. Moses sat down, still clutching the shotgun. I didn't know who was more mad – the old woman for treating him like a kid, or Moses for visiting Ma Boyle with a sawn-off shotgun as his calling card.

'Cup of tea?' she asked, and then, without waiting for a reply, shouted, 'Mary, put the kettle on.' I could hear rustling in the kitchen, but that was the only noise. Moses and Ma Boyle just stared at one another. She seemed to be drinking in every detail of his face. After several long moments she pushed her great bulk up from the chair, waddled over to a cabinet in the corner and pulled down the top lid to search inside. I eyed Moses, warning him to be careful. I assumed that Ma Boyle was looking for a gun. But he shook his head, dismissing me. After she found what she was searching for, she sat back down in the chair; it thumped back against the wall.

'What brings you here, Moses?' she asked.

I stiffened. The old bitch knew fine well what the

problem was. She had ignored me from the minute I got in, yet the order to torch the Fat Boy and Kenny Cameron's house must have come from her. None of her family acted without her say-so.

'Where's Glasgow Joe?' Moses asked. His voice was calm and reasonable.

Ma Boyle stared at him. 'Are you sure that's what you want to talk about?'

'Where's Glasgow Joe?' Moses asked again.

'Listen, so . . . do I look stupid?' she asked, answering herself quickly, 'No, and neither is Glasgow Joe. There's no way he would start a war over a bike. It was necessary that the stupid bitch behind all of this knows that she was out of order and Joe understands that. He also knows it won't go any further.'

Moses eyed her up and down as I remained invisible to Ma Boyle. Then he stood up and went to walk away. I stopped him.

'Brodie, she doesn't have Joe,' he said, then he shrugged me off. 'Let's get out of here fast, we're wasting our time. Joe hasn't called, he hasn't been in touch – there's something wrong.' Ma Boyle moved faster than I would have thought possible and, before I could stop her, she grabbed Moses's arm.

'Please stay son . . . just for a cup of tea.' She stroked his head, seemingly oblivious to the fact that the leader of the Dark Angels had waltzed into her home with a gun – getting him to be sociable wasn't the option I would have thought she'd go for. Her next words made it all much clearer. 'Your Auntie Mary's making it, Moses lad; she'll be through in a minute.'

Moses pulled away from her. 'You had your chance when I was seven; I wasn't good enough then so I'm not good enough now. Granny.' He hissed the final word and ran out of the door. Ma Boyle pressed a photograph into my hand, clearly deciding that I was real after all. I turned it over to see a young man in a tank top and bell-bottoms.

'That's my Jimmy. He died in Barlinnie six years ago.'

Ma Boyle did not need to tell me it was Moses's father. The features were the same. Moses had been taken into care when he was seven. The Boyles must have refused to care for him, and if Ma Boyle had taken him then, he would not have endured years of abuse at the hands of my father. I left, my departing gift to the old woman a look of pure disgust.

'Don't say a fuckin' word,' Moses warned as I climbed into the back seat. I handed him the photograph and he tore it into little pieces, throwing it out of the open window where it scattered behind us like confetti. 'Try Joe's mobile again,' he said, but we both knew in our hearts that there would be no answer. 'Let's go back to Cumberland Street; he might be waiting there.' Moses put his head down. He wasn't going to speak unless it was necessary. I knew that he would have already put an order out for the Dark Angels to scour Edinburgh looking for Joe; he would have also phoned Kailash, who would put out her own feelers.

The house was cold and dark when we arrived. I wandered into the kitchen to put on a pot of espresso; it was going to be another long night. The sink was full of breakfast dishes and it was soothing to turn on the hot water and plunge my hands into the soapsuds. Joe had left the porridge pot soaking. My breath caught in my throat as I thought of him making sure I had a good start to the day. When it was left to me I grabbed a chocolate bar on the way into the office. The hot brown coffee spurted out of the coffee maker; I grabbed a towel, placed it on the handle and poured out two cups. Moses wandered into the kitchen carrying the morning mail; he laid it on the table.

'Do you never read your letters?' he said. I was never much interested in the junk that came through my letterbox. The important stuff went to the office. 'What about this?' He handed me a yellow padded envelope. I picked up the scissors and snipped the top of the package off. Tipping it upside down I shook the contents out onto the table.

I don't know which one of us screamed first.

I felt Moses squeeze my hand very tightly – or maybe it was me squeezing his. We stared at a finger in front of us. A wedding band had fallen out of the package too, with nothing to cling on to; the golden Celtic knot design I had bought for Joe when we married.

I sat down and stared at it. The digit looked fresh and I didn't stop Moses when he popped Joe's finger in a glass filled with ice.

'You never know,' he said, picking up the package and sticking his hand inside, searching for a note. 'Look on the bright side,' he said.

'There's a bright side?'

'He's still alive.' Moses pulled out a note on plain A4 paper with bloody fingerprints all over it. ***Meet me at the entrance to Leith Docks eleven pm. Come alone.***

'The entrance to Leith Docks is slap bang in the middle of the red-light district,' I said.

'I know that,' said Moses.

'But what you don't know is it's also in the centre of Cupid's killing field,' I said as he looked cluelessly back at me. 'So whoever I'm meeting tonight is probably the real killer – and it's not Graham Marshall.'

Fear curled Moses's lip. 'So you're saying Joe was taken by this fucking serial killer that's going around? Christ, Brodie – you'll have to throw Marshall to the wolves to save Joe.'

I stared back at him.

'Did you hear me? You'll *have* to throw Marshall to the wolves. No choice. Joe's what matters, not some scumbag kid-killer. Marshall is going down anyway, Brodie,' said Moses. I nodded, but years of training and dedication were pulling me apart. 'And you're not going alone,' he said.

'It's past eleven, Moses . . . perhaps they will have gone?'

The only transport we had was Joe's trike. Moses hated going on any type of motorbike and, as he pointed out, if we were going in under stealth the noise of the trike would blow our cover. The cold wind blew through our hair as I started up the machine. A few curtains twitched this time. Maybe the residents of Cumberland Street weren't so different from those in West Pilton Circus after all, or maybe they'd just had enough of me, their very own neighbour from hell. The streets were quiet, and the traffic lights were at green. The only thing I needed now was for Sam Jones to be waiting at the entrance to the Docks. She was the one with most to gain.

Moses got off the trike at the Shore and I turned left at the traffic lights and parked in front of the Malmaison, once the old seamen's mission. The moon hid behind the clouds. The streets were deserted, apart from a few prostitutes who poked their heads out of closes, then, when they saw I didn't have a car, melted back into the shadows. I walked over the cobbles towards the gates. Over my shoulder I saw the ships docked against the quayside. Out of the corner of my eye I saw a woman leaning against the large ship's anchor, an ornament that architects had left behind to remind the people of Edinburgh that Leith had once been a thriving Docks. True Leithers just wished they still had the Docks instead of the fancy waterfront restaurants and flats that they could not afford.

Bizarrely, I was disappointed that DI Sam Jones had not brought Joe along, although in my head I knew that was ridiculous. The police officer was holding him to ransom to make sure I did whatever she wanted – and she wanted Marshall to go down. When I was ten feet away from my blackmailer, the moon came out from behind the cloud and for the first time I saw the woman I was supposed to meet – and it wasn't Sam Jones.

Patsy Barnes.

'Brodie. I'm sorry it had to come to this.'

'Fuck off with your apologies. Is Joe safe?'

She nodded. 'But he won't be if you don't call off the tail.' She pointed to the dark shadows where Moses was hidden. 'Moses!' I called. He stepped out under a streetlight and walked towards us. 'Such devotion,' Patsy said as she stared at Moses. 'I approve of devotion; it's the only thing that has kept Joe alive.'

'Spare me your sentiments,' I said.

'I'm not a fool, Brodie,' she smiled. 'And I don't dislike you. Don't make me kill him. There are so few good men left in this world, don't you think?'

'What do you want, Patsy?' I said.

She smiled again. 'I told you what I want; I want a face-to-face interview with Dr Graham Marshall.'

'Is that really what this is all about? You've got Joe just so you can get a crappy interview with someone? Anyway, I've told you – it's not possible. He won't see you and I can't make him.'

'Then arrange for me to see him when he comes into court.'

'That's not possible either . . .'

'Make it happen.' She handed me a mobile phone. 'I'll ring you tomorrow. I'll be expecting good news.'

Chapter Fifty-Nine

The cold wind was driving rain into our faces, stinging the skin on our cheeks and turning them red raw. The weather was coming in off the River Forth, and the Docks are exposed. Gusts blew around our legs, spraying water from the puddles up over our shoes; my feet were soaked. Moses pulled me by the arm and dragged me across the cobbles to the quayside. He lifted his legs and straddled the thick black iron chain.

'No point in us catching our deaths,' he said, climbing up the gangway to a deserted herring trawler that had been converted into a restaurant. It had failed. Slipping his tools out of his pocket, he slid open the lock. I was beyond caring. Buffeted by the wind, I dared God to do his worst. Our feet clanked against the polished oak floorboards. Moses led his way into the galley as the gale blew the boat against its mooring, bumping it off the side of the quay, jolting my stomach. I suspected we both had the same thoughts. Who was Patsy Barnes? Certainly not, I now knew, a journalist – unless she was also a psychopath. The two weren't mutually exclusive. And how had she managed to capture and assault Joe, whose very appearance could put the fear of death into Edinburgh's hardest men?

'It's nearly midnight. What the fuck are we going to do, Brodie? You heard what she said. You have to arrange a face-to-face meeting for her with Marshall tomorrow or . . .' Although Patsy Barnes hadn't said what would happen if we ignored her instructions, the threat was clear enough for us to understand. If I didn't arrange a get-together between her and Marshall, Joe was history.

I had several problems in front of me. The first insurmountable hurdle was that Marshall wasn't due back in court for another seven days. I could think of no reason the prosecutor would bring him out of prison for any reason other than court. If I tried to arrange for Patsy Barnes to see Marshall in Saughton Prison, he'd refuse to come out of his cell for the visit and there was nothing I could do about it.

'Do you have any influence?' I asked Moses. He knew people inside every jail in Scotland, and for the price of a packet of fags he could arrange most things. 'If you wanted the bastard dead,' he sniffed, 'it would be easy to get him in the shower with a pair of scissors or a sharpened comb.' He stared up into the sky. The moon broke its cover and shone down on us, highlighting the worry lines on his face. He shook his head and continued. 'This requires coercion, and I don't know the bastard, don't know his weak spots. Would he be bothered if I threatened his wife?' he asked hopefully.

'No way. He'd probably pay you,' I said.

'That's the problem with bastards like Marshall – he's got nothing to lose. It's very difficult to negotiate with someone like that.' Moses rested his chin in his hands, and his eyes looked up at me, like the kid he still was, waiting and just hoping that someone would somehow fix everything one day.

'There is just no way I can fix this, Moses. I can't phone the authorities and ask them to bring Marshall out. There's paperwork, procedures and protocols that have to be followed.' He said nothing, just puffed his lips out. He had thought of something, and it was difficult for him to swallow. The same idea had occurred to me but I dismissed it, all the while hoping I could come up with something else.

'Bancho,' we said in unison. Moses stopped slouching, sat up straight and pushed away from the table.

'Bancho cares about Joe,' I said, listing the pros of the solution.

Moses rubbed his nose, a sure sign he thought I was lying. 'No, forget it. Bancho cares about Bancho, even if they did work together on that sex trafficking thing last year. You know the rules – Joe doesn't involve the police in his business.' I opened my mouth to speak. 'No police,' interrupted Moses.

'Okay smartarse, what's your solution?' I snapped.

'Follow Patsy Barnes, find out where she has him?' he asked.

'That was the original plan, then you fucked up and she spotted you!' I snipped at him.

'I know. That was weird. No one spots me in the shadows. It's how I survived all these years. Do you have any idea who the fuck this woman is?' I shook my head. 'The only photograph I've seen of DI Sam Jones was out of focus and taken ten years ago. With hair dye, make-up, weight gain or loss and age . . . it's difficult to know who you are dealing with.'

Moses nodded. 'I still can't believe anyone was able to take Joe,' he shook his head. 'I mean . . . it's Joe for fuck's sake. It's Joe.'

'I'm responsible; I introduced them. By doing that I vouched for her,' I said, my voice cracking.

'Don't beat yourself up about it. Let me do that if we don't bring him home. How did she do it though, Brodie?' A sigh escaped my lips. 'If she is Cupid, then she's using drugs to sedate him just like she did the others,' I answered. Moses started to laugh a long slow rumble. 'Well, I hope she's got an elephant gun, because if that big crazy bastard wakes up and finds out what she's done to him . . .' He stopped laughing and handed me his mobile. 'Bancho. Make the call.'

Chapter Sixty

Bancho had worked fast. I guessed that he didn't want to think how bad the situation was if he was my last resort, so in the early hours of the morning he'd pulled together a group of people – an elite, powerful, influential gathering. I had crossed swords with each and every one of them at some point in my career and was acutely aware of this fact now that I approached them with my begging bowl. I wasn't concerned that my ego would be dented if they refused to help me; I would do anything to secure Joe's safety.

This meeting had to be kept secret. If the word got out on the street then lives would be at risk, especially Joe's. It was why we could not take the chance of meeting anywhere official. My first suggestion was Kailash's brothel; whores know how to keep their mouths shut. Bancho thought I was taking the piss, but I wasn't. Half the secrets of Edinburgh are known only to women and men who make their money on their backs and knees. Still, I took Bancho's point, and as I walked into the Dean of Faculty's house, I was alone. There was no way Moses would be invited into this hallowed salon. It was one of the most prestigious addresses in the city – I was lucky I was getting over the doorstep of 333 Moray Place myself. David Menteith QC, dean of the Faculty of Advocates, was exhausted after a night of interrupted sleep. Agnes Sampson, Procurator Fiscal, sat in a chair beside an empty fireplace, and she too looked less than pleased at having her slumber disturbed. Ranald Hughes QC was mildly amused at my discomfort.

DI Bancho hovered anxiously, flitting from foot to foot. He had gone out on a limb and I wasn't sure how much he had told them, but I had to give them what they wanted to get them to help me. The death of a known assassin and former IRA sympathizer like Glasgow Joe would make their day.

Duncan Bancho joined me on the Persian carpet in front of the fireplace. 'We have a situation.' He blew out a breath and an apologetic smile flickered across his face. 'Yesterday, Cupid struck again. This time the victim was in London.'

'The MO was the same?' Agnes Sampson asked.

Bancho nodded.

'The victim was Renee Smith,' I added, ever helpful. 'So Marshall's contention that he was being set up is looking more credible as each hour passes.' The dean snorted. The trial had already raised too much media interest for his liking. Scots law and crime prevention was on show. Ranald Hughes QC looked scared. He didn't want to harm his career by being caught up in this matter. Usually the Faculty of Advocates would not be involved in a prosecution at this stage, and Agnes Sampson had pulled them in to prevent this kind of catastrophe.

'Jesus,' he said. He just sat there for a minute, and then said, 'Oh, Jesus Christ.' Then he shrugged his shoulders, glanced at his Rolex once more, and said, 'Listen, I'd like to help out here, but this is . . .' Hughes spread his hands and dropped them on his lap. 'I don't think there's anything I can usefully add to this discussion.'

'I have an idea,' I said. They all looked at me gratefully. 'I was the last person to see Renee Smith alive. Well, not the last obviously . . .' I let that information sink in. They turned and nodded at one another knowingly, as if I, Brodie McLennan, must be the root cause of all the ills befalling the Scottish justice system.

'Let's hear your idea, Brodie.' The Dean of Faculty lay back in his comfortable armchair and crossed his legs at the ankles, as if he knew that this was going to take some time. He was wrong.

'I know the identity of Cupid,' I said, watching the dean uncross his legs, sit up and take notice of me – as well he might. I was about to pull his arse out of the fire as well as save Joe's. 'Her name is Patsy Barnes. Either she's a psychotic journalist or she's just using that as a cover, but, either way, she wants a face-to-face with Marshall.' I looked at the dean. He didn't seem particularly encouraged by my information, and I had to admit it was a bit short on facts, but it was all I knew. I cleared my throat, drew myself up to my full height and continued. 'We need to bring Marshall back into court,' I said.

Agnes Sampson studied her nails. 'He's not due back for another six days,' she said, rubbing her hands together like an undertaker. 'In the meantime, Cupid could go on a killing spree.'

I was nodding my head, willing them to agree with me. 'Precisely,' I said, taking one step towards them. 'So, what we have to do is charge him with something else and bring him in from Saughton this morning, and I'll tell Patsy Barnes she can have her "interview" with Marshall, which, she claims, is all she wants.' The dean studied me. Every instinct he had was telling him that I was pulling the wool over his eyes, but he couldn't figure out exactly what was going on. In the end he let out a sigh. A long, slow sigh of a man resigned to his fate. He had to throw in his lot with Arbuthnot's bastard, or lose his chance at gaining his place in posterity by taking his seat in the College of Justice.

'What charge did you have in mind, Ms McLennan?' he asked.

I turned to Agnes Sampson and said, 'Charge Marshall with the abduction of DI Sam Jones.'

Bancho smiled.

Chapter Sixty-One

Moses and I stood at the entrance to an almost deserted Edinburgh Sheriff Court. I stood and stared up at the terrace of The Tower restaurant and I felt sick. If only I had worked Patsy Barnes out earlier, Joe would be safe. It was entirely my fault. Jesus, Lavender would never have let things get this far – she'd have called magazines, confirmed with editors; Barnes would have been checked out long before I'd even heard her name. I missed Lavender in all areas of my life. Lois just wasn't in her league.

It was all arranged. Graham Marshall was to be brought into Edinburgh Sheriff Court with the rest of the custodies from Saughton, but his case wouldn't be heard until the afternoon. Bancho was expecting trouble, as well he might, and he wanted the courts to be clear.

The difference between 10 a.m. at Edinburgh Sheriff Court and 2 p.m. is like the difference between an ant hill and a mole hill. In the morning the courts teem with life, scurrying here, there and everywhere. In the afternoon, the odd client, policeman, or lawyer stalks the halls with purpose. Bancho's risk assessment was that, whatever was going to happen, the fewer spectators and bystanders the better. My watch showed it was two fifteen and I still hadn't heard from Patsy Barnes. Fear ran riot through my system. I was doing a damn good job of convincing myself she knew about our plan and had disappeared back to London taking Joe's where-abouts with her. Bancho also needed the time to get together the armed officers who were going to be watching the court. They were put in place in the early morning before business commenced. Teams of gun-toting cops might have alerted Barnes to the fact we had our own plan to rescue Joe.

'Have you been down to see Marshall yet?' Moses asked. It was my usual practice to see every client when they arrived in court, discuss the criminal charge with them, and generally hold their hand. I shook my head. 'I couldn't go through with the whole Judas thing,' I said. 'He'd rumble me straight away and refuse to go up to the court. I'm only going to see him when Patsy Barnes is in the room.'

Moses glared at me. 'D'you think that's wise?' he said. 'I mean, who's going to protect you?'

I shrugged my shoulders and sighed. I'd been holding my breath without realizing it. 'Bancho and the armed police officers are protecting me,' I said. 'Duncan's also got something up his sleeve he won't tell me about in case I inadvertently reveal it to Patsy.' By now I was feeling tired, tense, and frustrated that I had to leave these details to Bancho without any input from me. It was agreed that the only person I could be seen talking to was Moses because Patsy Barnes had already seen him.

The mobile she had given me started to ring.

'Hello?' I said. There was complete silence except for the sound of her soft breathing – she was waiting for me to speak. 'It's all arranged.' I spoke quickly, anxious to get this conversation over with. 'The fiscal had to serve new charges on him for the abduction of DI Sam Jones.' She giggled. I waited for it to stop, tapping my foot. 'Graham Marshall—' I began. 'Kevin Milne,' she interrupted, the giggling stopping as suddenly as it had begun. 'Kevin Milne,' I appeased her, 'will be brought into Court Ten at two thirty. There will be you, me and Sheriff Clerk Alex Grant. It was the best I could do.'

'I'll be there,' she said, and hung up the phone. I had no doubt she would be, just as I knew she would tell me where Glasgow Joe was afterwards. If she didn't tell me I would beat it out of her, whether Bancho was watching or not.

Moses and I walked into the courthouse in silence. The guards at the entrance made us walk through the metal detectors. As usual I set it off. I put the office keys I had forgotten I was carrying into the plastic tray, and walked back through. This time it stayed quiet – it seemed like a warning. We walked to Court Ten in silence. Moses had insisted on accompanying me, and, since Patsy Barnes was aware of his existence, I couldn't see any harm in it. I glanced at Moses. A smile was on his face; he was going to enjoy himself regardless.

'What's so funny?' I glared at him. 'What's so funny?'

He swallowed hard. I knew it was taking all his self-control not to laugh again; nerves affected him like this.

'It's like the Wild West, guns at noon,' he said.

'Get in,' I said as we stood facing the heavy new oak door of Court Ten. Moses always had a flair for the dramatic. He lifted his foot and kicked open the door of court. It swung with the force, hitting itself back off the wall; one quick glimpse told us that the court was empty except for the clerk, Alex Grant, who was busy sorting his papers from the morning. Everything looked normal. Moses stepped back and let me go first. That was the order of things – lawyers led the way.

At two thirty precisely, the prisoner Dr Graham Marshall was brought up from the cells. The staircase led directly into the courtroom and I could only hear one set of footsteps. He wandered up into the dock on his own; his head appeared first and he looked around, his eyes searching for me. When he found me the muscles in his face relaxed. The movement was almost imperceptible. Marshall was a man well used to controlling his emotions.

In spite of his criminal notoriety, he had less courtroom experience than a Niddrie shoplifter. If one of them had been allowed to walk unguarded up from custody they would have vaulted out of the dock, for they would have smelled a rat. Dr Marshall, regardless of his Mensa IQ, did not. The only sound was of Alex Grant shuffling through his morning court papers. In my imagination, a clock was ticking. Everything was slowing down and a fly buzzed lazily by the agents' table. Moses was seated in the public benches. I was forced by this charade to wander over to the dock to reel off a tissue of lies to my client. Irrational anger against Patsy Barnes, or whoever she was, consumed me. Our heads were soon locked together as we discussed procedural matters. I was explaining to him that the papers would be served when the prosecutor arrived down from Crown Office. She'd sent me a message that she had been delayed.

The door creaked open.

He turned, expecting to see the fiscal.

What he saw was the face that should have haunted him every night since he was ten.

If he'd been reasonable; if he hadn't been the monster he was.

The face that told him he had gone too far, crossed one of the few women he shouldn't have. The face that I'd been chatting with, having coffee with, discussing fancy fucking articles with – the face of Patsy Barnes.

'Long time no see, Kevin,' she whispered, pulling a handgun from her pocket. 'I've waited a long time for this – so has my boy, so has my son Matthew.'

My eyes widened as I stared at the weapon that the woman I now knew was Donna Cook held in her hand. I couldn't get through security with a bunch of keys, but she'd managed to smuggle a gun in. She was going up in my estimation every day.

'Donna, put it down,' Marshall said with authority, well spoken and assured. 'Please. Do it. You know this isn't the way to go about things. You think this will bring you peace? Help you to sleep at night? Stop the night-mares? It won't. It definitely won't.'

Donna Cook stared at him, never blinking, never moving. Could she hear him, or was she too far away in her own world of revenge for that?

Marshall decided to try another angle, deciding to let his London accent out too as part of the act. 'I was just a kid, Donna. I'm a different person now. You, better than anyone, know how I was brought up – the fighting and brutality . . . what chance did I have? If only I had known any experience of love, I would never have touched your little boy. Your angel. I was a victim too, Donna.'

At those words, Donna Cook walked up to the dock. In accordance with normal procedure, the door at the bottom of the stairs was locked. Heading back down the route by which he had come would simply mean Marshall was a cornered rat, but I'm sure he must have considered it.

'Your chances? Your chances? What chance did Matthew have?' she asked, waving the gun in his face. 'When you took him, you should have murdered me too. You weren't as clever as they all said, after all.' Donna Cook's eyes were wide with hate. 'Do you know – at first I tried to join him, but no one would let me. No one would let me die.' She waved her free hand around the court. 'Then I decided, so be it, that I'd wait for you. Maybe that's what I was being kept alive for.'

Marshall's eyes flicked wildly around the courtroom – did he really think anyone was going to help him? 'It wasn't easy; of course it wasn't easy – you'd taken my only reason for living,' Donna said. 'Whilst your family were given therapy and new identities, I didn't get any help until I decided to help myself.' She smiled at him and stroked the gun over his cheek, which was slick with sweat. 'Then the papers started running stories about what a clever boy you were, Kevin.' She smacked the gun off his forehead until a tiny trickle of blood ran like a scarlet ribbon down his face. 'All those exams you kept passing. Matthew would have passed exams. I wouldn't have let him rot in Shank Town. He would have got out – I would have worked my knuckles to the bone, scrimped and saved every penny. I would have done everything for him, but you took all of that away – and you took it for yourself. You got given the life Matthew should have had by killing him.'

She walked into the dock beside Marshall. 'I knew then I'd have to make something of myself. So I started my plans. My long . . . term . . . perfect . . . fucking . . . plans. I made something of myself just as you had done. I needed to wait, wait until you were this big, respected, fancy doctor. You have your life, your home, your business, your wife, your mistresses, your reputation – well, say goodbye to it all, Kevin. The world is going to see you for what you are and what you've always been.' Donna Cook started to smash the butt of her gun off his face, as if she was trying to obliterate his features beyond recognition.

'Donna!' I shouted, trying to break through into her frenzied state. 'If you kill him, then you're just as bad as he is.' Donna Cook had one hand around Kevin Milne's throat. His blood had splashed back onto her, and she glared at me. 'Is that it, Brodie? Is that how you think this will end? You'll trot out some shit clichés and I'll let that bastard live?'

She was right – I had offered nothing. 'Okay, okay, maybe if you kill him it won't make you a monster like him because he took the life of your baby. But he's made you into a killer too,' I said. 'You killed those men, and Kelly Adams. Have you killed Sam Jones? Joe? All those innocent people?' For a moment she didn't move. I thought I'd got through to her. Although it looked dangerous, I had begged Bancho not to interfere until she had told me where Joe was. I feared we were still miles from that point.

'Innocent? Those men betrayed their families by fucking around. Kelly Adams was dispensable – she was nothing, worth nothing. Christ, she loved *that*...' She pointed at Marshall.

I reached out for the gun. 'Joe never betrayed his friends or family. Never. Tell me where he is. It's your part of the deal, Donna. I got you your meeting with Graham Marshall.'

She never had time to answer me. A shot rang out and pinned her to the floor as a large red stain soaked through her blouse like a dark red poppy. Alex Grant, the sheriff clerk, was marching towards us.

'You stupid fucker!' I screamed at him. Kneeling down I picked up Donna Cook in my arms. 'Where is Joe? Where is Joe? Tell me, tell me! Where is Joe?' I shrieked, but she had already slipped into unconsciousness.

Chapter Sixty-Two

The courtroom was now in chaos. DI Bancho, and armour-clad, armed officers stormed up the stairs, taking them two at a time. The noise and shouting was deafening. The officers just kept on coming, and I was pushed back into the periphery of the scene. Alex Grant looked unrepentant and his free hand was steady as he pushed back his black hair. He still held the smoking gun.

Bancho checked me over with his eyes. A doctor was soon on hand to stem the blood flowing from Donna Cook's chest. They wouldn't let me near her. I stormed across to Bancho who was locked in conversation with the clerk, who thought he was Billy the fucking Kid.

'Who is he?' I said pointing at Alex Grant. My finger was shaking with fury.

Bancho glanced at me, deliberately misunderstanding my meaning. 'He's the sheriff clerk.'

'Clerks don't go around shooting people,' I said, poking Bancho in the shoulder. 'Who is he?'

'Sorry,' said Grant, who looked anything but contrite. 'I was in Special Forces in Northern Ireland during the Troubles. When the Lockerbie hearing was on I was sent undercover. No one questions a clerk, and since nine/eleven I've kind of been on standby – it's the case in a lot of city courts actually,' he offered sheepishly.

Bancho shrugged his shoulders. 'If I'd told you about him your eyes would have given it away. Donna Cook would have picked up on it and he would have been compromised.'

'Bancho, you have to find out where Joe is! Let me speak to her, she might see sense,' I said, pulling on the front of his jacket, dragging him towards where the medics were still working on the woman. She had killed at least four people, butchering their corpses, two victims were still missing, and I had chatted with her over coffee without suspecting a thing. I caught myself studying her features out of the corner of my eye, wondering if I'd ever trust my own judgement again. 'What went on in there? How could she have waited so long?'

Bancho stood quietly by my side. 'The impulse to kill,' he said. 'Does everybody have it, do you think?'

I glanced at him and nodded resignedly. 'It's the mark of Cain. If I don't get Joe back safe, you'll certainly have no doubt about my fucking impulses.'

Graham Marshall was backed up in the dock. The medics had refused to allow the police to interfere in the scene until they had stabilized Donna Cook. He watched me approach with an undisguised look of hatred in his eyes. I pretended not to notice. I stared straight ahead of me through the mass of armed police officers and, as I bent down over Donna Cook, he turned away.

'Give me five minutes,' I said to Bancho. He in turn sought permission from the police doctor, whose nod was faint but enough for me. My knee cracked like another gunshot as I knelt down beside the dying woman. Other people have lived with more severe injuries, but this one had no will to carry on. Her desire for life had been lying rotting in a cold grave in Edmonton Green cemetery for twenty years.

I held her hand.

'Stay with me, Brodie,' she whispered. It was a request. Time slowed down and people melted into the background. 'I just want to go to sleep,' she said. Her fingers were cold and damp, the life seeping out of them.

'You can't,' I said. 'You can't go to sleep until you tell me where Joe and Sam are. Do it, Donna. Save something out of all this.' I stroked her hair. It clung to her pale forehead; her breathing was shallow and so light I wondered how she was hanging on.

'I didn't mean it to turn out like this,' she said, her eyelids flickering. 'He had to be punished and death was too easy. He had to be marked. People needed to know who he was; he needed to be abused in the street, killed like an animal for his atrocity – he needed to suffer.'

'Breathe, Donna,' I commanded. 'Where is my Joe?' I begged. 'Tell me now. I don't know if you believe in God, but now's not the time to take chances. Tell me where they are, Joe and Sam, and you can sleep easier.' The spark of life was fading from her eyes. She coughed and blood flowed from the corner of her lips, dribbling down her chin. I rubbed her hand, willing life back into her, but the tears streaming down my face were for Joe, not Donna Cook. She coughed again, spattering my face with droplets of ruby red. 'Please,' I whispered, elongating the word as my desperation grew. Just as her eyelids began to close, before they shut completely, her eyes flickered onto her handbag.

The handbag lay open, its contents scattered across the floor. I dropped her hand and sprang across the floor to grab it. Poultry cutters caught my eye. They were stained at the tips with blood. Joe's? Sam's? Hot bile burned my throat and, as I raked through the other items, I knew I was destroying important evidence but didn't care. What was that compared to Joe's life? It was an odd and inexplicable assortment of stuff: a travel-sized vacuum cleaner used in caravans, bags filled with a clump of hair, and a child's drawing.

In amongst the detritus of her life was a small black journal. In childish writing she had inscribed her name and address.

Donna Cook, Logie Green Farm, Midlothian.

It made sense that she would keep a hostage in the country where no one could hear his screams while she amputated a finger.

'Bancho!' I shouted. 'Send a squad car to this address!' I threw the book at him. He caught it as I lifted my eyes and locked onto Graham Marshall's gaze. 'Tell me,' he hissed. 'Did you sell me out?'

I nodded.

If he was cursing me to hell, fair enough – I'd see him there. I'd make him pay for all eternity if Joe was harmed.

Chapter Sixty-Three

I sat beside Bancho in the passenger seat as he drove me out to Midlothian. The car smelt of peppermint chalk as Bancho chewed his way through yet another packet of indigestion tablets. My fingers gripped the edge of the passenger seat as he drove straight through the third set of traffic signals at red; I prayed he'd been on skid training as water lay in pools across the road. The blue light was flashing but I wasn't convinced it could save us. Relentless, horizontal rain tried to delay our progress; nonetheless, we stayed in the outside lane on the bypass heading towards North Berwick.

Bancho had his foot welded to the floor. I felt hollow. It was a strange and unsettling experience needing Bancho's help. The muscles in his jaw were clenched tight and I could hear him grinding his teeth. The patrol car had radioed over ten minutes ago that Joe was alive but in a bad way, drugged and tied to a bed, lying in his own filth. There was no mention as yet of Sam Jones, but I assumed she was in the same condition. I didn't care what Joe looked or smelled like as long as I could hold him. In those last few moments with

Donna Cook, I had almost given up hope of ever seeing him again.

We drove through the beautiful East Lothian villages but, for once, they failed to stir me as I stared out of the windscreen at the driving rain, counting down the minutes and guessing how much longer it might take us to get there. At least I could solve one mystery for Bancho. Graham Marshall's wife, Alison, was wrong about the burglar not stealing anything when their Morningside home was broken into. She clearly, and quite understandably, hadn't inspected her husband's hairbrush, the detritus from which was probably still lying on the floor of the courtroom, along with the other contents of Donna Cook's handbag, unless it had all been bagged up already and given to forensics.

The countryside was flat, except for Berwick Law, a hill that stuck straight up into the grey, cloudy sky. On the horizon I fancied I could see the farm track that would take me to Joe, a narrow, private road more used to tractors than cars. It was muddy and wet; spray covered the windscreen. Bancho put the wipers on but they only spread the muck, making it impossible to see down the twisty lane. I tried to focus on the things I *could* see. On my right was a waterlogged field filled with sludge, the type of terrain on which it would be almost impossible to walk without losing your shoes, home to free-range pigs who snorted happily as they rolled in the muck.

We turned into a well-kept courtyard. On our left was a large, open barn stacked high with round bales of hay. A clean, new tractor was parked inside. Where was the farmer? Why had he rented a working farm to Donna Cook? A million questions filled my mind, but Bancho wouldn't know the answers to them so there was no point in asking him. I stored everything away for later when my main question had been answered: 'How was Joe?'

I jumped out of the car while it was still moving. My ankle twisted slightly on impact but I didn't let it slow me up as I ran towards the front door.

Joe.

My Joe.

He lay there, unconscious. The fear and panic and love all poured out of me at once and I screamed. When it was out of me, the racking sobs began and I laid my hand on his chest. His heartbeat was so, so slow. Two paramedics scrambled around him trying to insert an IV line, but they couldn't find a working vein – Joe's body was shutting down. They were very tolerant and I tried to hold on to their quiet confidence. They worked around me whilst I held his hand and tried to bring him back to life. His skin was cold and colourless, as if all the blood had been drained from him, but I couldn't let him go. I focused all my love on him. If I had to go into hell itself, I would carry him out. A glimpse of what my life would be like without him flashed before my eyes. A shudder ran through me. His breathing reminded me of Donna Cook's. It wasn't a helpful connection but, unlike her, I knew Joe wanted to live.

I leaned across him and kissed his lips. They were dry and unresponsive. A fat tear splashed onto his cheek but I didn't wipe it away as I put my arms around his neck and whispered in his ear. The paramedic murmured something, and gently nudged me a few inches to the side so they could have access to another vein. He tapped down on the inside of Joe's arm as I crouched down, still holding his hand.

'Joe? Joe, can you hear me?' What could I say? There were no words that could bring him round, nothing that could reach him. As I bent down, next to him, I felt as if I heard Joe himself breathe into my ear. 'God, you're a stubborn cow, Brodie McLennan,' his voice seemed to lilt. 'Put me out of my misery – say what I really want to hear.' I lifted my head, wiped my tears on my sleeve and looked at the body of the man I adored as much now as I had on the day I met him.

'Joe,' I laughed through my tears, 'Joe, will you marry me? Will you get your lazy arse up off that bed and make an honest woman of me – again?' I asked.

The paramedic at the side of my arm smiled at me. 'What do you think his answer will be?' he asked as the IV started running freely. 'Should I buy a hat?' he shouted as he carried my man out of the front door.

Chapter Sixty-Four

Duncan Bancho and the officers first on scene carried
out a search of the premises for the unknown farmer
and Sam Jones. There were no other addresses in Donna
Cook's address book, so the search was centred on the
farm. The paramedics had requested I remain behind
at the farm rather than go with them in the ambulance.
They'd be working on Joe for some time – it would be
easier on him and me if I wasn't present. I needed Bancho
to drive me back into Edinburgh for visiting time that
night – where the hell was he?

At the side of the farm was a patch of ground measur-
ing around thirty by sixty feet, covered in netting, and
at the bottom was a small polytunnel. It was a well-
tended kitchen garden. The rain had stopped. The wind
blowing from the west brought with it the scent of mint.
Herbs were growing along the side wall of the house in
outsized terracotta pots: basil, rosemary, oregano. A cold
sensation crept up my gut and was slowly making its
way to my throat. Now that I knew Joe was in safe hands,
Sam Jones was in my mind – and I had a horrible feeling
I'd be meeting her very soon.

'Bancho!' I screamed, but the wind carried my voice away. 'Bancho!' I shouted again, harder. I climbed onto the wire fence and threw my leg over. Thank God it wasn't electrified. 'Duncan!' I shouted, still failing to get his attention. With my first step, my shoe was sucked into the mud and the cold, wet dirt squelched up through my toes. I'd already lost one shoe and I knew the other would soon follow, so I kicked it off. Marching across the field, I was grateful the pigs gave me a wide berth. They were larger up close. I was forced to go too close to the corrugated shelter and a sow with a litter of ten piglets snorted out a warning at me. I picked up my pace but not by much, the mud making my progress torturously slow. Bancho and the two junior officers stood on the corner of the field nearest to the house. They were huddled together and then they spread out like a fan, scouring the ground before them. They showed no signs of coming in, their heads bent staring at the grooves and ruts in the ground.

Dragging my right foot out of the slime, I flung it forward. My hip clicked, locking in place, and I wobbled precariously. I trembled, and my first thought was that my unsteadiness was caused by the clicking of the joint. Sticking my arms out like a plane, I tried to regain a sense of balance.

Something was under my foot. I wriggled my toes around it and over it – it wasn't hard like a stone. I used my big toe to dig it out so I could kick it out of the way. The obstacle had been trampled into the mud, and was larger than I had initially thought. Bending from the waist, I reached into the mire and tugged.

By the time I found myself shaking hands with a corpse, even Bancho could hear my screams.

From his position further up the field, Bancho had a clear view of my feet as they danced up and down out of the mud.

'He's dead, Brodie. Whoever he is, he's dead. Has been for ages, by the looks of things – don't suppose it matters to the poor sod now, but at least the pigs didn't get him. Now, calm down . . . you're destroying a crime scene,' Bancho told me.

The police sergeant accompanying Bancho was older and more compassionate, his dark brown eyes peering out from a lined and baggy face. He took my arm. 'Ssssh,' he said. 'Everything is going to be all right.' I knew he was lying, but the tone of his voice was soothing. Duncan Bancho looked at the setting sun. 'Let's get back inside,' he said. 'The temperature's dropping.'

The walk back across the field seemed to go faster. Maybe it was shock. I held on to the fact that Joe was alive and that I was still breathing – right now that was enough for me. The brush with death, and with whom I presumed was a dead farmer, had clarified my priorities. A taxi back to Edinburgh Royal Infirmary, and then a hot bath and a scrub-down with carbolic soap.

The door to the farmhouse was open when I got there. I could feel its warmth on my cheeks as the heat escaped out into the cold night air. Even though the downstairs looked like a spread from *Homes & Gardens,* it was a crime scene. The ID boys had arrived in their transit van, so we had to be careful. Gerry Cornwell had cadged a lift with them, and new deep lines of grief and fear were etched upon his face. We still hadn't found Sam. His eyes, damaged by days of drunkenness and crying, half hidden behind his glasses, had sunk into his skull. He wasn't a man who looked as though optimism was an option.

My legs were covered in stuff I couldn't bear to define; a quick trip to the downstairs toilet meant I could wash my legs. I filled the hand basin with warm water and, perched on one leg, I stuck my right foot into the sink. The water felt warmer than it actually was and stung my cold, scraped skin. Out of the bathroom window I could see the crime-scene boys in the field, struggling to put up their tent. The mud was treacherous and the officers were slipping and sliding as the heavy blue plastic flapped in the wind. The arc lights highlighted the field as the boar roamed around agitatedly, disturbed by the strangers invading his territory.

Someone had made me a cup of hot, strong, sweet tea. I sipped it gingerly and watched as Bancho opened up the computer in the study and scrolled down the history. 'Farmers fucking dating site,' he said, clicking on the search engine. I could hear him breathing short and shallow. 'Well, now we know how the poor bastard met Donna Cook.' I looked over his shoulder. The home page promised countryside love. If I'd had any tears left, I'd have shed them there and then.

Chapter Sixty-Five

The taxi ride back to Edinburgh was uneventful, but a quick call to the Edinburgh Royal Infirmary to enquire after Joe's health gave me bad news. Upon regaining consciousness, he had discharged himself. The charge nurse described the idiot who had driven him away – and from that moment Moses Tierney was off my Christmas card list.

The lights were on in Cumberland Street and, as I drew up outside, the door opened and Moses's face peered round. He'd been watching for me. 'Before you start,' he said, stepping out to greet me, trying to cajole me but no doubt seeing the look in my eyes which should have told him everything, 'you know what a stubborn big bastard he is, and if I hadn't been prepared to take him he would have walked on his own.'

Louisa joined him on the front step, her twisted frame leaning against the doorjamb. 'No one could stop him,' she said. 'You know that.' Louisa grabbed my arm, pulling me inside the hall, but there was a desperate look in her eyes that frightened me. Her pupils were dilated, making her eyes great black saucers in her bloodless face. She

333

stared at me, her hand on my arm, preventing me rushing into the bedroom to scold Joe and scoop him up into my arms. 'Go easy,' she warned. Louisa had suffered herself, so she recognized the depths of Joe's pain in a way that I could never pretend to. Her eyes were locked onto mine; she flicked over me, assessing the situation. I slumped back against the wall, almost defeated, and she nodded, releasing her grip.

The floorboards creaked as I walked along the hall. I doubt Joe heard, but when I turned the door handle it rattled, alerting him to my presence. I walked into the bedroom but he did not look up. He sat in a large chair by the window, staring out with unseeing eyes, keeping guard against unknown assailants. I knew what he would be thinking – the worst thing had happened. He would think that he had failed me, failed to protect me and others that he had deemed needed his protection. The room was in darkness but a shaft of moonlight shone into the room, illuminating his profile, the roman nose that had been broken and inexpertly set on more than one occasion. The faint scars on his high cheekbones, forehead and chin were all badges of honour in Joe's world. The left hand strapped across his chest was not.

I moved closer, careful not to alarm him.

I laid a hand on his forearm. His skin was cold and clammy; he didn't turn to look at me. Joe was in shock, the state of being in limbo, suspended from the real world. 'Come to bed, Joe,' I whispered. 'Please come to bed, let me hold you.' I tugged at his arm but he wouldn't budge. After five minutes I released my hold, and backed away to the bed. I lay down fully clothed and pulled the covers over me. Although I didn't expect to, I fell into a deep sleep, a nightmare world inhabited by murder victims. Presiding over the realm of the dead was Kevin Milne or Graham Marshall, a procession of his prey lining up before my eyes in some macabre pageant. It started with Matthew Cook, and in my dream state I saw his last moments – just as Donna must have, every single time she closed her eyes. I included all Donna's known kills, the death of the farmer, Renee Smith, and the attack on Joe.

I gathered them up and laid them at the feet of Graham Marshall.

Then the truth hit me.

My client was innocent. He was not the killer known as Cupid. These were the charges that held him in Saughton Prison, so by now the governor would have released him. He was free as I slept and his mind would be focused on one thing – revenge. There was no doubt in my mind that he intended to kill me. Marshall was not, and never had been, sane as most people would define the word. His innocence had been proved, albeit in a dramatic and violent way. But all he would be able to see was that I had set him up for Donna.

I woke with a start and threw my feet over the side of the bed.

The first thing I noticed was that Glasgow Joe was gone.

The second thing was he had left me his knife.

Chapter Sixty-Six

I stood in the Grassmarket looking along to the Cowgate. Even in daytime it was dark and dank. Straight in front of me was the arch that supported the South Bridge. The first body to cross the bridge was in a coffin and the citizens of Edinburgh have been wary about this area ever since. With good reason – it was one of the haunts of the body snatchers, Burke and Hare. I was surrounded on all sides by high tenement buildings that shut out most of the natural light, and the wind was howling into my back, blowing me towards the Mission. I was aware I was dragging my feet, but it wasn't just because I was exhausted and suffering from the effects of stress. I had the creeping sensation that I was being followed.

Six long nights had passed since I had last seen Glasgow Joe. Despite scouring the streets of Edinburgh with Moses and the Dark Angels, he was nowhere to be seen. We had pulled out all the stops, but we all knew that Joe would not be found until he wanted to be; nevertheless, the hunt would continue. The underground jungle drums were buzzing with the news that Moses had approached the Boyle family for help in the search. No one was more surprised than me, but in a way it was troubling that Moses considered he needed to use his last resort to find Joe. He had traded his personal freedom to buy Ma Boyle's cooperation but, once he had crossed that line, there was no going back. Ma Boyle was a stubborn, nasty old bitch, but she was crucial to our cause. As one of the country's major drug dealers she had contacts in every major city, town and village in Scotland, and to find Glasgow Joe we had to be prepared to grease palms we normally wouldn't spit on. And it was effective. Ma Boyle had got her contacts on the West coast checking out Joe's old haunts in Govan, Parkhead and the Gorbals, but no one had seen him. It was as if he had dropped off the face of the earth.

Unfortunately the same couldn't be said for my former client.

All charges against Graham Marshall were, as was to be expected, dropped, and he walked out of Saughton Prison an innocent man. My former client certainly had access to his computer. He wrote to me within an hour of his release. It was an aggressive, threatening email, demanding the retainer back on the grounds that I had breached client confidentiality and completely disregarding his current free status. Two hours before I received his communication, I had written a cheque payable to him for the full amount, drawn on the firm's account, but when I received that email, plus his threat to report me to the Law Society, I took great pleasure in tearing it up. It was the first time since Joe had gone missing that Lavender smiled.

I had my best friend back. Now I just needed my man.

Joe wasn't the only missing person in my life. Kenny Cameron was homeless and it was obvious that no newspaper story was going to be written, so there'd be no pressure put on the council to rehouse him. He had fallen through the net and I needed to set things right. I made a deal with the powers that be, heavenly powers, that if I found Kenny Cameron they would send Joe back to me, and that's how I came to be parking Joe's chopper outside the homeless shelter known as the Mission.

I really didn't want to bump into Graham Marshall but I had no choice. However, I couldn't be responsible for my actions if he was there, and I was pretty sure Bancho would let me get away with anything where Marshall was concerned. Rationally, I wasn't convinced my ex-client was the root cause of the whirlwind of grief I found myself in, but emotionally I wanted to punch the bastard's lights out. My hatred for him steeled my resolve and I tightened the muscles in my jaw, threw back my shoulders, and marched into the Mission.

The world was the same: lunch was still served at noon and the queue was already starting to form. My eyes searched for familiar faces. Mack the dreadlocked tramp was nowhere to be seen, but his dog Lucky was being carried by Wee Elvis.

'Hey Brodie,' Wee Elvis shouted. 'D'you like my dog?' He carried the white Jack Russell terrier under his arm and lifted Lucky's paw and waved it at me. Wee Elvis had been brought up in care and abused by resident social workers. He was a chronic alcoholic, and on more than one occasion he had cowered under my desk fighting imaginary beasts as he suffered from delirium tremens. He was one of life's victims. I didn't want to accuse him of stealing Mack's dog, but I couldn't see why the huge tramp would have let him go when he had told me in great detail how much that dog had meant to him. However, there were only so many battles I could fight. I waved back to Lucky the dog, pushed my way through the queue and made my way to the kitchen. By the time I reached the gunmetal grey shutters, I'd removed my jacket and rolled up my sleeves. I knew the score before I walked into Ina's domain. Information would be traded for work, so for the next hour I'd be dishing up soup. It wasn't Sunday so there would be no roast dinner, just plain old soup.

'Hullo there, hen,' Ina said. A smile lit up her face as I hung my coat on a peg and took down a clean white apron. I tied it round my neck and walked over to her.

'What do you want me to do?' I asked, knowing that she'd not let me be idle. The canteen was filling up. Untidy queues of unwashed, bedraggled human beings gave the room a depressed air. Posters showing pictures of missing people, loved ones, lined the wall. I stared and learned that Andy Mullen, who left home at sixteen, would be twenty-six now. He just walked out of the house after a family row. If anyone saw him, would they tell him to contact his mother who was very ill. 'They've just fallen or been pushed through the cracks, hen,' said Ina, watching me. 'We can't fix everything – but we can feed them.'

The older ones milled about, holding their trays in front of them like a shield. The younger ones buzzed and chatted, throwing their hands around like puppets. 'Drugs,' hissed Ina. 'If I got my hands on their dealers . . .' The old woman's lips formed a thin, unforgiving line; I wondered if she had lost someone that way and she was working it all out through her work here. Ina handed me a ladle and pointed to an outsize pot of thick Scotch broth. 'There, hen, mind and scoop from the bottom.' The pot weighed a ton. Ina bought all the ingredients for the soup herself, never asking for a penny from the charity, and the carrots, onions and barley must have taken up most of her pension. I could see bits of lamb floating in the rich soup – nothing but the best for Ina's lost boys and girls. 'Now that one,' she said, pointing to the canteen door, 'he restores my faith in humanity. He's a bloody angel, a saint the way he looks after them as if they were his own.'

A snort escaped from my lips and the shock of seeing Graham Marshall meant the hot soup splashed up my arm. 'Shit,' I hissed, and banged the pot down on the counter.

Mary McLennan would have agreed with me that a leopard doesn't change its spots. I watched as Marshall walked into the centre of the room with a stethoscope round his neck. He was scanning the crowds, searching for a particular patient. I wasn't prepared for what happened next. Led by Wee Elvis, the lunchtime crowd raised their empty trays above their heads and banged them with their free hands. Loud whistles accompanied the round of applause to make it raucous and ear-splitting.

340

Marshall took a bow. Like a magician, he bent deep at the waist and swept his arm out, swan diving forward. The good doctor had done time. Like most of them, he had spent some of his life in Saughton – it made him one of their own. They seemed undisturbed by the fact that he had ended up in this life by torturing and slaughtering a baby.

I wanted to vomit.

Then the bastard, the cheeky, arrogant bastard, went one step too far. Marshall himself started to clap. He half turned towards me and clapped loudly, saluting me, letting the crowd know my part in his acquittal.

A tear came to Ina's eye. The pensioner manhandled me, pushing, shoving me out of the kitchen into the canteen. So it was that I ended up standing side by side with the man I hated most in the world.

He put his arm around me.

'Take a bow, Miss McLennan,' he said. 'My case only adds to the legend that is Brodie McLennan.'

My flesh crawled. I had to get away from him. Stepping forward into the crowd I held my hands up; a fake smile forced my lips apart. 'Enough, enough,' I said.

'You're the best, Brodie, the best!' shouted Wee Elvis. He turned to the toothless woman standing next to him, saying proudly, 'She's ma lawyer too.'

'Thank you,' I shouted. 'But I think it's time we fed your bellies. The grumbling noise is making me think the South Bridge is about to collapse.' I scurried back behind the open roll shutters and took up my ladle. The time passed quickly as I doled out the soup and stale rolls, hatred for Marshall brewing all the time. Silence fell as, one by one, the tramps sat down to enjoy their lunch. Marshall took a seat by Wee Elvis and Lucky. They were locked deep in conversation, and I had a horrible feeling Marshall had chosen to give attention to the man because I was fond of him. Marshall glanced up at me out of the corners of his eyes and a shiver ran through the nerves in my spine. I tilted the pot on its side to scrape the last bowlful of soup out. It was mainly barley and water, and the waiting youngster with a navy baseball cap on looked at me reproachfully. I took a fiver out of my pocket and slipped it under his soup bowl.

'Buy yourself a Big Mac later,' I whispered. Ina didn't believe in giving them money. It was too easy to spend it on drugs, and the price of cocaine on the streets of Edinburgh had fallen so low that a fiver would get him what he wanted. I shooed him away before she noticed. I turned my back on the diners. The noise of their chomping, slurping and chatting infiltrated the kitchen. Ina was a bit deaf so I raised my voice.

'Ina,' I said. 'I need your help. Do you know a guy named Kenny Cameron?' Ina wiped her thin, wrinkled hands on the white apron and looked up at me. 'Wee guy,' she said. 'Ugly, skinny, under nine stone, about thirty-seven, thinning hair, moustache?' I was nodding, my heart felt warm as Ina described him exactly. 'Where is he?' I asked. 'He's not here today, I was looking for him.'

'Last time I saw him was a couple of days ago,' she said. 'I told the other guy who was asking about him.'

'What other guy?' I said.

'Big fella, in a hurry, wanting to know everything like

yesterday was too late,' Ina nodded. I didn't wait to hear the rest. Grabbing my jacket from the hook by the door, I ran.

'What about the dishes?' Ina shouted after me.

I didn't have time for niceties. If big Billy Boyle was asking after Kenny Cameron, then the poor wee man was toast.

Without stopping to say goodbye, I ran for the front door.

Chapter Sixty-Seven

The early afternoon traffic was busy. The lunchtime crowd from the Mission were making their way to various park benches, alleyways and street corners, but a significant number of them huddled together outside the shop doors, in groups of twos and threes, hunched against the prevailing north wind. I studied their weather-beaten faces, searching for Kenny Cameron. He was nowhere to be seen but, as I looked for him, the small hairs on the back of my neck stood on end. My stomach clenched and, turning my head, I made no effort to disguise the fact I was looking over both shoulders. I was sure someone was watching me – if it was that bastard Marshall and he knew I was on to him, maybe he would bugger off and leave me alone. Maybe.

Scouting out the immediate area for my stalker, I spied the very man I thought was stalking me. Marshall wasn't alone. Wee Elvis and Lucky stood by his Mercedes, which was parked up in the Grassmarket. Wee Elvis looked distressed. I made a move to see what was what when a rusty white transit van pulled up at the kerbside and blocked my view. Irritated, I headed for Joe's custom-made chopper. It wasn't the best undercover vehicle. With its coffin-shaped tank and red leather upholstery, once you spotted it in your rear-view mirror, you didn't quickly forget it.

The driver pulled down his window and someone hissed at me to get my attention. I ignored whoever it was. There was no way I was wasting time giving anyone directions. Walking away from the van, as if I wasn't aware the driver wanted to get my attention, I heard the hiss again but turned a deaf ear and started undoing the lock on the chopper's wheel. Three or four alcoholics in thin tracksuits lolled against it, shivering and drinking cans of Special Brew. They parted to let me get on with my business. They chatted amongst themselves and offered pieces of advice, like that the crankshaft was cracked, as if they knew what a crankshaft was. 'Oi, hen,' said a young man with dull, matted hair the colour of mouse fur and red-rimmed eyes. He pointed a nicotine-stained finger at the dirty white transit van. 'The gadge in there wants to speak to you.'

I nodded, ignored him, and turned my back on the group, concentrating on turning the stiff lock. It needed some WD40. A hand went over my mouth. I tried to sink my teeth into the callused skin but my assailant's grip was too tight. He bent down over me, crunching my back against his chest. He was a big, heavy bastard. I breathed in a deep lungful of air, and amongst the odour of unwashed skin was a smell I loved. There was only one big bastard who smelled like that and he was mine.

I stopped struggling.

Glasgow Joe was back.

As I relaxed, Joe released his grip and stood up. The watchers formed a small crowd round us but I didn't give a fuck about the crowd. I leapt up and wrapped my legs round his waist. Kissing Joe felt like a homecoming. He stroked my hair and tried to stem my tears.

'Ssssh,' he said. 'There'll be plenty time for that later. Right now we need to follow Marshall. I've been tracking him for days; that's why I disappeared. I thought it was the best way to protect you. I've got to look out for you, Brodie – if I can't do that, I'm nothing.' Joe held my hand and, crouching down, pulled me back to his white transit van. Jumping into the driver's seat, he pointed out the window to the chopper. 'Tell me,' he said, 'tell me you weren't going to follow a psycho like Marshall on that?' I shrugged and turned my attention to the dashboard where he had a family-sized bag of assorted crisps. I reached out and stuck my nose in the bag. There was one cheese and onion left; it was our favourite flavour. I handed the bag to him; he glanced at it out of the side of his eye.

'D'you miss me that much?' Joe asked, and I nodded. Words were stuck in my throat, a squash ball of emotion preventing me saying what I wanted to. It was easier to give him crisps.

He smiled and squeezed my knee. We set off in the direction of the Grassmarket, Marshall three cars ahead. As we drove past his parking spot, I saw Lucky sitting on his own on the pavement, Wee Elvis in the passenger seat of the Mercedes. After that I didn't bother to watch the road ahead, instead half turning in my seat to look at Joe's profile. He had lost weight since he was captured by Donna Cook. I wasn't sure if he wanted to talk about it, but I needed to.

'What happened with Donna Cook?' I asked. 'I mean, Joe, how could you be captured? How did she get you?' The muscles on his cheeks tightened, his skin paled, and he stared straight ahead. The knuckles on both hands were white and bloodless as he gripped the steering wheel.

'You introduced me,' he said. There was no accusation in his voice. 'Then I met her in MacDonald Road.' MacDonald Road was close to his boxing club; she must have lain in wait for him. 'Her car had broken down.' He rolled his eyes. 'I can never resist being a knight in shining armour. She said the latch for the boot was under the passenger dashboard. I bent in, next thing I knew there was a needle in my arse and the steering wheel was coming to meet me.' Joe rubbed a fading bruise on his forehead. 'I went out like a light; she'd used enough tranquillizer to drop an elephant.'

'What did she do when you got to the farm?' I asked. I covered his left hand with mine. He didn't try to pull away but I could feel the muscles in his arm tense.

'She bundled me onto a trolley, you know the type, a big bit of wood on casters,' he said. 'It was just like I was a hunk of meat. Funny thing with her was, it was nothing personal. Her hatred of Kevin Milne, or Marshall, whatever the fuck you want to call him, had knocked any sense she had out of her. I was just a cata- lyst to get what she needed.' We travelled along Corstorphine Road, heading for the private hospital where Marshall sometimes worked, when Joe pulled the van over and parked. Sitting in the loading bay we watched Marshall's car turn right up to the building. Wee Elvis was still beside him.

The hospital was a former convent school set high on top of Corstorphine Hill. It was surrounded by mature parkland and the oak, elm and horse chestnut trees were beginning to bud. The car park was busy; patients parked their BMWs for free and climbed the old stone steps to see their consultants. Everyone was preoccupied with their own troubles and ailments, too busy to notice two disreputable-looking characters in worn bike leathers sneaking up the driveway searching out Marshall's car. Joe spotted it first. The Mercedes was parked way off, further up the hill outside a set of outbuildings that, although old, looked as if they had been newly renovated.

'Since Marshall was released from prison he spends all his time here or at the Mission,' Joe said. He grabbed my hand and pulled me closer to what I guessed was the old stable block. The lichen-covered grey stone was beautiful; what few windows it had were set high up in the walls. It seemed horses didn't need daylight but human beings, especially sick ones, did. It didn't surprise me. The Edinburgh District Council planning authorities were notorious; if a building hadn't had provision for letting in daylight in the seventeenth century, well, it wasn't going to today: they couldn't allow an extra pane or skylight, or where would it all end? We crouched down beside Marshall's Mercedes. There were no other cars parked outside this building. Joe reached up and tried the handle. The door was open and the keys were still in the ignition.

'Careless,' Joe said.

'Arrogant,' I said. 'He thinks he's untouchable . . . he could be right.'

'We'll see,' said Joe. His right eyebrow was raised – always a danger sign. His lips were set in a grim line, as he inched nearer and nearer to Marshall's lair. It was surprising how easy it was. No one paid any attention to what was going on up the hill. They were all focused on the comings and goings in the main hospital. 'The back door,' Joe said. 'Run for it and no mucking about. Do exactly what I tell you to, Brodie. Trust me.'

Keeping my head down, bent in half, I ran towards the green stable door. By the time I got there, Joe was already working on the lock. He pulled out a set of tools and with a deft flick of his wrist the door swung open. The first room we came through was a disposal unit. Hospital waste, bagged up, stood ready to be burned. One of the sacks had burst open and items of old dirty clothing burst out. My heart stopped. A green, yellow and black beanie lay on the floor. Mack, the dreadlocked tramp who used to own Lucky, had worn one exactly like that. I didn't stop to examine it closer. Joe was already heading down the corridor. I had to run to keep up. He knew where he was going and I could sense he had been here before. Adrenalin pumped through my system. The wing of the hospital was bright and sterile but unwelcoming. There were no friendly nurses' stations, or vending machines dispensing chocolate treats to visitors, no crappy artwork on the wall.

The stable block was very small. The first room with the waste in it was the old tack room, and there were only three more doors and a cubicle that had been converted into a small kitchen. Joe opened up the door on his right. It was in darkness, except for a night-light that highlighted the bed and the patient in it. Wee Elvis lay on a bed in a hospital gown, hooked up to an IV. Next to him was another bed, covered in bloodstains. There was a body covered in a sheet and I had no inclination to remove it.

'Did you hear that?' I asked, turning to look over my shoulder. But Joe didn't answer me. He grabbed my jacket and pulled me into Wee Elvis's room. Joe stared through the crack in the door. Wee Elvis's hair was still damp; he had been showered quickly, I guessed. I looked at him in a clean, warm bed for the first time in years, and I knew I had to get him out of it.

'Brodie,' whispered Joe, breaking me out of my thoughts. 'Look!' Through a two-inch crack in the door, I saw the brightly lit corridor. Joe couldn't take his eyes off the motorbike courier dressed all in black and carrying an organ transplant box. The bold red writing on the side declared: *Human Heart – for transplantation*

'We have to let the courier go,' said Joe. 'It could all be above board and, even if it isn't, whoever the heart belongs to . . . it's not going to do him much good now.' I nodded, clenched and unclenched the fingers of my hand. The courier walked away with the organ. He was good at his job. He wasn't hanging around because the surgical team were waiting for the arrival of the organ. The recipient already had his old heart removed, and his family would be in the waiting room, pacing the floor, praying for his survival and anxious to begin their new life.

Just as my thoughts drifted back, Marshall walked into the room and up to Wee Elvis. Joe and I were still out of sight, but it didn't matter. 'Hello, Brodie,' said Marshall without turning around. 'And . . . Joe, is it? I believe I've been to your delightful hostelry in the past. How kind of you both to drop in.' Marshall finally turned round. If he was at all surprised by our presence, it didn't show in his eyes. My knees felt weak as Joe marched up to the doctor and swatted him away. Marshall fell against the operating table. I tried not to look. The sheet fell off the body, revealing a corpse with a huge hole in his chest – right where his heart once lived.

'So what was it, Marshall? Do you take their hearts out because you just like it? Do you do it because you can? Or do you have a nice little business going here?' asked Joe. 'I've been watching you for the past week. Your clinic at the Mission allows you to spot the down-and-outs who are healthy and, with a little care, their organs are suitable for transplantation, I'd guess. There's a huge market out there, isn't there, Doctor?'

Marshall's face tightened. 'There's a need and I fill it.'

'Your need, I take it?

Marshall was circling Joe; his anger was increasing. 'Does anyone care what happens to these people?' he said. 'No one even noticed they were missing.'

'Oh dear God,' I said, finally finding my voice. 'Kenny Cameron? Have you killed Kenny Cameron?'

'Do you need to know?' Marshall asked.

'Yes, yes I do.'

'Well then . . . I rather suspect I won't be telling you.'
Everything went still. White-hot fury ran through my
veins. I pulled Glasgow Joe's knife from my pocket and
ran hurtling towards Marshall. Lifting the knife high above
my head, I brought it down in a slashing move and stuck
the blade in his left anterior jugular vein. His eyes bulged,
surprised at last. He held on to my arms, gurgling. Blood
running out of the side of his mouth, he fell to his knees,
almost pulling me over. Bent double, I watched as the life
slipped away from the murdering bastard – was this how
Kailash felt when she killed my father?

Blood will out, as they say, and I was my mother's
daughter. A mixture of Kailash Coutts and Mary
McLennan.

I thought I saw Marshall's fingers move in an attempt
to crawl towards freedom, help – or me. We didn't hang
around to find out, only calling Duncan to let him know
where to find Wee Elvis. We drove in silence through
the dark streets of Edinburgh, heading for the Docks,
where we could both see where we had been raised.
Glasgow Joe and I walked hand in hand down by the
Shore. I took a deep breath in, and stared around the
Docks and the streets of Leith, drinking in every detail.
It all looked beautiful to me, from the hookers in the
doorways and the empty pleasure boats to the swans
swimming on the Water of Leith.

'I think it's time we got out of here, darlin',' he said,
holding me tight as my heart broke. 'We've got the future
waiting for us.'

Epilogue

I wished Kailash was there to tell me I looked fat. My hair would have been nicer if Malcolm had done it. I wanted Lavender to give me something to borrow.

My wedding day – again. Same man, almost the same place, but everything else so different.

At the first service station we had stopped at to fill up, Joe had halted just long enough to allow me to phone home. Lavender cried when she realized I wouldn't be there to be godmother to her baby. The blow was softened when I told her that I would be signing over my side of the business to Eddie – that was a better present than a teddy bear, I thought. As I hadn't given Marshall back his cheque, it meant the firm was debt-free too. She told me that everyone, thanks to her, thought that Joe and I were off on our bikes doing a world tour – she'd even set up a fake blog for us.

The next call was calmer. Kailash greeted my news with her usual style, promising to meet us in America – one day. I guess she assumed that Glasgow Joe would be in regular contact through their Internet gambling company and it would all work out; she had no idea what we were really running from. Kailash would break the news to Connie and Grandad. This hurt – I knew that Connie would track me down one day, but with Grandad's age, I worried. It wasn't very long since I'd found him, and now I feared I'd never see him again. I also couldn't bear to disappoint him. His dream of me becoming a judge was gone. I was leaving law, and at the moment if I evaded arrest I would be grateful.

Glasgow Joe only spoke to Moses, and he gave him firm, clear, unequivocal instructions on how to cover our tracks, and to put pressure on Bancho not to look too hard for Marshall. I couldn't imagine a grown-up Moses, but this might force him into it. I wondered if his Granny would look after him at last.

Now, today, I looked at Joe and thought about all we had been through. We were such different people to the last time, but we still loved each other. I missed everyone so much, but it felt right to be alone with him. It would be a small ceremony – just us and the two strangers we'd drag in as witnesses. We didn't need our past but it still called to me. I wanted Mary McLennan more than ever . . . but I knew that I needed Kailash too.

Joe was on his elbow looking at me. 'Ready for your present?' he asked, reaching down the side of the bed and handing me a newspaper tied with red ribbon. 'I love you, Brodie McLennan, I love you with all my heart – now, let's get on with the rest of our lives.'

A bloody newspaper? No diamonds? No grand gesture?

Thanks Joe – thanks . . .

354

The Scotsman

8 February 2009

News, Edinburgh

A news conference was held in Edinburgh yesterday to mark the close of the killing spree known as the 'Cupid' murders. Detective Inspector Duncan Bancho of Lothian and Borders Police led the conference with his colleague DI Sam Jones of the Met. During the investigation, there had been concern that DI Jones herself had been abducted and killed by Donna Cook, the mother of toddler Matthew Cook who was murdered in the late 1980s by notorious child-killers Kevin Milne and Renee Smith. DI Jones did not go into detail about her own ordeal, but thanked DI Bancho and his team for their thorough investigation which, sources tell us, led to her discovery, close to death, in a Midlothian farmhouse. Bancho said that the case had proved to be a challenging one for his officers, but that perseverance and professionalism had resulted in success.

BIRTHS, DEATHS & MARRIAGES

Lavender and Eddie Gibb are delighted to
announce the birth of
Jodie Ironside Gibb
at Simpson's Memorial Maternity Pavilion,
Edinburgh
at 2.17 a.m. on 28 January 2009
Mother and daughter doing well – father
just about coping.
Love to everyone who has been with us on this
amazing journey – especially Auntie Brodie and
Uncle Joe.
Hope to see you soon xxx

PERSONAL ANNOUNCEMENTS

She loves you. She will do anything for you, no matter
what you need, no matter what you ask. She will always
be there for you. Anything she has done so far is nothing
– you are all that has ever mattered to her. She wants
me to tell you this – from the moment she saw you, you
were locked in love together. We all miss you – Malcolm
says he hoped you packed the conditioner, Louisa says
the flat's never seen action like it, even Duncan says that
things are boring now you're not here. Me? I'm off to
my granny's. Take care, doll, and say hiya to that big
ginger bastard from us all. M xxx

Infamous Killing Duos – Maria Thomson

From Jack the Ripper to Harold Shipman, some names are instantly recognizable. But even more terrifying are those serial killers who hunt as a pack . . .

Myra Hindley and Ian Brady

Responsible for committing the infamous Moors Murders, Myra Hindley and Ian Brady murdered five children aged between 10 and 17 in the 1960s. They worked as a team, with Hindley luring the children to their brutal deaths at the hands of her partner Brady. They abducted, sexually abused and tortured their young victims before killing them and burying their bodies on Saddleworth Moor in Lancashire. The British public were horrified at the murders, the first widely publicized child killings in UK history, particularly at the hands of a woman. Hindley and Brady were sentenced to life imprisonment in 1966, and were recommended never to be released.

Fred and Rosemary West

This husband and wife duo tortured, raped and murdered at least 12 young women between 1967 and 1987. Married when she was just 17, Rosemary committed her first murder the following year, killing Charmaine, Fred's daughter from his first marriage whilst he was in jail for theft. When Fred was released from prison not long after, he immediately went on to kill Charmaine's mother, his ex-wife Rena. Rosemary worked as a prostitute from the couple's home, and had eight children, five of whom were Fred's. The couple were found guilty of the killings brought against them in 1995, which included one of their daughters, Heather, who they had killed when she was just 16 and buried under the patio.

The Ken and Barbie Killers

Paul Bernado and Karla Homolka, also known as the Ken and Barbie Killers, were notorious Canadian serial killers. Together they killed three girls, including Karla's sister Tammy. Soon after they first met, they became sexually obsessed with each other, and fed off each other's twisted sexual fantasies. Paul carried out a series of at least 12 violent rapes, which Karla allegedly supported, becoming known as the Scarborough Rapist. Soon after his twelfth rape, Bernado and Homolka moved on to murder, torturing and sexually assaulting their victims before killing them. Although questioned and linked to the Scarborough rapes, it was some time before the pair's crimes were revealed and were eventually brought to justice in 1995.

SHADOWS STILL REMAIN

Peter de Jonge

When a gifted student mysteriously disappears from a New York bar, Detective Darlene O'Hara unravels a chilling story of murder and deception.

Running from a troubled past, Francesca Pena's come to New York to reinvent herself, earning a scholarship and the admiration of her more privileged friends. But none of them knows the real Francesca.

Following a night of partying with three friends, she's reported missing. Detective Darlene O'Hara from New York's 7th Precinct and her partner Serge Karamanoukian – 'K' – investigate.

A week later, Francesca's body is discovered severely mangled in a toilet by the East River. The case quickly becomes a high-profile hunt that the Homicide Unit are quick to snatch away.

Covertly, O'Hara and K continue their own investigation in the city's seedy underbelly. And they could never have predicted what they would uncover.

From Peter de Jonge, who previously joined forces with the *New York Times* bestselling author James Patterson to write two No.1 bestsellers, comes a tense and electric thriller set in the rotten core of the Big Apple.

ISBN: 978-1-84756-056-8

Out Now

What's next?

Tell us the name of an author you love

| Grace Monroe | Go ▶ |

and we'll find your next great book.